DREAMER

The Seeker Series: Book Two

By Amy Reece

DREAMER

Limitless Publishing, LLC
Kailua, HI 96734
www.limitlesspublishing.com

Formatting: Limitless Publishing

ISBN-13: 978-1-68058-160-7
ISBN-10: 1-68058-160-0

DEDICATION

For all the girls who are brave enough to follow their dreams. And for the boys who hold them through the nightmares.

CHAPTER ONE

*"And there was a large, dark blankness in my mind,
a deep fog of unknowing."*
-Madeleine L'Engle

December 22
Galway City, Ireland

The darkness was utter and complete. I was awake but could see nothing. I tried to wave my hand in front of my face, but I discovered both hands were bound together tightly with what felt like duct tape. I tried to move my legs and realized they were unbound, but wedged against something. I began to panic, trying to scream, but my mouth was taped shut. What was happening to me? Wait, was it me? Was I me? Suddenly, my body was thrown against the wall in front of me; I realized I was on the floor of the backseat of a vehicle of some sort. Was I being kidnapped? Why? Who would want to kidnap me? Was I going to be killed? I went into full-blown freak-out mode, sobbing and beginning to hyperventilate. Would I ever see my family again? My somewhat odd, but always loving grandmother, my devoted mother, my best friend in the world, Tara? And Jack. I choked on a sob as I thought of him, more of a prayer than anything else. I mourned the life we might have had together; the love, maybe even the children we would someday have. What would happen to the tiny life I carried within my womb? What would Scott do when I wasn't waiting for him? Wait...what? I wasn't pregnant! And who the heck was Scott?

I woke myself up, sobbing and covered in sweat. I looked around, momentarily confused by my unfamiliar surroundings. *Where was I?* Was I still in the hospital? No, now I remembered I was in my hotel room in Galway City, Ireland. Cassie and I had arrived early this evening and after a quick, yet elegant meal in the hotel dining room, I had wanted nothing more than to fall into bed. This horrible nightmare was no doubt a result of jet lag after flying from New Mexico to Ireland and eating right before bed. I stopped to listen for movement from Cassie, occupying the suite's adjoining bedroom, but heard nothing. Good. She had been as exhausted as me and didn't deserve to be disturbed. The bedside digital clock read 3:30 a.m., but I knew I wouldn't be getting back to sleep anytime soon, so I got out of bed, shivering in the December chill. I don't even know what time my body thought it was. I got myself a glass of water from the bathroom, then went to the window and pulled back the curtains to look down into Eyre Square. I could barely make out the tents and canopies of the

Christmas Market. When we had checked in this evening, the young woman at the reception desk had let us know that tomorrow—now today—would be the last day of the market, so we should be sure to save some time to explore.

As I looked down into the city center, I found myself thinking back over the incredible chain of events that led me to spend my Christmas break here in Ireland instead of with my family and friends back home in Albuquerque. It all started in late October with a vision in the middle of my English class; a vision of a pregnant Veronica Albluth. Well, she was no longer pregnant. That steroid-shooting monster, Coach Trevino, also her baby daddy, had seen to that when he beat the crap out of her. He beat the crap out of me too, and I had the stitches in the back of my head to prove it. I also had a really unattractive bald spot where the ER doctor had to shave my head to put in the stitches. I know I shouldn't be so upset over this, but it was my freaking hair! I should have hit him a lot harder. Anyway, the visions continued and intensified. Now I was even having visions of the future, both of which had already come true, exactly as I had seen. Well, one of them wasn't an earth-shattering vision or anything, but still! I had seen Jack's little sister lose her first front tooth weeks before she actually lost it. And Jack…yeah. He was new to my school this year, and although we were in the same grade, he was two years older than me because of some bad decisions during his first year of high school, which caused him to fall behind. He never even spoke to me until I started freaking out in class, nearly passing out—actually passing out once, but Jack wasn't there—during a vision. One thing led to another, Jack finally got off probation, and we were now dating. Okay, that's a bit of an understatement, because I am completely and totally in love with Jack Ruiz. He says he loves me too. I smoothed my fingers over the charm bracelet he gave me for my birthday last Saturday. And now I was here in Galway to meet with the Seer Council to find out why I was developing some really crazy powers, thanks to the fact that I have druid blood flowing through my veins.

I shivered again, wishing I had packed a robe, and decided to crawl back under the covers. I reached over to pick up the book from the nightstand I had started to read before I went to sleep, more out of habit than anything else; I hadn't made it through a full paragraph before drifting off. I couldn't even remember what I had read, so I decided to start again. *A Ring of Endless Light* by Madeleine L'Engle. I had borrowed the dusty old hardcover from my English teacher, attracted by the poetic title. I had thrown it in my carry on, thinking it would be a good idea to have at least one real book in addition to my Kindle. As I opened it now, I noticed an inscription I hadn't seen before: *Merry Christmas, Ashley 1983 Love, Mom and Dad.* On the inside cover was a bookplate stating This Book Belongs to Ashley Hayes. The first line of the book was one of those that drew you in and made you want to keep reading: *I saw him for the first time at the funeral.* This time I lasted for at least ten pages before I found myself drifting back to sleep.

***

I woke up late the next morning with the weak winter sunlight streaming in from the window. I guess I had left the curtains open when I couldn't get back to sleep the night before. I looked over at the digital clock, which I couldn't read because of the note propped up against it.

Decided to let you sleep in. Get some rest and meet me downstairs in the lobby when you're ready.
Cassie

I moved the note and saw it was already 10:00 a.m., but I appreciated Cassie letting me sleep in. It was a bit awkward traveling all the way to Ireland with her; I mean, I didn't really know her very well, after all. I had met her last month when my grandmother took me to see her in sort of a counseling role. Cassie and I (and my grandmother and mother, for that matter) were all psychics because our ancestors were druids. This psychic power was passed on to the females in the family; it was most often a type of enhanced intuition of one sort or another. But then I came along, and apparently I was like the most powerful Seer in several generations or something. Anyway, Grams, Mom, and Cassie all thought it would be a good idea if I came to Ireland to meet with the Seer Council, a group of women with this same type of psychic power who kind of watch out for all the families. I was really dreading the whole thing. I would much rather be at home in good old Albuquerque, NM, spending the holidays with my family and with Jack and his family. Sigh.

I got up, took a leisurely shower (only washing my bangs because of the stitches—so disgusting), dressed in layers so I'd be ready for sightseeing, and strolled down to the lobby of the hotel, enjoying the ambiance along the way. We were staying in the historic Meyrick Hotel, right in the center of Galway City. It was beautiful, with lots of marble and warm colors everywhere. I walked across the black and white marble tile of the lobby and found Cassie sitting in an easy chair in front of one of the many fireplaces, typing busily on her laptop. She looked up as I sat down in the adjacent chair.

"Oh, good morning, Ally." She looked up from her computer. "Are you feeling more rested today? I'll order some tea and scones to tide you over until lunch, okay?"

"Yeah, sure. That sounds great. Thanks."

She typed for a moment more, then closed her laptop and hailed one of the many hovering waiters. She ordered tea and an assortment of goodies and then took a good look at me. "You still look tired, Ally. Didn't you sleep well?"

I considered telling her about my nightmare, but decided it was pretty lame. Why would she want to know about that? It was simply the result of jet lag, and oh yeah, the absolutely horrific week I had leading up to this trip. "I never sleep very well the first night in a new place. I'm sure I'll catch up tonight. I'm fine." I tried to brush off her concern.

"Okay. Well, after we have some tea, why don't

we go and explore the town a bit?"

"Sure. It might be fun to check out the Christmas Market. I didn't have a chance to do any Christmas shopping before we left and I'd love to find some really different gifts here."

"Oh, my dear, yes," a small, older woman said as she approached our sitting area. She was wearing an extremely floral dress ensemble complete with matching hat. She also wore a "Hello My Name is Caoimhe" nametag. I was staring at her name, trying to figure out how in the world to pronounce it when she held out her hand, and said in a lovely Irish lilt, "So sorry to interrupt, but I heard you talking about the Market. I live in a little town outside Galway, so I know all the best sights to see. My name is Caoimhe." She pronounced it 'Kwee-va'.

I shook her hand saying, "Wow, that's a really cool name."

"Ah, thank you, my dear. That's very sweet." Only it sounded more like, 'Ah, thanka m'dear. That's verra sweet." I was completely charmed, thinking she was a dream grandma. I mean, I love my Grams, but she has a few quirks. This lady looked like the kind of grandma who would authentically greet you after school with tea and cookies. My grandmother only does that when she's fishing for information.

"Lovely to meet you, Caoimhe," Cassie said. "Are you here with the gardening convention?"

"Oh, yes. There's quite a group of us here. We have to meet in the winter since we're all so busy actually gardening in the spring." She chuckled.

Cassie and I both laughed politely. Cassie introduced us, simply saying we were on vacation.

"Oh, and here's Fionnuala. Come and meet these lovely Americans, Fionnuala!" Caoihme called to another woman walking toward us.

We invited them to join us for a cup of tea, which they did, proving to be a wonderful source of information for sights to see around Galway.

"Now, be sure to stop by the Spanish Arch and the Lynch Window. You surely don't want to miss those," Fionnuala said.

"And do stop by Dillon's Claddagh shop on Quay Street. What a perfect gift a Claddagh ring would be for your young man!" Caoimhe enthused.

"How do you know…?" I began. I noticed Cassie giving her a rather sharp look.

"Oh, my dear! A girl as pretty as you surely has a young man, now don't you?"

I know I blushed. I also didn't say anything.

"Ah, there now. I knew it. What's his name? Do you have a picture? Tell me all about him, dear," Caoimhe urged.

"Well," I stammered. "His name is Jack and, um, I don't know. He's really nice and very good-looking…"

"Surely you have a picture? What kind of girl doesn't carry a picture of her young man?" Fionnuala chimed in.

I reached into my back pocket for my iPhone and scrolled through the photos until I found a good picture of Jack I had taken a few weeks ago. I handed it to the ladies.

They oohed and ahhed over his picture in a way

sure to win my approval. They were both rather sweet. Caoimhe handed my phone back saying, "He's a keeper, all right. Well, thank you for the tea, but we'll let you get on with your day of sightseeing now. Have fun. Come along, Fionnuala." They were gone with a whiff of floral perfume.

"Well, they were interesting," I said.

"Yes." Cassie sniffed. "Shall we take their advice and do some sightseeing and shopping this afternoon?"

"Sounds good. Give me a few minutes and I'll meet you back down here."

CHAPTER TWO

"Who is it that can tell me who I am?"
Shakespeare–King Lear (1.4.230)

Cassie and I spent a wonderful, if chilly, afternoon searching through the stalls at the Christmas Market, finding some unique gifts to take home to our family members. Grams and Mom aren't much for trinkets, but I bought some beautiful Celtic design pendants I knew they would love. Grams prefers simple jewelry, so I chose a lovely Celtic knot design in sterling silver for her. For Mom, I found a lovely tree of life pendant I knew she would like. I picked out a bracelet with linked Celtic crosses for Tara. I was suddenly glad I hadn't had a chance to do any Christmas shopping before I left; I wouldn't have found anything this cool at the mall back home. I had downloaded an app before I left Albuquerque to figure out the euro to U.S. dollar conversion and figured I was keeping fairly well within my budget, all things considered. I was making some serious inroads into my babysitting money, but Grams and Mom had both slipped me some extra spending money for the trip. Cassie and I decided to devote today to shopping and save the sightseeing for tomorrow and the next day.

I told Cassie I wanted to check out the Claddagh shop Caoimhe had told us about. Jack had given me a beautiful charm bracelet for my birthday, and I thought it might be nice to get him one of the rings for his birthday, which was in a few weeks. I had to decide if I had the guts to buy him a ring. Was it too cheesy? Was I presuming too much? Did he even like jewelry? I have never had to buy a present for a man since I don't have a father, uncle, or grandfather in my life. What did I really know about Jack, anyway? I knew he liked cars and that was about it. Aagh! I was freaking out right there on Quay Street. I stopped on a nearby bench, put my head into my hands and tried to breathe. Cassie sat by me, reaching over to brush my hair back, as it had fallen over my face.

"Hey, what's wrong, sweetie? Are you tired? Do you need to go rest? I know you probably haven't fully recovered from your injuries yet."

I looked up at her with a horrified expression. "How on earth do you pick out gifts for a guy, Cassie? I want to get Jack a Claddagh ring but I'm afraid he'll think it's stupid or lame..." Yep. I verbally vomited a rant of insecurities for a good two minutes. When I finally stopped to suck in a breath, Cassie laid a hand on my arm to calm me down.

"Stop, Ally. You are working yourself into a

froth."

I looked at her and nodded.

"Now, why don't you tell me why you want to buy Jack one of those rings? What's your reasoning?"

"Well, I've always thought they were beautiful and I really like what they symbolize: love, friendship, and loyalty. I think it's a perfect description of what I feel for him, and then there's the whole Irish aspect to it. Is it lame? Will he think I'm pushing?"

She laughed a little bit. "Oh, I really doubt he'll think you're pushing. Didn't he get you a bracelet with a compass rose on it? And I don't think it's lame at all. We'll make sure to find a nice masculine design. If it truly symbolizes how you feel about him, then it's a perfect gift. And don't worry too much about future shopping for him, or any man in your life. A man who's in love with you usually doesn't care too much at all about gifts. I find they almost always prefer you wrapped up in something sexy for them to unwrap," she finished with a knowing smile.

"Cassie!" I exclaimed. "Really? I mean, it's good to know, but Jack and I don't...I mean, we haven't...well, yet...but someday...if everything... you know."

She laughed and pulled me up from the bench. "Come on. Let's find this shop. I think I might need to buy one of those rings for Gregory as well," she said, referring to her gorgeous fiancé, whom she was planning to marry in June. "And tomorrow, we desperately need to find a hair salon for you because, damn girl, those doctors did a number on your hair. No offense, sweetie."

"None taken," I said ruefully while reaching up to straighten my slouch beanie, which had nearly fallen off my head, prompting Cassie's rude, yet truthful comment about my hair. I had to have 17 stitches in the back of my head, courtesy of a close encounter with a glass trophy case. The doctors had shaved off a healthy chunk of hair to clear the area and I didn't know if any salon would be able to disguise it. I would finally be able to give myself a gentle wash tomorrow morning. I had been carefully washing my bangs since Friday, but a full wash was forbidden until tomorrow. My head had never felt more disgusting and itchy, and now I was going to have to find a new hairstyle. I had been wearing my bright red hair curling well below my shoulder blades with longish bangs I would sweep to the side. I was hoping I didn't end up with some butch-looking haircut, because I really, really didn't think I could pull it off.

We found the jewelry shop, Thomas Dillon's Claddagh Gold, on the corner of William Street and Quay Street and entered the bright yellow door set in the red-painted brick wall. We decided to look into the attached museum before shopping, thinking some background info might be a good idea. The museum had displays for many of the various legends of the Claddagh ring, but the one I liked the best was the story of Richard Joyce, who was captured by an Algerian corsair on his way to the West Indies and sold as a slave to a Moorish goldsmith. In 1689, when King William III of

England demanded all the slaves be set free, the goldsmith tried to convince Richard to stay and marry his daughter. But Richard refused, determined to return to Galway to the girl he had left behind. He set up shop as a goldsmith and made her the first Claddagh ring. Now there's romance for you. It should be made into a movie. Sigh. Well, I quickly discovered my true love would have to settle for sterling silver, rather than 18 carat or even rose gold. I did not have 500 or so euros to spare, no matter how much I loved him. I found a beautiful ring for about 60 euros, including the engraving 'love, Ally.' Apparently Cassie had more disposable income to throw around than I did because Gregory would be getting a gold ring. Oh well, it's the thought that counts. I splurged and bought a matching one for myself, caught up in the romance of the whole thing. If Jack poo-pooed the idea of us wearing matching rings, well, I was screwed. Before I could freak myself out again, Cassie steered me out of the store and down the street to a charming teashop called The Secret Garden so we could warm up with afternoon tea and scones.

I stayed up late that night so I could Skype Jack, calculating if it was 1:00 a.m. in Galway it would be 6:00 p.m. in Albuquerque and he would be home from work. I kept myself awake by reading more in the book I brought, *A Ring of Endless Light,* which turned out to be a story about a girl who was dealing with a lot of deaths in her life. Sounds depressing, I know, but it wasn't. The girl was a little younger than me and found out she had the ability to communicate telepathically with dolphins, which was really cool. I wondered if I would be able to do that, what with my burgeoning psychic powers and all. Hmm, where could I find a dolphin to try it out on? Reading about the protagonist's emotional journey was helping me think more clearly about what I had been through over the past few months. Anyway, it was turning out to be a pretty good book. I texted Jack to let him know to log on and then there he was—I missed his handsome face so much! I wish I could have the real thing, but this digital version was good in a pinch.

"Hey, beautiful. What time is it there?" Jack asked.

"It's about 1:00 a.m. Jack, are you naked?" Darn this pixelation! I could make out an expanse of brown chest, but not much else.

He laughed. "No. I have pants on. I'm not into naked Skyping. I just got out of the shower. Let me grab a shirt real quick." He stepped away from his monitor.

"Don't get dressed on my account," I called to him.

I could hear him chuckling as he came back to the computer, pulling a white t-shirt over his head. "I'll get naked as soon as you do, querida. Now let me look at you. How are you feeling? I still think it was too soon for you to hop on a plane overseas. Are you tired? Has Cassie let you get any rest? And why are you staying up so late to talk to me?"

"Calm down, Jack. One thing at a time. I'm fine. Cassie let me sleep in late and we did some shopping this afternoon. I'm staying up late because

I miss you like crazy."

"Yeah, I miss you too. This sucks."

"I completely agree." We stared at each other for a minute, which seemed weirdly awkward on Skype, although we could spend lots of time together at home not talking.

"You still look tired, babe," he said with a worried look on his face.

"Oh, I'm fine. I need to get used to sleeping here, that's all. I miss my pillow." I told him about the hotel and meeting the cute little old ladies this morning and how pretty all the Irish accents were. I didn't tell him about the ring I had bought, since I wanted to keep it secret until his birthday later in January. I told him Cassie was taking me to get my hair fixed the next day. "Will you still love me if I come home with freaky hair?"

"You know I will. I love your hair, but it doesn't matter what you do with it. I would prefer, however, if you don't mess with the color. At least we'll still have that. And even if they mess it up, it will grow out, sweetheart. Don't worry, okay? Please?"

"Yeah, I know. It's stupid. It's only hair. It makes me mad."

"Believe me, I understand. That asshole Trevino better hope I never get a chance to be alone with him," Jack fumed.

"I can't tell you how much I wish we were together right this second so I could wrap my arms around you and kiss you really, really good."

"Back at you. Go to bed, okay? I love you."

"Love you too. Bye." I finished on a yawn, disconnected, and fell back on my pillow, pulling the comforter up as I went.

***

December 26

I had spent the last few days exploring Galway with Cassie. Caoimhe and Fionnuala even took us to see a few of the sights they especially recommended, including the Spanish Arch and the Lynch Window, where in 1493 the mayor of Galway hanged his own son for murdering a young Spanish man. Apparently the mayor's son thought there was more to their friendship than just friendship—wink, wink—and stabbed him when the feelings were not reciprocated. Jeez, drama much? Find a new boyfriend and move on. Anyway, this is supposedly where the word 'lynching' originated. I was going to return to Albuquerque full of useless little tidbits like this. The ladies were wonderful tour guides; if you want to get the inside scoop on a new city, find some locals to hang around with. They took us to lunch at a friend's house and we got to sample some real Irish cooking; no touristy stuff for us. Their friend's name was Maire—pronounced Myra—another very sweet elderly lady, who prepared some very tasty little hand-held pies stuffed full of vegetables, a mashed potato dish with cabbage and leeks called *colcannon,* and a delicious lemon tart for dessert. I wondered how Maire knew I was a vegetarian. Maybe she was, too, and it was simply a happy coincidence.

Cassie made good on her promise to take me to a

salon to get my poor hair fixed. She found a high-end salon and treated me to a spa day, including a facial, mani-pedi, and haircut and style. I walked out of there polished, buffed, and with a lot less hair. I ended up with a short bob with a shorter, layered back—the stylist worked really hard to disguise the giant missing chunk—long front, and side-swept bangs.

"Wow, Ally. You look…so sophisticated. I can't believe how much older you look. Wow," Cassie enthused. "Do you like it?"

"I don't know yet. I never planned to go this short." I ran my hands through the short, short back. The stylist had been very careful around my stitches and you really couldn't tell from the back there was a missing chunk—as long as I styled it correctly, which she had shown me. "I'll have to get used to it. Like Jack said, it's only hair and it will grow back."

"That's the spirit. I bet he's going to love it."

***

He did say he loved it on when I Skyped to thank him and Megan for the cheerleader charm to add to my bracelet. Megan had handed me the small package at the airport and made me promise not to open it until Christmas morning. Jack made me model my new haircut from all the different angles and said he could hardly wait to run his fingers through it, which made Megan giggle. She told me I looked like a grown-up, so I guess I could live with it. It's not like I had much choice, anyway. Jack then sent Megan out of his room so we could talk privately. I could hear her singing, "Jack and Ally, sitting in a tree…" as she skipped out of the room.

"I am so sorry about that," Jack said, shaking his head.

"Oh, don't worry about it. You know I think she's adorable."

"So, how are you doing? Really doing, querida? Are you nervous about the meeting tomorrow?"

His sweet concern did much to calm my nerves. "Yeah, I'm a little nervous, but I mostly want to get it all over with. I'm seriously ready to be with you, Jack, and not only see you onscreen."

"Right back at you, babe. I need to have you here in my arms. For now, I'm going to let you go and get some sleep. I love you, you know."

"I do know, but it's good to hear. I love you too. Good night."

***

I had to get up early on the morning of the 26th because we were scheduled to meet with the council at 8 a.m. sharp. I was pretty nervous and had no idea what to expect. I realized I didn't even know where we going to meet them. I was picturing a medieval castle and a huge, round table when Cassie began steering me toward the conference room right here in our hotel. I was sputtering my surprise when she stopped and turned me to face her.

"Listen, Ally. I know this is probably going to make you angry, but please believe they had a really good reason for it."

"For what, Cassie?" I asked.

Instead of answering, she opened the door of the conference room and ushered me inside.

Sitting around a perfectly normal hotel conference table were Caoimhe, Fionnuala, Maire, and four other ladies cut from a very similar cloth. Seriously? Maybe I should have seen this coming, but apparently the stress of the last couple of weeks had dulled my normally suspicious nature.

"Welcome, Ally," Fionnuala began. "Please come in and have a seat so I can introduce the rest of the council."

"Gardening conference, huh?" I said a bit petulantly as I flopped down in the chair they indicated.

The rest of the ladies chuckled, but Caoimhe actually had the grace to look somewhat penitent. "I'm sorry, dear, but we wanted a chance to meet you and get to know you a bit before we had you before the formal council. Forgive us, please. It was in your best interest."

Fionnuala completed the introductions. In addition to the three I had already met, there was Aine (Anya), Eithne (Enya)—which wouldn't be confusing or anything—Bridget, and Iona. Today, as they were not masquerading as garden conference attendees, they were dressed in what I guess could be described as trendy business casual. They looked sharp and even somewhat funky. I was impressed, although I didn't want to be since I was still a little pissed.

Fionnuala appeared to be the leader or

spokesperson for the council and called the meeting to order. "Council members, we have gathered today to begin the examination of a new Seer, Alethiea Grace Moran."

I raised my eyebrows in alarm at Cassie, who shook her head slightly.

Caoimhe must have noticed, because she turned to me and said, "No, Ally. We don't drag every new Seer to Ireland to stand, or sit really, before the council, but your grandmother and Cassie have reported your powers seem to be more powerful than usual."

"And you are developing more powers as time passes," added Iona. I grudgingly appreciated the ladies were all wearing the 'Hello My Name Is…' name tags still, or I would never be able to keep them all straight. "That is very unusual. Most Seers manifest one simple power. Your case requires extra examination."

The first thing they asked me to do was give them a rundown of the events of the past few months, ever since my first vision showed up. So I rehashed the whole thing, starting from seeing Veronica was pregnant and getting beat up, to my weird future visions of Megan losing her tooth and of Veronica and myself covered in blood. I noticed them all shifting in their seats and looking nervously at each other when I told them about these visions. I also told them about how I was able to block a vision as it was happening, which I still felt guilty about. I ended my story by telling them what had happened in Coach Trevino's office a little over a week ago. They all expressed horror and Caoimhe actually got up and came around the conference table to examine the stitches in the back of my head. I was touched when she smoothed my bangs back and kissed my forehead.

"You poor child. It's so much to bear, and at your young age. It's a shame!" she exclaimed before returning to her seat.

They produced a few miscellaneous items and asked me to touch them, like I had done for Cassie. I concentrated and was able to see in my mind where each item came from and to whom it belonged. For some reason, it seemed so much easier this time than when I had done it for Cassie.

"Very well, my dear," intoned Fionnuala. "We have much to discuss this afternoon. Cassie, bring her back here tomorrow morning at the same time. You may go now."

Well. We were clearly dismissed. Cassie and I gathered up our things and left to enjoy the rest of our day in Galway.

***

December 27

The next day the ladies wanted to see more of my 'powers', for lack of a better term. I certainly wasn't comfortable referring to them as such, but whatever. It turned out Bridget was the one with the ability to touch me and see, like Cassie had done. The room was deathly quiet while Bridget held my hand, nodding and humming a little.

"Yes, yes." She set my hand back in my lap and

patted it. "There is so much going on in your head." She turned back to the council. "It's as Cassie told us, sisters. She has remarkable powers, and I sense much more to come. It's waiting in her mind, ready to spring forth!" she enthused.

Aw, crap. I really, really didn't want to hear that. I am seriously freaky enough, thanks anyway. More powers showing up were really going to cramp my style.

"But could she be the one?" asked Iona.

Wait, what?

"That's not at all clear yet, but she is the most promising Seer in many years. We will have to wait and see," warned Fionnuala. "This will take a lot more time before we can be sure. She has barely turned 17. She has an entire year to finish developing her powers."

I was pretty close to losing it by now. What in the heck were they talking about?

Caoihme noticed my distress. She seemed to be the one most attuned to my feelings. Perhaps it was part of her gift? "Sisters, it's time to tell her. She needs to know."

"Yes, yes," said Fionnuala. "Eithne, you tell the story better than any of us." She nodded to one of the ladies I had yet to hear from.

The thin lady wearing black leggings and a red tunic cleared her throat and began to speak. "The Celtic Seers trace their lineage back to the time of Oliver Cromwell and the Wars of the Three Kingdoms, when Cromwell and his forces landed in Ireland. Their brutality was legendary. Cromwell hated the Catholics and absolutely refused to tolerate anything he considered pagan, including the Druids. The Druids were the keepers of the ancient knowledge, the true intellectuals of the Celtic world. They refused to write anything down, so much of what they knew has been lost forever. A priestess, whose name has been long-since lost to history, escaped the siege of Galway in 1650 and found sanctuary with a local farm family. She was very beautiful and kind and she and the farmer's son fell in love. They married and had several sons, although nobody remembers exactly how many. The priestess lived the rest of her life as a simple farmer's wife, all her Druid knowledge and power apparently lost when she passed. But the couple had one daughter. She began to show astonishing mental powers when she reached young adulthood. Those powers were passed on to her daughters, who passed them on to their daughters. This continues to this very day, however weakened and diluted the powers have become. Every few generations, however, one daughter is born who has the powers of the original Druid priestess. We call this woman the Oracle. Our last Oracle was born 75 years ago."

"Who is she? What happened to her? Is she one of you?" I looked around at the elderly faces surrounding me.

"No, dear. None of us are the Oracle. It is a very sad story, the saddest story we have experienced since the time of Cromwell. Fifty-five years ago, when our beloved Oracle was 20 years old, she was taken from us," Aine responded.

"How did she die?" I asked in a hushed voice.

"Oh my dear, she didn't die, at least not then.

She was literally taken from us. She was stolen, kidnapped by the Gaulish Seers. We have never heard from her since, and all of our requests for her return have been ignored. We have no idea whether or not she still lives."

"What? Gaulish Seers? There are more of us out there? What does that mean? And how can they just steal our Oracle?" I was outraged.

"So many questions." Fionnuala shook her head. "Yes, dear Ally. There are more of us out there. Wherever there was a significant group of Druids, there appears to be some vestige left in the form of Seers, although not everyone calls them that. We used to have a tentative relationship with the Gaulish clan, but it ended when they stole our Oracle. We continue to send missives every few years requesting her return, but we have been ignored completely," she ended with a disgusted sniff.

"Well, why doesn't someone go get her? You know, rescue her? Who are these Gaulish types, anyway?"

"It's not that simple, Ally. There is quite a rivalry between the two clans, made so much worse when they stole the Oracle. But maybe we can finally begin to recover now."

"Oh, how are we going to…" I let my words trail off as I noticed them all staring at me expectantly. "Wait, you don't think I…I mean I couldn't…" They stared at me, eyebrows raised, some of them nodding slightly. "Do you seriously think I should go rescue her?"

They all exploded into peals of laughter. Even

Cassie joined in the apparent hilarity. I sat with my arms crossed, staring back at them. I didn't see what was so funny. They finally laughed themselves out and Fionnuala said, "No, sweet girl. We don't expect you to go rescue her. I'm sure she's long gone by now. No, Ally, we are hoping you *are* the next Oracle."

Talk about dropping a bomb. I can honestly say I didn't see that one coming.

CHAPTER THREE

"When the mind's free, The body's delicate."
Shakespeare –King Lear (3.4.11)

The plane ride home seemed endless. I desperately wanted to sleep, but it wasn't going to happen. I couldn't seem to turn off my mind since the council had dropped the enormous Oracle-shaped bomb on me. What were they thinking? I can't possibly be the Oracle. I can barely manage to keep my own head straight, much less be the example of wisdom for an entire group of people! I was starting to hyperventilate even thinking about it. After the ladies sprung their little surprise on me, they proceeded to tell me all about what an oracle does. She is all about interconnectedness and communication with plants, animals, and all kinds of nature. An oracle knows how to move in and out of altered states as a vehicle, and a birthright. Most importantly, an oracle is a prophet. I don't even know what half of that means, and they think I might be their Oracle? Yikes!

That wasn't the worst part, either. I mean, it's bad enough, but no, the worst part was they wanted to get to know me much better over the next year, to figure out whether or not I'm really the next Oracle. And by "get to know me better" I mean they want me to spend all my vacations in good ol' Ireland. Actually, they really wanted me to stay there and forget about Albuquerque. Yeah, whatever. It's so not happening. I was only able to get them off my back by promising to spend a good portion of my summer with them. I was planning to make sure it was the same eight weeks Jack was at basic training for the army. They also wanted to see me for spring break, but I had plans for putting the kibosh on that. I let them think I was fine with it so I could get out of there. I was completely done in and so needed to get back home to some sanity. This was a bit too much for me right now.

I guess I was more exhausted than I realized, because about an hour and a half before we landed I fell asleep. Unfortunately, I found myself back in the middle of the recurring nightmare, which had plagued me since arriving in Ireland. Every night I would "wake up" in the back of a vehicle of some sort, bound and gagged, knowing I was being kidnapped. Since the first time I had this nightmare it had evolved from flashing back across the memories of my loved ones, wondering why I was in this predicament, to trying to figure out the glaring "who" question. Who would do this to me? Now when I had the nightmare, I could hear and feel the vehicle driving, bouncing along an uneven road. I was starting to get really irritated by this nightmare. Disconcertingly, I still felt like I was pregnant in the dream and longed for someone named Scott.

I woke to my seatmate poking my shoulder and saying, "Miss, are you all right?" Apparently I had been sort of crying or whimpering in my sleep. That's a bit embarrassing. Cassie had elected to stay a few weeks longer in Galway to spend more time with the council researching the chances I was the Oracle, so I was seated next to a stranger. By some miracle I had been bumped up to first class, which made this flight home so much better than the flight to Galway. Overseas flight in economy class? Yeah, not so much fun. The flight attendants brought around warm washcloths for us to refresh with and I took the opportunity to duck into the bathroom to brush my teeth and freshen up my makeup a bit. I was about to see my boyfriend after nearly two weeks apart and I sincerely hoped there would be some serious kissing involved. I didn't want to scare him away with manky breath and a shiny face. As I stared into the mirror, applying cherry-flavored lipgloss, I wondered what on earth these horrible nightmares were about. They were really starting to bug me. I was also beginning to regret not mentioning them to the Seer Council or at least to Cassie. Well, if they didn't stop after I got back home, I would talk to Grams about them.

We finally landed at the Albuquerque Sunport and I made my way towards the baggage claim, wondering who would be there to pick me up. I exited the revolving doors from the secure area of the airport and saw a beautiful sight: Jack leaning against a pillar, hands in his pockets, watching the disembarking passengers. His face lit up in a huge smile when he saw me, mirroring the giant one on my face. Within seconds I was in his arms, my carry-on bags forgotten in a heap next to me, being hugged and kissed within an inch of my life.

We finally came up for air and Jack held my face between his two big hands. "Let me look at you for a minute. God, Ally. I missed you so much." And he was kissing me again. I'm really glad I thought to pack my toothbrush in my carry on. It felt incredible to be back in his arms. I had almost forgotten how good he smelled and how wonderful it felt to be surrounded by his strength, held securely against his hard chest.

"Where's Mom and Grams?" I asked when we finally got our momentary fill of each other and we were on our way to the baggage claim, my tote bag over his shoulder.

"I'm it for your welcoming committee. Disappointed?" he asked with a crooked smile.

"Not even a little bit," I said with an answering grin. "But how did you manage to pull it off?"

"Well, I had to practically swear on a stack of bibles I would take you straight home where they are preparing a homecoming feast for you. Tara and Megan are both there, supposedly helping."

"You're staying for the feast, aren't you?" I asked anxiously.

He grabbed my hand. "Of course, querida. Don't worry; wild horses couldn't drag me away from you tonight."

I filled him in on the lighter details of my trip on

our way home. I decided to wait until we had a more significant chunk of time to tell him about the whole oracle thing. That would take some explaining and I needed his undivided attention. It was barely dusk as we exited the freeway toward my neighborhood and Jack pulled into a church parking lot set off from the busy street.

"I thought we had to get straight home?" I asked curiously.

"Yeah, well, I know I won't have you to myself for the rest of the night, so I'm stealing a little time now. I figure I can fudge about ten minutes into our trip home by claiming a traffic jam on the freeway. It can be our secret." He turned off the ignition and leaned over the center console to kiss me. I was having none of that and climbed over the console to sit in his lap, straddling him. We had perfected this over the last few months. We spent a few precious minutes getting reacquainted. Suffice it to say I would need to reapply my lipgloss and comb my hair before we got home. I did, giggling a bit as Jack also had to comb his hair and tuck his shirt back in. Don't judge me. I needed to have my hands on his skin a wee bit. He, as always, remained a perfect gentleman. Mostly. My world was back in alignment.

Mom and Grams had really pulled out all the stops for my homecoming. They took turns nearly squeezing the life out of me and telling me I couldn't be gone for such a long time again. There was a "Welcome Home, Ally" banner Tara and Megan had collaborated on, probably to get them out from under foot in the kitchen, and way too much food for six people. They had prepared all my favorites: labor intensive spinach lasagna, garlic bread, a strawberry-feta salad, and a wondrous, gooey chocolate cake for dessert. It was so good to be home. Everyone admired my haircut, Megan embarrassing both Jack and me by asking if he had run his hands through it yet. Tara said it made me look at least 19, except for the fact I'm still as short as most middle-schoolers. She's sure not one to sugarcoat anything.

After dinner, I sat by Jack on the couch, his arm around me, as I told everyone about the trip. Since Megan was there, I left out all the details about the council and the true purpose for the vacation, focusing instead on the sightseeing we had done and all the beauty of Ireland. I gave everyone the small trinkets I had chosen for them, but I was holding the Claddagh rings back for Jack's birthday in a few days. It was close to 9:00 p.m. and I was beginning to droop when Jack kissed the top of my head and suggested I get to bed.

"Come on, sweetheart. You're exhausted." He pulled me up off the couch and dragged me toward the stairs to my bedroom. I said goodnight to everyone, kissing my mom and Grams and thanking them for a wonderful homecoming dinner. I hugged Tara and Megan, promising to catch up more in-depth with Tara the next day. As soon as we were out of sight of the others, Jack pulled me into his arms for a sweet kiss. "You get some sleep, okay? I don't like the look of those dark circles under your eyes. I don't think you got enough rest over the past couple weeks." He kissed my forehead, a worried look on his face. "Call me when you wake up. I will try really, really hard not to call you, no matter how antsy I get."

I laughed, kissed him again quickly, and went off to my own bed with my own pillow, which I had sorely missed.

***

I woke late the next day, appreciating that Mom and Grams had let me sleep in. I'd had a wonderful night's sleep without a trace of the awful nightmare. I tried to remember what day of the week it was, but gave up when I couldn't grasp it. I headed downstairs, following a mouthwatering smell. Mom was at the stove, flipping pancakes. I grabbed a cup of coffee and asked her what day it was.

"Sunday, sweetie." She chuckled a bit. "Jet lag's no fun, huh?"

"Yeah, it's a bitch, Mom." At her raised eyebrows I muttered, "Sorry."

She came over and hugged me. "I'll forgive your potty mouth this once, since I missed you so much," she teased. "Your grandmother is not the best influence on your language." We shared a secret smile over my audacious grandmother, whose language could, indeed, be colorful. She held my face in her hands, her thumbs running gently over the dark circles under my eyes. "You still look tired, Ally. Did you not rest well over there?"

It was the perfect moment to tell her about the awful nightmares, but something held me back. "I really missed you all," I said as I hugged her, tears close to the surface. Later, I would need to analyze why I was reluctant to talk about these dreams. Hopefully they were a thing of the past, anyway.

"Okay, enough of this." She stepped away, wiping her eyes. "Let's get you fed and then I think you better call your boyfriend. He may have promised not to call, but I have a feeling he'll be here pounding on the door before too long. And when your grandmother gets up, we want to hear about what happened with the Council."

We feasted on blueberry pancakes, Grams deigning to join us halfway through, making her entrance wearing a purple silk caftan. "Darling, you still look exhausted! Why don't you go straight back to bed after breakfast?" She had a mischievous look on her face. "I'm sure Jack won't mind."

"Cute, Grams. I already texted him." When Grams was seated with her breakfast and coffee, I filled them in on the details of my meeting with the Seer Council. They laughed at how the ladies had tricked me by pretending to be at a gardening conference, but were shocked by what I told them about possibly being the next Oracle. We hashed it out for a while, but were ultimately unable to come up with anything new or useful. They related all that had happened while I was gone and how they had spent their Christmas, Grams at the senior center and Mom with her boyfriend, whom Grams and I had yet to meet. It was so good to sit and talk with them; I am lucky to have such a happy, if somewhat unusual, home life. After about an hour I had to call an end to the fun. "Jack's picking me up in about an hour, so I need to get ready. I smell bad and I'm stewing in my own filth, so if you lovely ladies will excuse me?" I rushed upstairs to shower, shave my legs, buff, polish, powder, and otherwise make myself kissable and touchable.

Jack had let me know he was at Mass and would pick me up right afterward and take me to lunch. When he showed up driving my car, the VW Bug he had restored and given me for Christmas, I assumed we would resume our driving lessons. I had made some progress in regaining my behind-the-wheel confidence, but had a ways to go with the whole stick-shift thing. I had lost my nerve for driving right after I got my license when I got in a nasty fender-bender, but Jack was determined to help me regain my confidence, and thus my independence. I opened the door before he even had a chance to ring the doorbell and launched myself into his arms, sealing my lips over his, letting my tongue invade his mouth to taste everything I had been missing for the past two weeks.

"Hey, beautiful," he said huskily when I finally pried myself off of him. "That's quite a greeting." He was adorably flushed. "Let's get out of here before I change my mind and find somewhere dark and private to take you. We could stay there about a week." He drew me back for another kiss.

"Ahem," Grams coughed, purposely disrupting us. "Ally, let the young man up for air."

I smiled against Jack's lips. He smiled back, putting his arm around my waist and pulling me close to his side. "Hi, Mrs. Moran. Sorry about that. It's been a while; I mean…" he said.

"Oh, Jack, calm down. I understand. I was in

love once or twice myself. And please, please call me Adele. Mrs. Moran makes me feel so old." If 58 isn't old enough to be called 'Mrs.' then I don't know what is.

"Okay, Adele. Thanks. Ally and I are going out to lunch and then I'm taking her driving, if that's all right?"

"Of course. You two have fun." She pulled me close for a hug. "Don't keep her out too late. You do look more tired than usual, Ally."

We went to Mannies on Central Avenue for lunch. It's a homey, old-fashioned diner and one of the most famous grammatical mistakes in Albuquerque. Their lack of a possessive apostrophe aside, it was a great place. Over homemade vegetable soup for me and a giant burger for Jack, I filled him in on what the Seer Council had said about me possibly being the next Oracle.

"So, wait," Jack said as he put his burger down. "I thought you went there to find out if you were really a Seer? What happened to that? How did it turn into this oracle thing? And what the hell is an oracle?"

I pushed my soup away, my appetite gone. If I was having a hard time with this, what did I expect from Jack? How could I expect him to keep on accepting all the new freaky stuff that keeps happening to me? Was this the point when he finally decides to walk away?

"Ally? Hey, what's up? You got real quiet all of a sudden. Not a good quiet, either. What are you thinking?"

I shook my head. "No, it's nothing. I get it. I

understand."

He looked at me for minute and then sighed. He got up and came around to my side of the booth and took me in his arms and kissed the top of my head. "You've got that look on your face. You know, the one that says you think I'm not going to be able to handle any more weird stuff and this is it for us. Huh? Admit it—it's what you were thinking, isn't it?" I nodded, trying to keep the tears in. "Okay, look at me." He pulled my face up to look directly in my eyes. I could stare into his beautiful, deep brown eyes all day. "First, and most importantly, I love you, Ally. I'm in this for the long haul, no matter how freaky things get. If it means I get you, then count me in. You gotta start believing in us, babe." He stopped to kiss me briefly and thank the waitress for refilling our coffee cups. "Secondly, you're giving me, and all guys in general actually, way too much credit for deep thinking. When I say 'what the hell is an oracle?' that's all I mean. No hidden meaning. I just want to know what it is. Guys are actually pretty simple and we tend to say exactly what we mean." He kissed me again and then returned to his side of the table, placing a napkin in my hand so I could mop my face. Poor guy: it seems like all he ever did was watch me cry. I was such a girl. "Now let's finish eating while you tell me all about this oracle stuff, okay?"

So I wiped my eyes and told him about how the Seer Council had tricked me into believing they were simply a group of innocent little old lady gardeners, but they actually held my fate in their hands. I told him about the last Oracle being stolen away from her people by the Gaulish clan, never to be heard from again. And I told him how the council was very interested in my abilities to see the future and seemed to think it was possible evidence of my oracle-ness or whatever. I finished with, "And they didn't want to even let me go. They made me promise to come back over spring break and in the summer."

"Spring break? Ah, Ally, no. I can't stand not having our last school vacation together. You gotta tell them no, querida. I'll probably go nuts if you're gone."

"Don't worry. There is no way I'm going back over spring break. I'll go in the summer as long as it's while you're gone to basic training." I grabbed his hand across the table and rubbed my thumb over his knuckles. I told him what the council had told me about oracles, how they were messengers between worlds or something.

"Ally, what do you think? Do you think you could be this oracle?" He looked at me with concern.

"I don't know, Jack. I think there's a lot more to the story than what they're telling me. I don't trust those little old garden-seer ladies. I can't even think about being an Oracle before I know what's really going on."

"That was a very Oracle-like thing to say," he said with a laugh.

"Shut up." I smiled. "Does this lunch include pie?"

***

38

The lunch did include pie, strawberry for me and chocolate cream for Jack, after which he took me to practice my driving. I had forgotten some of my technique on the stick shift, but Jack was patient and I finally started to get the hang of it. We were driving around the same church parking lot he had taken me to before Christmas.

"Great job, sweetheart! You'll be ready to drive to school next week."

"Jack, I haven't even driven on a real street yet." I was starting to hyperventilate.

"We'll get you out on the streets tomorrow. You haven't stalled out in at least five minutes."

"No, no way, Jack. I'm nowhere near ready for the streets!"

He reached over and took my hand. "Calm down. You're freaking yourself out!"

I rolled my eyes at him. I didn't feel like I'd ever be ready for actual streets with real cars.

"You need to start believing in yourself, Ally. You can do this." He kissed me as we switched seats so he could drive us. "So, what do you want to do for the rest of the day? I am entirely at your disposal."

"Really?" I gave him what I hoped was a lascivious look, but was probably merely pathetic. "Anything I want?"

"Let me qualify my offer: anything PG-rated," he countered.

I stuck my bottom lip out at him.

"Stop pouting. Maybe PG-13, depending on where we go. Happy?"

"Yes. Supremely happy. Would it be super-lame

if we went to one of our houses and watched a movie? I'd really like to curl up on a couch with you."

"Not even a little bit lame, *querida*. Let's go to my house since Trina wants to fix dinner for you anyway," he said.

"That's sweet of her. And this way I get to spend time with Megan too."

"Do you only love me for my little sister?"

"I love you *and* your little sister. And you've got some special attractions all your own." I let my hand tip-toe across his chest.

He captured my hand and brought it to his mouth, kissing it and laughing at the same time. "Come on. Let's head over to my house. I guess I can share you with my family for the evening if I have to."

We ended up watching *The Princess Bride* with Megan and Jack's blue heeler, Sodapop, curled up between us. Jack and I both fell asleep before the Rodents of Unusual Size made their appearance. I woke up right as Wesley and Buttercup were sharing a final kiss and couldn't resist starting a tickle war with Megan, which in turn woke Jack up. He joined in, albeit a bit sleepily, until Megan skipped off to see if dinner was going to be ready soon. I took the opportunity to curl up right next to Jack, inhaling the spicy, warm scent, which was so much a part of him. The smell alone did warm, wiggly things to my insides.

Trina had, as usual, outdone herself with dinner. I don't think she had it in her to not go overboard when entertaining. Mat showed up about halfway through dinner, apologizing to his mother with a kiss on her cheek.

"Good thing you're finally home, Ally," Mat said around a mouthful of enchiladas. "My cousin was cranky while you were gone. All that pent-up energy. He seems so much calmer now."

"Mat!" exclaimed Trina.

"I will literally punch you in the face, you a—"

"Jack!" both Trina and I broke in, hoping to save Megan's tender ears. Mat laughed.

"Sorry, Trina." Jack slitted his eyes at Mat, which made him laugh harder.

"It's okay, Jack," began Manny. "Mat's just jealous. He's got nobody to spend his…energy on."

Score one for Manny. Even Trina laughed. Mat rolled his eyes.

"So, speaking of energy…where's your little friend, Ally? What's her name? Tia? Tammy?" Matt pretended to be stumped over my best friend's name.

"Are we really going to do this, Mat? What do you want to know about Tara?" I laughed.

"Pathetic, huh?" The rest of us, including Megan, nodded. "Fine. Please tell me if she's seeing anyone."

"Not that I know of, but I haven't had a chance to talk to her much since I got back. I'm spending the day with her tomorrow. I'll find out for you, but Mat, I don't think it's gonna happen with you guys. I'm sorry." I actually felt bad for him.

"Oh, you wait and see," Mat said. "I haven't even started yet. Tara and I are destined for each other! She just doesn't know it yet." I envied him the confidence I was sorely lacking in so many areas of my life.

CHAPTER FOUR

*"...he had a kind of light within that drew me
to him like a moth to a candle."*
–Madeleine L'Engle

The first day of a new semester dawned and I woke with mixed emotions. I had squeezed every bit of enjoyment out of the last week of vacation, spending every second I could with my family and friends because I felt a little bit cheated out of this Christmas break. This was Jack's last semester in high school before he would head off to basic training for army ROTC. We were heading towards such big changes and I felt like things in my life were fast slipping beyond my control. I was still plagued by the awful nightmare of being tied up and kidnapped, although I had hoped it would cease once I got home from Ireland. Instead, it had returned my second night home and nearly every night since. The dark circles under my eyes had taken up permanent residence and I knew my mom, Grams, and Jack were really starting to worry.

I had, against all odds, driven myself to school this morning—I only stalled out twice—and was now standing in the counselor's office, trying to get information about signing up for the ACT before the first bell rang. He was with another student, so I sat in a green vinyl chair, waiting.

"So, Ren, uh, Rem?" My counselor, Mr. Grant, stumbled over the name of the young man he was ushering out of his office.

"It's Rémy, monsieur," the young man replied. He was very good-looking and, judging by his accent, French.

"Ah, that's it, yes. Well, here is your schedule. I'll try to find someone to help you find your first class," he said and then spotted me. "Ah, Miss Moran. Perfect. Can you help this young man find his classroom? He's new." The new guy looked surprised, or maybe interested is a better word, when he heard my name. Odd.

"Uh, sure. I was wondering if I could get information on signing up for the ACT? And could I make an appointment? I'd like to talk about my credits." The new student was staring at me with what could only be described as a smirk. It made me vaguely uncomfortable, although I wasn't sure why.

"Of course. I'll get you a packet and find a time slot for you." He disappeared back into his office. The new kid and I stared at each other, but whereas I felt awkward, I'm pretty sure he didn't; he seemed to exude confidence out of every pore. Was I the only one having a confidence crisis?

"So, you're new here?" I launched the first

conversational volley when I could no longer stand the pregnant silence. "Did you just move to Albuquerque?"

"Ah, oui," he said with a shrug. "I'm on exchange for the rest of the year."

I am not gonna lie and say his deep voice with the accent wasn't the teeniest bit sexy. I may have a boyfriend and all, but I'm not dead.

Mr. Grant came out of his office with an official looking packet. "Here you go, Miss Moran. The deadline for the March test date is this Friday, so be sure to go online and sign up." He handed me a slip of paper. "And here is an appointment."

"Thanks, Mr. Grant. I will." I turned to new exchange kid. "So, uh, you ready to go? I can help you find your class."

"Oh, yes, let me introduce the two of you," Mr. Grant seemed a little flustered and rushed. "This is Ally Moran," he gestured to me. "She's a junior also, and a member of our varsity cheerleading squad." Wow. I had no idea my fame was so widespread that even the counselors knew who I was. "And this is Rémy Giles, a new exchange student from France."

He reached out to shake my hand, but I suddenly knew, without the least shadow of a doubt, I should not let this boy touch me. Something inside me screamed to keep my distance. So, I awkwardly stared at his outstretched hand until Mr. Grant coughed and Rémy slowly withdrew it. Better he think me a rude American than I let him touch me. Trying to cover the awkwardness, I asked to see his schedule, which he handed me with a knowing smile. "Well, we have 1st, 4th , and 7th together. Come on. I'll show you the way and introduce you around a bit, if you want."

"Merci," Rémy said with a slight smirk.

"So, where are you from? And why Albuquerque of all places?" I had my hands stuffed deep in my jacket pockets as we walked so he couldn't 'accidentally' brush up against my skin. I can't explain—well, rationally anyway—why I did not want him touching me; I knew I couldn't let that happen.

"I'm from Rouen in Normandy." At my confused look, since I'm not up on my French geography, he continued, "it's about 130 kilometers northwest from Paris."

First geography and now the metric system? Yikes. "So, how did you end up in Albuquerque? It's kind of off the beaten path."

"Ah, oui." He shrugged again. It seemed like it might be a signature move with him. "There weren't many other choices this late in the year. If I wanted to come to the U.S., I had to be happy with New Mexico. Once I found out it was actually in the United States, I was fine with it."

I chuckled a little, as he seemed to expect. Yeah, we New Mexicans get that a lot.

"So, Ally. That's a very pretty name," he said. "Is it short for something? Alexandra, maybe?" Eww. I think he was starting to hit on me. Maybe. I don't have a lot of experience with hot French guys hitting on me. Or any guys, actually. Jack was the sole exception, and I, sadly, pretty much had to chase him down.

"Nope. Not Alexandra."

"Let's see…Allison?" He was still smirking and I really needed to smack the smirk off his smug face. Hot he might be, but it doesn't excuse annoying in my book.

"Nope, not even close. Here we are: 1st period, pre-calculus." I led the way in and found a few of my cheerleader friends to loose Rémy on. Maybe they would appreciate his French charm in the way he was obviously used to. I sank gratefully into my desk chair. Whew! I was not made for this flirting crap! I took out my cell phone and texted a brief good morning to Jack.

Me: Hey. Good morning.

Jack: Hey beautiful. How r u? C u 4th period. Luv u.

Me: I'm ok. Love you too.

"So, a boyfriend? That's too bad." Rémy was peering over my shoulder, reading my texts. Intrusive little creep!

"Do you mind?" I glared at him, hiding my screen.

He laughed and turned back to the girls who were, as expected, going nuts over him. I guess I couldn't blame them; he truly was very good-looking with golden brown hair, which fell over his forehead in a sexy just-rolled-out-of-bed look and piercing blue eyes. He was dressed differently than the rest of the guys too. His jeans were cut in a way that made them look, I don't know…European, I guess. And he wore a scarf. Yeah. No guys in my high school, and maybe all of Albuquerque, wore a scarf, unless they were gay. Nothing wrong with being gay, but it was pretty obvious Rémy wasn't. And the scarf looked good, damn it. I could appreciate his physical beauty without being attracted to him because my reaction to him was definitely more on the irritated side than anything else. Something about him set my teeth on edge.

At the end of class, Rémy thanked me for showing him around and said he'd see me in 4th period. Then he headed off with a girl named Meredith. Good riddance. I tried not to think about him through 2nd and 3rd periods.

Jack was waiting for me outside of physics. I was so happy to see him after the morning experience with Rémy I couldn't keep myself from giving him a hug and a fairly decent kiss, even though neither of us was much for PDA at school. It simply wasn't classy. There's always an exception, however, and Jack certainly didn't seem to mind my kiss, returning it with enthusiasm.

"Hey, are you okay?" he asked as he pulled away. He ran his thumbs gently over the dark circles under my eyes. "I'm starting to worry, querida. You're not bouncing back like you should."

"I'm fine, Jack. I'm not sleeping well." Before I could elaborate, I heard a throat clearing behind me. Rémy, of course.

"Ah, Ally, this must be the boyfriend. Bonjour, my name is Rémy Giles." He extended his hand to

Jack.

Before I could think to step between them, they were shaking hands.

"Jack Ruiz. Uh, nice to meet you." Jack made it sound almost like a question, which amused me. "So, how do you know Ally?"

"Ah, we met this morning when she was so kind as to show me around the school and introduce me to everyone. I thought we had such a connection, *un coup de foudre*. Love at first sight. But then I find you have a boyfriend and I am desolate, chérie," he addressed me at the end of his ridiculous speech.

"Whatever," I said rudely in response to his cheesy comments. "Rémy is an exchange student, Jack. There was no connection. Let's go." I walked into physics, leaving both Jack and Rémy to follow or not.

Mr. Chiszowski paired Rémy with Veronica, as her former lab partner had dropped out at the semester. As we worked our way through a lab on series circuits, which, as usual, Jack understood and I didn't, I watched Rémy and Veronica across the room. She was so much more subdued since her near-death experience at the hands of Coach Trevino right before Christmas. The old Veronica would have been at the front of the pack flirting and showing off for the hot new guy. This new Veronica sat hunched over her lab table, talking to no one, working quietly on the assignment. I hadn't talked to her since I got back, which I regretted now. I was surprised to see Rémy was different around her: he was quiet and seemed to show her a great deal of deference. It was a different side to him and I didn't know what to think about it.

"That guy bugs you, huh?" Jack looked up from our ammeter and voltmeter.

"Yeah. We didn't hit it off this morning."

He went back to recording the voltage of our circuit. "Well, good. I may not need to kick his ass, then."

I laughed a bit and turned back to help him with the circuit.

***

After physics, Jack and I walked hand-in-hand toward the cafeteria. Annoyingly, Rémy walked alongside, ignoring the fact we hadn't invited him to join us. He kept up a steady stream of inane chatter all the way to the cafeteria. I looked up at Jack, biting my lip to hold back a smile as he rolled his eyes.

"Ally, you are so kind to introduce me to all your friends," Rémy said.

"I never said I would do that. You're simply following us."

"Being the new guy is not easy," he continued as if I hadn't spoken. "I'm so lucky to have found you, chérie."

"Please stop calling me that," I requested through clenched teeth.

"I may have to kick his ass, after all," Jack muttered as we entered the cafeteria.

Rémy again turned on his considerable charm as he was introduced to Tara, Travis, and Dustin. He took Tara's hand and, I kid you not, kissed the back of it, murmuring, "Enchanté, mademoiselle." She clearly bought it, which was disappointing. They sat next to each other and I watched her completely fall under his spell. She actually simpered at him. Great. I was really hoping to find a way to distance myself from him, and he goes and immediately charms my usually taciturn best friend. Did she just giggle? Yuck. Why did he seem to be so intent on worming his way into my inner circle?

"Hey, let's all go to the movies tonight," suggested Tara, prying herself away from him momentarily. "Rémy's never been to an American movie theater. Come on, it'll be fun."

I was having a hard time thinking of something less fun than going on a group date with annoying euro trash. I gave Tara a look that, I hope, said 'forget it, not happening.' She responded with a pleading look.

"Yeah, come on, you guys," added Travis. "We haven't been out together for ages, except after games. I want to hear all the details about what happened with you and Veronica."

Rémy, of course, picked right up on this and wanted to know what he was talking about. Tara and Travis were interrupting each other to tell him all about the steroid scandal from last semester when I happened to glance over and noticed Veronica sitting by herself at a table. She looked depressed and miserable, so I got up and went over to her.

"Hey, Veronica. How's it going?" I sat down next to her.

She looked up from playing with her food. "Oh,

hey. Ally. It's, um, going fine, I guess."

"I'm glad to see you back. I didn't know if you'd be able to come back this soon." Then I wondered if maybe I shouldn't bring up what had happened. Maybe she was trying to forget. I hoped I hadn't stuck my foot in my mouth.

"Yeah, I'm okay to come back to school as long as I take it easy."

"Are you coming back to cheerleading?" I asked hesitantly.

"I don't know," she began. "I'm not sure if I'm allowed. Or if I really want to," she ended on a whisper.

"Well, I hope you decide to come back," I put my hand on hers. "Veronica, come sit with us. Please?" She had said, when I visited her in the hospital, that she wished we could be friends again, so I needed to at least try.

She looked over at our table and sighed. "I don't know. I—"

"Please?" I asked again.

She said nothing, but stood up and began to gather her lunch and followed me back to where my friends were sitting. Rémy stood up and pulled out the chair next to him for her. Jack muttered 'kiss ass' under his breath. Rémy was extremely solicitous to Veronica while still managing to flirt outrageously with Tara.

"So," began Dustin, before it could get too awkward. "Where are we going tonight? Why don't we catch a movie and then walk across the street to ABQ Uptown? We can eat somewhere there, like maybe Elephant Bar. How does that sound?"

The others were amenable and I was about to make up an excuse for Jack and myself when I noticed Tara mouthing 'pretty please' at me. I sighed and looked at Jack, raising my eyebrows. "So how about it? Any chance you're free tonight?" I was praying he'd say no.

He looked at me, completely unenthused, but also having seen Tara's plea. "Yeah, I guess so. I get off work at 6."

"Perfect!" exclaimed Dustin, checking times on his phone. "There are several movies that start at 6:30. We'll all meet by the ticket booth, okay?" We all nodded with varying degrees of enthusiasm.

"Veronica, you want to come with us?" I asked hesitantly.

She shook her head. "Thanks, but I don't think I'll feel up to going out tonight."

Jack walked me to my next class, pulling me into a quieter side hall. He backed me up against some lockers and swooped in for a good kiss. We were trying our best to make up for all the kisses we had missed while I was in Ireland.

"I think you're going to owe me big time for putting up with that French douche bag tonight," he said as he nibbled his way along my jaw to my ear, which he knew pretty much rendered me incoherent.

"Well, you can name your price. I promise to make good on my debt," I whispered with a delicious shiver. Jack sure can kiss. He laughed and sent me off to my next class with a light swat on my rear end.

CHAPTER FIVE

"The pattern is closely woven."
–Madeleine L'Engle

We ended up watching the newest Marvel comic book story to be made into a movie. I usually love this kind of movie, but tonight I was too distracted by the teen drama surrounding me. Jack apparently thought it was a great idea to invite Mat to come along on our group date and Mat thought it would be a great idea to bring a date.

"I didn't invite him, querida," Jack said as the previews were ending. "I told you, he invited himself. He just showed up here with that girl."

I sat stewing in my seat, refusing to hold his hand. I had been cranky since Mat and his date showed up and was taking it out on Jack. We were surrounded by people dedicated to outdoing each other with their flirting and cute-couple behavior. On one side were Tara and Rémy, feeding each other popcorn and giggling. On the other side was Mat and his girl—I think he introduced her as

Jeanette or Lynette—drinking from the same soda cup at the same time with twin straws. Whenever Tara did something cute with Rémy, Mat would counter with something equally nauseating with his date. I was thoroughly disgusted and sat with my arms crossed, staring grumpily at the screen. Travis and Dustin, however, sat holding hands. obviously enjoying the movie, oblivious to the tension around them. It must be nice. Why should I care what Tara did? Why did it bother me so much? And why was I wasting time worrying about it when I could be holding hands with *my* boyfriend? I looked over at Jack; he was slumped in his seat, chin in hand, pretending to watch the movie. This was no more his fault than mine; neither of us had wanted to be part of this awful group date. There was no logical reason for me to take it out on him. I sighed and scooted closer to him, reaching out to take his hand. "I'm sorry."

He sat up and interlaced his fingers with mine. "Yeah, me too." Both couples were still at it: flirting, giggling, and other barf-inducing behavior. "Come on," Jack said as he gathered up our popcorn and soda. I followed him as he chose new seats in the top row of the theater, far enough away to not have to deal with the ridiculous teen drama happening down in the front.

"You're pretty smart, you know that?" I said as I leaned closer to kiss his cheek, staying to run my lips right under his jaw line.

"Behave yourself, minx," he said, holding my face captive in his hands. He looked into my eyes for a moment. "Aw, screw it." He leaned back in to kiss me deeply, his tongue seeking mine. We let ourselves enjoy it for a few minutes, sinking into the kiss, before finally breaking apart, panting slightly. "We should fight more often," Jack said huskily.

I couldn't even speak, so I simply nodded.

***

Later, as we sat in a back corner of the Elephant Bar, across the street from the movie theater, the teenage drama show continued. It was excruciatingly clear to most of us at the table that Mat was simply trying to make Tara jealous and had no feelings at all for Jeanette/Lynette. Well, maybe it wasn't clear to her, since she seemed to be lapping up all the attention from Mat, who was at his most charming tonight. I watched Rémy carefully to see what his reaction would be, if he was picking up on the underlying currents. He met my gaze, gave me an amused smirk, and even had the audacity to wink. This guy confused me. Was he really interested in Tara? Had he really hit on me this morning and then by lunchtime switched to my best friend? And why had I felt such a strong compulsion to not let him touch me? I got the distinct impression, psychic or not, there was much more to Monsieur Rémy Giles than met the eye, and I was determined to figure out what it was.

"So, where did you two disappear to during the movie, huh?" Tara took a break from flirting to ask Jack and me.

I squeezed Jack's hand under the table. "Oh, I

didn't like sitting so close to the screen."

The others all either smirked or snickered. Tara laughed outright. "Whatever. Liar. You always want to sit right in the front. Did you guys even watch the movie? Or did you make out the whole time?'

Jack laughed and put his arm around me, hugging me close, and kissing my hair. "Yeah, well I still haven't made up for all the time I missed while she was in Ireland."

"Why were you in Ireland?" Rémy asked, accompanied by a rather sharp look.

I met his stare for a moment. "Oh, you know. Just a vacation." I didn't look away from him, although I could feel Jack looking between the two of us, confused.

"Where did you go? Dublin?" he asked, continuing our staring contest.

"No. Galway." I would not be the first to blink.

"It's a beautiful city, no?" He stared for what seemed like several minutes, but was probably shorter. Finally, he gave me another one of those damned smirks and looked away, picking up Tara's hand and turning it over to kiss her wrist. God, I really did not like this guy.

"What the hell?" Jack whispered in my ear.

"Later," I whispered back.

***

Before Jack dropped me off later, I told him about my weird reaction to Rémy in the counselor's office when I felt like I should absolutely not let him touch me.

"Yeah, that's weird," he agreed. "And at dinner he asked *why* you were in Ireland. It was kind of strange, you know? I mean, most people would ask about where you went, what you did, stuff like that. This French dude just asks 'why' in a creepy way. And what was with the staring contest?"

"I don't know. I do know he creeps me out. I don't trust him and I don't like how he's suddenly all over Tara. He was hitting on me and then all of a sudden he switches to Tara?"

"Hey, you're not jealous, are you?" He kissed my neck, which usually puts a hold on our conversations.

"Hmm, no. I have no need of pretentious French euro trash when I have you, Jack."

"I don't know," he teased. "Maybe the whole exotic foreigner thing turns you on. He could probably whisper to you in French. Don't girls like that?"

"Well, you can whisper to me in Spanish. Why don't we see if it turns me on?"

He obliged, alternating whispers with nibbles on my earlobe.

"Yeah. That'll do the trick." I sighed and pulled his face to mine and kissed him in earnest.

***

I was about halfway through *A Ring of Endless Light*. I'm usually a faster reader, but I hadn't had a lot of time to read since I got back. Plus, due to my nightly nightmares, I was so sleepy I wasn't able to

58

read more than a few paragraphs before I fell asleep. The girl in the novel, Vicky, had three guys after her and she was able to communicate telepathically with dolphins, which was very cool. One of the guys, Zack, was deeply troubled and selfish, but they had great chemistry. The guy who introduced her to the dolphins, Adam, reminded me a lot of Jack and I was rooting for them to get together. It was much more than simply a romance, however. She was dealing with her grandfather's impending death and the recent death of a family friend, the father of the third guy. I really liked how she wrote poetry, which I, like every other teenage girl, had tried when I was in one of my more angsty, melodramatic phases. Let's just say I suck at poetry. It was comforting, somehow, to read about how this girl was trying to come to terms with all the crap in her life. It made me hopeful I could do the same.

I fell asleep and, once again, found myself in the midst of the nightmare.

I fought my way to consciousness, my head still fuzzy. Where was I? I tried to remember what had happened, but I couldn't focus. I tried to move and discovered my hands were bound. My heart pounded in terror. I tried to scream, but I was gagged. I was having such a hard time concentrating. Had I been drugged? The vibrations and bouncing reminded me I was in a vehicle. Was I in the trunk? No, it seemed more like I was on the floor of a backseat. The car turned and I bounced painfully. Were we on a dirt road? The bumping and bouncing went on for what felt like hours. Then the vehicle came to a stop.

I woke with a choked scream, sitting up in bed, my heart pounding, and I was covered in sweat. The nightmare was the same as always, but it had never gone on for so long; I always woke while the vehicle was still moving. I was absolutely terrified of what I would learn the next time I had the dream. It was several hours before I was calm enough to get to sleep.

***

I fell asleep in physics the next day. Mr. Chiszowski was showing us a film about electric cars, and the combination of a dark room and my sleepless night equaled lights out for me. I awoke to Jack softly rubbing my back and whispering in my ear, "Wake up, sweetheart. The movie's over and Mr. Chiszowski is about to notice you slept through it."

I reluctantly sat up. "I think I drooled. I must disgust you," I said while wiping my mouth. I had been deeply asleep, not an easy task while sitting at a lab table.

"Nah, it was cute," Jack said.

On the way to lunch, after I finished putting away my morning books, Jack turned me around with my back to my locker. "Why are you so tired lately, querida? Are you working a graveyard shift I don't know about?" His concerned look belied the light teasing.

I laughed briefly and hugged him. "No. I'm not sleeping well. I'm, uh, well, I'm having a recurring nightmare and it's keeping me awake. It sucks. I'm so tired."

"Well, with all the shit you went through last semester, it's no wonder. What's the dream about?"

I sighed. "I keep dreaming about being kidnapped. It's probably leftover stress, but the dream goes a little bit farther each night, which stresses me out even more."

He pulled back to look in my eyes. "Can your grandmother give you a prescription for some sleeping pills or something? I'm starting to get worried, Ally."

I pulled away and took his hand, walking toward the cafeteria. "She probably could, but I haven't talked to her or my mom about it yet." I saw he was about to protest, so I preempted him, saying, "I will, I promise. If the dreams don't go away by the end of the week I'll talk to her. You worry too much. Hey, your birthday is this weekend," I changed the subject. "What does Trina have planned? Can I steal you for a night?"

"Sure. Let me talk to Trina. She probably wants to have a dinner. I'm going to see if I can get her to minimize the occasion. I don't want her to fuss."

"Good luck with that. She's a born fusser."

***

"All right, question number 8," Tara said. We were lounging in her room later in the evening as she administered the latest *Cosmo* quiz, 'What Kind of Sexy Are You?' "For the ultimate holiday present, you'd give your guy: a) Tasteful nude photos of yourself, b) Surfing/golfing/skydiving lessons, or c) A classic silver watch?"

"Hmm. Well, if it has to be *tasteful* nude photos, I'm gonna have to go with surfing lessons. Those will come in so handy here in Albuquerque," I answered.

"B then," she said, oblivious to my sarcasm. "Next question: Fill in the blank: If I were reincarnated as a bra, I'd be…a) plain white cotton with a T-back, b) a red satin, cleavage-maximizing, diamond-encrusted bustier, or c) pale pink lace with a tiny bow?"

"Gosh, I don't want to be boring, but I have no cleavage to maximize and those diamonds sound itchy. Let's go with the pink bow."

"C it is. Last question. Your favorite sex pose is: a) you on top, frontward, b) you on top, backward, or c) him on top. You like the feeling of being enveloped?"

"This got uncomfortable," I said, flushing.

"Don't be a prude." She tapped her pen on the magazine. "I'm waiting."

"Yeah, yeah. I'm trying to figure out if 'frontward' is really a word. In lieu of actual experience with any poses, I'll say c."

"Great. Let me tally your results." I waited while she tallied and counted. "Okay, you are 'fun-lovin' sexy.' You're the quintessential natural-yet-naughty chick," she read. "What men find so appealing about you is that you're rough-and-tumble yet tender. He has his best friend whom he can still open doors for and have a terrific sex life with. Wow, sounds great, huh? You're really lucky, you know?"

I caught a rare glimpse of her vulnerable side as she looked out the window for a moment. "Hey, it's a dumb quiz. It doesn't mean anything," I said as I put my arm around her shoulder.

She chuckled without any mirth at all. "Oh, I know. It's not that. It's seeing you with Jack, so happy. I mean, I'm not jealous…okay maybe a little." She laughed and laid her head on my shoulder. "I wish I had something like that too."

"Hey, you will. I mean, you've got two guys after you right now. I'm pretty sure you could have your pick of either of them."

"Ha. I mean Rémy is fun and all, but I don't think it will ever go anywhere. Even if it did, he lives in freaking France."

"What about Mat? He lives right here in good ol' Albuquerque."

"Forget it. He's not my type. Did you see the floozy he brought to the movies? Her eyebrows were painted on! And she was hanging all over him." She tried to appear casual, putting the magazine back on her desk and pretending to straighten up the items on top.

"Oh, and you weren't hanging all over Rémy?"

"Ouch. Hello pot, I'm kettle. You weren't exactly 'hands off' with Jack, you know. Didn't you two sneak off to make out?"

"Uh, yeah, but we're in a stable relationship. We weren't on a first date, you slut," I teased.

She laughed. "Rémy's fun, but that's it. I was mostly trying to make Mat mad. I can't believe he showed up like that! What a jerk!"

"Hey, go easy on him. He's not only Jack's

cousin; they're best friends. I'd like us all to be able to get along. I don't want awkwardness, okay?" I grabbed her arm and made her look at me.

"But he's so…ugh!"

I looked at her, eyebrows raised.

She sighed in disgust. "Fine. I'll play nice. But I don't like him!"

"Careful, chica. You might be protesting a bit too much."

"Shut up! Are you staying the night? We haven't had a sleepover in ages," she wheedled.

"Sure, but I may not be much fun. I'll probably crash way early. I'm so tired, Tara." I was holding back a yawn.

"Hey, you still having those nightmares?" I had told only Tara and Jack about the horrible dreams. I nodded.

"You don't think these dreams are, like, psychic, do you? You know, part of your powers?"

I hadn't thought of this, but now I sat on her bed, pondering the possibility. I didn't know if dreams could be part of my…repertoire? But I suppose they could. "I don't know. I've been assuming they were stress related, but now I'm not so sure. These dreams don't feel like any of my future visions, so I really hope they're not a warning I'm about to be kidnapped." I shivered.

Tara sat down next to me. "Hey, I'm sure that's not going to happen. Don't worry. You're probably right and they're simply stress dreams. I've got a great idea—why don't you start focusing on having sex dreams instead of stress dreams? Sounds like a lot more fun to me."

I laughed. "Yeah, it does. I'll work on it."

CHAPTER SIX

"Contending with the fretful elements;
Bids the wind blow the earth into the sea,
Or swell the curled waters 'bove the main,
That things might change or cease."
–Shakespeare –King Lear (3.1.4)

Trina couldn't be stopped. She definitely fussed for Jack's birthday, preparing a huge spread of food and inviting a slew of relatives who all brought food as well. In the Jimenez family, special occasions, or any reasonable facsimile thereof, meant family—lots of family. All of Manny and Trina's kids were there: Mat, of course; Shelly and her husband, Don, along with their young son, Nathan; Mat's oldest brother, Paul, and his wife, Elise; their kids, Josue, Becky, and Roberto; and his next older brother, Jason, with his fiancée, Jasmine. His grandparents and several aunts and uncles, along with at least ten other cousins were also there. It was very much like his post-probation party, but with presents. Trina baked a giant cake with nineteen candles, which

Mat had secretly swapped out for trick candles.

"Oh, Mat!" she cried, exasperated, while everyone was laughing. "When will you grow up?" She lightly smacked the back of his head. "Get these candles out so I can cut the cake!"

As Jack finished opening his presents, Shelly stood up to get everyone's attention. "Jack, sweetie, I know this is your birthday, and I don't want to take away any of your glory." Jack rolled his eyes. "But I can't pass up the chance to tell so much of our family at one time," she paused for effect, looking around at everyone. "Little Nathan is going to be a big brother!"

The room erupted in cheers, tears, and a complete hug-fest. Trina was a soggy mess. In the midst of all the chaos, Megan came over and quietly stood by me, saying nothing and looking too sober.

"Hey, munchkin. What's wrong?" I asked.

She shook her head, so I took her hand. She crawled onto my lap and curled up. "Is Shelly going to have a baby?" she whispered.

"Yeah, sweetie. What's wrong? Everyone's happy." It about broke my heart to see a tear trickle down her cheek. I didn't know what to do or how to comfort her, so I picked her up and carried her into the next room, away from all the noise, tugging Jack's shirt as I walked by him.

He followed us and sat down next to us on the couch in the family room, pulling Megan into his lap. "Hey, what are these tears for? What's the matter?" Megan shrugged. He met my confused gaze as I shook my head.

"Are you upset about Shelly having a baby?"

Jack asked. She shrugged again. Then she nodded slightly. "Tell me, Meg."

"Will Aunt Trina still take care of me?" she whispered.

"Of course she will," he said as he rubbed her back. "Megan, sweetie, Trina is excited she's going to be a grandma again. That's all. You don't have to worry. She will still love you and take care of you."

We managed to convince Megan, for the moment at any rate, she was not about to be replaced. Poor thing; she was so young when she was moved to Albuquerque, but she apparently had some deep-seated issues. Jack carried her upstairs to tuck her in while I returned to the party to make his excuses. Once he came back downstairs, we stayed for only about fifteen minutes before I asked him to take me home.

"Well, shit," he said as he settled behind the wheel of his Mustang. He scrubbed both his hands over his face in frustration.

"Hey," I said softly, reaching over to touch him. "She'll be okay, Jack."

"Yeah, I know. It's just…I don't know. It seems like my past keeps sneaking back in to kick me in the ass."

"Jack, it's Megan's past too."

"You think I don't know that?" he yelled. I flinched back in my seat, jerking my hand away from him as if I'd been burned. He let out a breath. "I'm sorry, Ally. I don't mean to take it out on you."

"Can we drive for a while?" I asked, crossing my arms in front of me. He nodded and put the car into gear. He drove us across the Rio Grande river to the West Mesa. We didn't speak until he pulled off to the side of the road on Nine Mile Hill where the view of the middle Rio Grande valley and the twinkling lights of Albuquerque stretched all the way to the Sandia Mountains in the east. It was breathtaking and we spent a few minutes to take it all in. We got out of the car and walked around to lean on the hood.

"I'm really sorry I yelled at you," he said quietly, linking his hand with mine.

"It doesn't matter, Jack."

"It does. You deserve to be treated better."

I turned to look at him and could see he wasn't done beating himself up over his outburst. "You're allowed to have a temper. So am I, and if you don't quit this self-castigating behavior, I'm gonna get pissed off."

One side of his mouth lifted, as if he was trying to hold back a smile. "Nice vocab. Okay, let me apologize once more and then I'll be done." He turned and took my chin in his hand. "I'm sorry, querida." He leaned in to kiss me softly.

"That's better," I sighed. "Let's not waste this perfectly lovely scenic overlook with arguing." So we didn't.

He kissed me all too briefly and then turned me around to lean back against him, his arms wrapped around me, protecting me from the cold wind. "Megan was so little when we left Taos—a baby, really. She doesn't even remember our mom and dad. I thought—hoped she would settle in with Trina and Manny, and she mostly has, but every once in a while she has one of these…panic attacks I guess you could call them. God, it kills me to see her like that."

I turned in his arms and held him tightly. "Jack, you are doing such a great job with her. Everyone has moments of insecurity. She's going to be fine. She has a great family, you know."

"Yeah, I know. I hate to see her so insecure," he sighed. "She shouldn't have to go through this crap."

I leaned back against his chest. "You can't fix everything, Jack. I love that you want to try, but this is beyond your control."

He turned me around to face him. "You're pretty smart, you know? You're also pretty sexy."

"You think so?" I teased. "Well, what are you gonna do about it?"

He showed me exactly what he was going to do about it.

***

The next evening, I took Jack out for his birthday. I picked him up in my VW, refusing to let him drive so it wouldn't ruin the surprise. He managed not to cringe too much at my rough starts out of first gear. He always spoiled me rotten, driving all the time, paying for every date we went on, so I dipped into my savings and splurged on a romance package at a fondue restaurant, The Melting Pot, complete with roses, surf-n-turf, and sparkling cider.

"Ally, sweetheart, this is wonderful, but

extravagant, to say the least. You don't eat either surf or turf," he complained. "What are you going to have here?"

"Says the guy who got me a car for my birthday. There are plenty of vegetables and bread I can cook and dip in the fondue. Don't worry about me."

"The car was for Christmas. I feel like a kept man."

I laughed. "Shh. Don't spoil my fun, okay?"

He sighed. "Fine." He poured us each some cider and handed me a glass. "How about we toast to my beautiful, amazing girlfriend, then?"

I raised my glass to touch his. Before he took a sip, he leaned across the table to kiss me. "You say the sweetest things," I murmured against his lips. "I want to give you your present now," I said, leaning back.

"All this *and* a present? We're going to have to set some rules in the future."

"Whatever. Like you'd ever abide by them. All right, I can do this." I took a deep breath and reached in my bag for his gift.

"Are you nervous, querida? Why?"

"Um, yeah. I'm not sure you're going to like what I got you. Do you have any idea how hard guys are to shop for?"

"Of course I'll like it." He rolled his eyes. "I'll like anything you give me."

"Yeah, I'll remind you of that when all I can think of is a tie or an ugly sweater. Okay, here goes." I handed him the box.

I had to practically sit on my hands as he unwrapped the Claddagh ring I had bought him in

Galway. I was so nervous. What if he hated it? What if he thought it was too presumptuous of me? If he thought it signified a more serious relationship than we had? But he had said he loved me, right? So, maybe…argh! Oh my God! Calm down already! "So, the crown stands for loyalty, the hands for friendship, and the heart for love. You wear it on your right hand facing inward to show you're in a relationship, so…" I couldn't continue and I couldn't look at his face.

"Like this?" He took my hand in his, the ring on his right hand ring finger. "You got a matching one?" I had put mine on for the first time tonight. "I love it, Ally. It's really special. Thank you." He got up and came around the table to pull me into his arms and kiss me deeply. "Why were you so worried? It's a perfect gift."

"I don't know. I didn't know if you'd think it was too girly or presumptuous or something."

"It's not girly at all, sweetheart. And what do you mean by presumptuous?"

I couldn't meet his eyes. "I mean, like, if you thought I was presuming too much about our relationship or something."

He raised my chin with his fingers, forcing me to look at him. "Ally, I am completely and totally in love with you. You are not presuming too much to give me a ring announcing to the world we are in a relationship. I wish I had thought of it first, actually."

"Really?"

"Really." He kissed me. "I don't think you realize how much I love you."

"I'm beginning to get the picture," I said and pulled him down for another kiss.

Later, over a dessert of fruit, cake cubes, and white and dark chocolate fondue, I decided it was time to drop the bomb I had been saving for several days.

"Jack, do you remember before Christmas, when you told me about graduating early and joining ROTC?"

He finished chewing and put down his skewer. "Crap. Is this going to be one of those conversations?"

"Yep. I'm afraid so." I put down my skewer and reached across to take his hand, looking him directly in the eye. "I saw my counselor this week. The short version is I signed up for the same eCademy online courses you did and I'm taking a community college English class my counselor signed off on to count for my senior English credit. I'm graduating this May with you, Jack."

"What? Ally, you're not doing this because of me, are you?" he said.

"No, not entirely. I will admit I got the idea from you, but I'm doing it for myself. Jack, I've never made a secret of the fact that I hate high school. And lately, with all this Seer/Oracle crap, I think it's a good idea not to be tied up there any longer than necessary."

"What about cheerleading?" he countered.

I looked him in the eye. "Fun, but not nearly enough to keep me tethered to all the teenage drama that comes with it."

He smiled wryly. "Yeah, I understand. Listen, I

won't lie—the idea that we can be in college together next year is awesome. As long as it's something you want for yourself. How are your mom and grandmother with this?"

"They took it surprisingly well, actually. Mom showed us an article, which proposes the idea that high school in general should only be three years."

"How did Tara take it?"

"She freaked out, of course. She hurled some truly impressive nasty names at me and then high-tailed it to the counselor's office to do the exact same thing," I admitted.

"So, will Tara be joining us at UNM next year, or is she going out of state, by some miracle?" he asked in a serious tone.

"Be nice." I laughed. "No, I'm afraid she is going to UNM with us. She's trying to talk me into rooming with her in the dorms."

"Sounds fun. Do you want to?"

"I'd rather room with you," I said with what I hoped was a seductive glance.

"Thanks for the mental image. I'm not going to be able to think of anything else now." He put his head in his hands and groaned.

"Good. I think it's a fabulous idea."

"Yeah, and I'm sure your mother would love it too. And I can imagine how hard Manny would kick my ass. Listen, sweetheart." He leaned forward and clasped both my hands on the table. "You will still be seventeen when we start college next fall. How about we shelve any discussion about moving in together until you're at least eighteen, okay? For my sanity, please?"

"God, you're noble. Are you sure you're actually human? Do I not tempt you in the least?"

"Ally," he said, sounding a bit dangerous. "If we were not in a public restaurant right now, I would show you exactly how much you tempt me. Now behave yourself. Besides, Mat is nagging me to move into an apartment with him as soon as I graduate."

"I know! Tara can move in with Mat and I'll move in with you. It's the perfect solution!"

"You're hilarious. It's not happening." He released my hands and sat back. "You know, Ally, sweetheart, I smell a rat. I think you totally distracted me from the main discussion by bringing up living arrangements. Confess, you little manipulator!"

I tried my best to look innocently down at the table, but couldn't keep from laughing and was relieved when he joined in. "I'm sorry, Jack. I didn't mean to be manipulative. Sorry for my pathetic seduction attempts."

"Your seduction attempts are anything but pathetic. But seriously, is graduating early really your decision?"

"Yes. Please stop worrying about it. I am absolutely sure about this. I am beyond ready to be done with high school. If you were to dump me tomorrow, I would still stick with my plan," I assured him.

He smiled. "Fine. I'll stop worrying. I'm really glad we are going to be graduating at the same time. And I have no plans to dump you tomorrow or any other day."

***

Sunday morning, as we divided up the chores for the weekly top-to-bottom housecleaning torture my grandmother had devised years earlier, my mom dropped a small bomb of her own.

"Oh, by the way," she said with studied casualness, "I'm having a friend over for dinner this evening. I would appreciate if you were both here and on your best behavior." She didn't even look up from her chore list.

Grams and I met each other's surprised gaze, which quickly morphed into evil grins. "So, we finally get to meet your boyfriend, Mom? It's about time," I said.

"Yes, Jen. I was beginning to think you had invented him," Grams said breezily.

"Or maybe," my mother said as she ripped off the list of chores and handed them to each of us, "I wanted to make sure I was serious about him before inflicting you two on the poor man. Don't embarrass me tonight." She pinned each of us with a sharp look that probably scared the crap out of the little kids at the school where she was the principal.

Grams and I howled with laughter as Mom gathered her list and left the room.

"Well, Grams, as tempting as it is to devise ways to have fun at her expense tonight, I really think we should be on our best behavior. She's never brought a guy home before and we don't want to scare him away." I looked at her sternly. "So, no wigs, tea parties, or anything else weird. I need you to be normal, or whatever passes for normal around here, all right?"

"Fine. Spoilsport," she muttered.

"Grams, did she really say she was serious about this guy? I don't know what I think about this. Have you seen him yet?"

"Nope. She's been keeping him on the DL for sure." Only my grandmother could pull off such a comment. "I'm going to go pump her for some more info so I can cyber-stalk him before he gets here."

***

When the doorbell rang promptly at 6 p.m., Grams and I were in place, both looking normal, but armed with the 411, as Grams put it, on one Brian Keller, 20-year decorated veteran homicide detective with the Albuquerque Police Department. I think she was actually disappointed not to find anything juicy about him.

Mom led him into the living room to meet us and I had to hand it to her: he was pretty cute for an older guy. He looked to be somewhere near 40, but I have to admit I'm not good with ages of people older than about 25. They all kind of look generic middle-aged. He was a lot taller than my mom and had light brown hair with a hint of gray around the temples. He had bright blue eyes that crinkled at the edges when he smiled, like maybe he knew how to laugh. For his sake I hoped so, since his day job was dealing with murderers. He shook hands with both Grams and I, looking us in the eye and not seeming awkward or stand-offish. So far, so good. He seemed nice and I got decent vibes from him, so I relaxed and decided to see how the rest of the evening went. Mom had prepared a great dinner of her signature pasta Puttanesca, making a special dish of it for me without the anchovies, capers, or olives, all of which are disgusting and which pretty much left tomatoes and garlic, but Brian seemed to be enjoying it.

"This is delicious, Jennifer. What's it called?" he asked. It was strange to hear someone call my mom 'Jennifer.' Everyone else called her Jen.

"It's called Puttanesca," Grams jumped in, "which means 'streetwalker.'" She watched him carefully for a reaction. "One story goes that the ladies of the evening would put it on their window sills to entice clients in with the smell."

"My favorite story is the one where the 'ladies' would fix it after a busy night at work to replenish their energy. Carb-loading, you know?" I added.

Brian smiled and said, "Well, it would definitely entice me. I don't think I'll even attempt to address your story, Ally."

Grams and I both laughed. Mom rolled her eyes. "What did I say about not embarrassing me? Honestly, you two!"

"So, Ally, your mom says you're a cheerleader. That's great. I played football in high school." Brian was definitely trying to change the subject for my mother's benefit.

"Did you go to high school here in Albuquerque?"

"No, I grew up in southern California, in Anaheim, actually."

"Wow. Did you go to Disneyland all the time?" I asked.

He chuckled a bit. "Not all the time, but probably a lot more than your average person. Have you been?"

"Once. Grams took us when I was 8. It was magical," I sighed. "But I think I would be able to appreciate it better now. I think we should definitely go this summer to celebrate my graduation. Hint, hint."

"I thought your mom said you were a junior?"

"I am, but I'm graduating a year early."

"Oh, so you're a smart kid, huh?" he asked, smiling, but in a nice way.

"More of smart ass, actually," Grams interjected. "So, you're a homicide detective, Brian? It sounds fascinating, yet morbid. How do you stand dealing with death every day?"

"Well, I don't really think of it like that. I think of it as bringing justice and closure to families."

"So, what kinds of cases have you worked? Anything we might have heard of?" Grams continued her interrogation. Brian might want to consider recruiting her.

"Well, I can't really talk about any active investigations, but I worked the case of the couple who were found in the trunk of the burned-out car a couple years ago. The guy got sentenced last month."

"Ugh, what a horrible case," my mom sighed. "Those poor people."

Brian reached over and took her hand in a sweet way. I was liking this guy; he seemed to treat my mom well. "And I recently picked up the Ashley Hayes case, which I'm sure you've heard about since it's been all over the news lately."

"That's the body they found a few weeks ago up by Sandia Man Cave, isn't it?" Grams asked.

"Yeah. It was a missing persons case, a thirty year-old cold case, until a hiker and his dog stumbled across her remains. I was assigned to it yesterday. It should be very interesting."

Where had I heard that name before? It sounded very familiar to me, but I couldn't think where I had heard it. It felt like a bell or something went off in my head, like I was supposed to remember something, but it was just out of reach. Well, this was going to bug me until I figured it out.

"So, Brian, tell us about yourself. How old are you? Have you ever been married? Do you have any children?" Grams continued. I could see my mother seething, but she was powerless to stop her mother from grilling the new boyfriend. It was actually enjoyable to watch when it wasn't a guy I had brought home. I had to admire my grandmother's chutzpah.

Brian seemed to have been forewarned, because he cast my mom an amused look before launching into his answers. "Well, ma'am, I'm 42. I was married once, briefly, when I was barely out of college, and I don't have any children."

"Oh, so you're divorced?"

"No, ma'am. I'm a widower. My wife died of a brain tumor," he said quietly. This time Mom reached over to take his hand.

"Oh, I'm so sorry, Brian," Grams apologized. "I

didn't mean to pry."

I choked a bit on a bite of bread. The day my grandmother didn't mean to pry would be a cold day in hell.

We rounded out the dinner with a beautiful tiramisu, which my mom certainly didn't make except on the most special of occasions. She was going all out to impress this guy, which I guess I understood after meeting him. He seemed pretty great. As we were getting started on dessert, the doorbell rang again.

"That's Jack," I said. "We're going to get started on our online classes tonight." I got up to let him in.

"Well, bring him in for dessert. There's plenty," Mom assured me.

I introduced him to Brian and they hit it off right away, discussing the latest NBA scores. I think Brian was relieved to have a momentary escape from all the estrogen.

After we finished dessert, I sent Jack into the living room to get set up for homework while I cleared the table. I walked into the kitchen, hands full of plates, and was shocked to see Brian and my mom kissing passionately. It gave me a funny feeling in the pit of my stomach. "Uh, sorry," I apologized awkwardly as I set the dirty dishes down and beat a hasty retreat. They broke apart guiltily, and I heard my mom giggle. Giggle! I don't think 36 year old women should giggle. I walked into the living room in a daze, flopping on the couch beside Jack.

"Hey, what's up?" he asked, noticing I was sitting there, not picking up my laptop. "Ally, querida? You okay?"

"No," I breathed. "I just walked in on my mom and Brian sucking face in the kitchen."

"Way to go, Brian," he responded, chuckling.

I punched him lightly on the arm. "No, not 'way to go.' It was deeply disturbing. Children should not have to see their mothers French kissing. I may need therapy."

"Therapy, huh? Sounds serious." He put his computer down and took my face in his hands. "I think I can help. I'm sure I can think of something to drive those awful memories away." He leaned in and placed his lips softly on mine. I would never get tired of the feel of his mouth against mine, the taste of him on my tongue. The funny feeling was back, but for entirely different reasons.

"Well, thank goodness you were here to save me," I whispered against his lips. He smiled and pushed me back against the cushions, deepening the kiss.

"Ahem," my mother interrupted, Brian at her side. "Uh, *sorry,*" she mocked me. "Brian and I are going out for a bit. Grams already left. So you two are on your own. I trust it won't be a problem, will it, Jack?" Her meaning was abundantly clear and embarrassing all at the same time.

"No ma'am. Not at all. You can trust me." He couldn't help but look ashamed. I rolled my eyes and shook my head at her.

They left and I sat up, my face in my hands. "I'm so sorry, Jack. That was embarrassing."

He laughed, taking my hands away from my face. "Not really. I will never be embarrassed about kissing you, sweetheart." He kissed me again. "And she was absolutely right to remind me to behave. Knowing we're alone in your house might be enough to make me forget all my good intentions."

"Ooh, that sounds intriguing and promising," I said as I kissed him back, this time pushing him back against the cushions.

He kissed me back for a moment before sitting up and gently pushing me away. "Homework time," he stated firmly.

"Fine." I huffed. It was sweet he felt this way, but it was frustrating, too. Although, if I was totally honest with myself, I was relieved my boyfriend wasn't pressuring me. If he ever called my bluff, I would almost certainly chicken out. I wasn't nearly as worldly as I pretended.

We spent almost two hours working on our online classes, economics and government, which were boring in the extreme, but at least we were spending time together. I guess that's how you know you really love someone: when even something boring is enjoyable because you're doing it with the right person.

Later, I walked Jack out to his car when he was ready to go home. As I was kissing him goodnight, I was swept into a vision.

A man leaned against Jack's car, his '65 Mustang. I was walking toward him and he stood up straight as I approached. As I got closer, I could see he looked familiar; he actually reminded me a lot of Jack, but about 20 years older.

I gasped and Jack said, "What, Ally? What did you see?" By this time he was used to my freaky visions.

"I think I saw a vision of you, in the future." I tried to catch my breath as I steadied myself.

"Hey, take it easy. Are you all right?"

"Yeah, I'm fine. It was nothing upsetting. I saw you, only older, leaning against your car. That's it; you didn't do anything except stand up as I approached. I guess you keep it for a long time, huh? I wonder why I would see something like that? Weird, isn't it?"

"Yeah, weird." He looked tense for some reason. "I gotta go, sweetheart. I'll see you tomorrow, okay?" He kissed me quickly and left rather abruptly. Was it something I said?

***

The next afternoon, Jack and I were walking out to the student parking lot together, making plans to get together after he got off work to do more online homework. I wasn't paying much attention to our surroundings and was surprised when Jack stopped suddenly about 50 feet from where our cars were parked side-by-side. I heard him curse under his breath.

"What is it?" I stopped beside him and looked around, quickly locating what he had seen. A man was leaning against his Mustang, standing up straight as he saw us approach. I looked up at Jack in shock. "But...it's my vision." I could see his jaw tense, anger beginning to ooze out of him, yet he didn't look nearly as shocked as I would expect. "Is that your father?" I asked quietly. He nodded. "You knew. Last night, when I had the vision, you knew, didn't you?"

"I suspected. Shit," he sighed.

"I can leave," I offered. "So you can…"

He clenched my hand tightly. "Please stay." I nodded and we walked together toward his father.

CHAPTER SEVEN

*"...it was as though two different worlds had
bumped into each other, and I was
shaking from the collision."*
–Madeleine L'Engle

Jack and his father stared at each other, neither saying anything. I don't think Jack realized how hard he was squeezing my hand, but I wasn't about to bring it to his attention. You've heard the expression about tension so thick you could cut it with a knife? Well, I never gave it any credence before, but this was a great example of it. As I looked between the two men, I was amazed at their resemblance. Jack's father had a slightly darker complexion and his hair had silver threads running throughout, but they had the same eyes, the same nose, and the same strong jawline. No wonder I thought the vision I had was of Jack in the future; I felt like I was getting a glimpse of what he would look like in twenty or so years. His father was almost as good-looking as Jack, but I hoped Jack wouldn't have the haunted, broken look in his eyes I saw in the older man.

"Jackson." His father finally broke the silence.

"Dad," Jack choked out. "What are you doing here?"

"I need to talk to you, son."

"Fine. So talk," Jack ground the words out.

"Could we go somewhere for a few minutes? Alone?" I noticed his father had a thicker accent than Jack and remembered he was raised in Mexico.

Jack shook his head. "No. Here is fine. And she stays." He stared hard at his father for a moment, then finally relented slightly, saying, "This is my girlfriend, Ally Moran. Ally, this is my father, Marcos Ruiz." We shook hands briefly.

His father nodded slightly, looking sadder and more defeated. "I wanted to let you know I've moved to Albuquerque. I've been hired as an adjunct professor at the university."

"That's great, Dad," Jack said in a completely flat voice. "Congratulations. I hope you'll be really happy. I didn't know they hired drunks to be professors."

I looked up at him sharply, shocked at his cruelty. His skin was drawn tightly across his cheekbones, his eyes hooded.

Marcos shut his eyes against Jack's verbal arrow. He opened them and looked his son in the face. "I deserved that. I spent eight months in rehab and have been sober for a year. I know I can't ever make it up to you, but I want to try. And I need to be a part of Megan's life. I'm so sorry, Jack. I can't begin to tell you how much I regret the past few years."

Jack looked away and I could detect the shine of tears in his eyes. "Yeah, well…you'll understand if I don't really give a shit."

His dad nodded again and looked away as well. "I do understand, Jackson. I needed you to know. Trina has invited me to dinner tonight so I can see Megan. I know you don't want to see me, but I hope you'll be there for her. This will most likely be very upsetting to her. She'll need you."

I hated Marcos in that moment; hated him for what he had done to Jack, and what he was doing to him now. I knew Jack would do anything for Megan, no matter how painful it would be for himself.

Jack, of course, nodded. "I'll be there."

"Good. Thank you, son," Marcos said.

"Are we done?" Jack asked. "I really need to get to work."

Marcos nodded. "Yes. I'll see you this evening. It was nice to meet you, Ally."

I watched him walk away, get in his car, and leave before I turned back to Jack. He had his hands in his pockets and was staring down at the pavement, the muscles in his jaw flexing. I didn't know what to say, so I silently wrapped my arms around his waist and held him tightly. After a full minute, he finally took his hands out of his pockets and hugged me close.

"Thanks for staying," he whispered.

"Always," I whispered back. "Will you come over after dinner?"

He nodded and pulled away. "I gotta go."

***

I worked on homework for my regular classes later in the evening while waiting for Jack to show up. We were reading *King Lear* for my CNM English class and I was supposed to be working on a character analysis for Edmund. The only thing I could come up with was he was a sadistic bastard and *King Lear* was probably the most depressing play ever written. I'm really more of a happily-ever-after fan.

I finished all my regular homework and glanced at the clock. I had begun to think Jack wasn't coming and I was worried maybe things hadn't gone well at dinner. When he finally arrived, he came in and flopped down on the couch, leaning his head back, eyes closed, and groaned. I curled up next to him, crawling under his arm and laying my head against his chest. He pulled me close and kissed the top of my head.

"You okay?" I asked.

"Yeah, I guess," he breathed. "This is not going to go down as one of my favorite days, however. It may even make my top ten list of days that completely suck."

"How did Megan do?"

"Better than expected. Better than I did, actually. She got real quiet and watched our dad throughout dinner. She sure didn't eat much."

"What did you do?" I was almost afraid to ask because he had been so angry this afternoon.

"Well, I didn't punch him in the face, which is what I wanted to do. I guess I kept quiet too. Any question I wanted to ask was something I didn't want Megan to hear."

"You probably didn't eat much, either. Wait here and get signed on the eCademy site." I kissed him quickly and headed to the kitchen. By the time I got back with a sandwich for him, he had both our laptops ready to go for our economics class. I grimaced; I had very quickly realized economics was not my cup of tea. If supply decreases and demand increases, what happens to prices? Who the hell cares? Certainly not me.

Jack took the plate with his sandwich from me, set it on the coffee table, and pulled me down on his lap for a kiss. "Thanks for taking care of me, querida. I love you." He kissed me again. "And I can tell you love me too."

"Oh, yeah? How so?"

"You actually touched meat for me." He gestured to the ham sandwich and then kissed me for a few moments. "All right. Stop trying to seduce me and let's get back to economics. I know how much you love those demand curves," he said as he set me down on the couch beside him.

"Seduce you? Hey, I'm not the one who started it this time." I said. "And I freaking hate economics. If it was up to me, we'd go back to the barter system."

He laughed and took a huge bite of his sandwich.

Two hours later, we had finished both our economics and government homework and were watching the news. One of the lead stories was the discovery of the identity of the remains of Ashley Hayes, missing since 1984. They flashed a picture of her. She was blonde, beautiful, and smiling. It was probably her senior picture and it made me sad to think of her never graduating, never going to college, or getting married.

"My mom's new boyfriend is the lead detective on the case," I told him.

"Really? Huh. That's cool, I guess."

"Yeah…" I said.

"What is it?" He turned to look at me.

"Well, I feel like I've heard her name before. I mean, before they found her body. It's bugging me, that's all. It's stupid."

He tucked a strand of hair behind my ear. I loved when he did that. "Just a feeling you get? Right?" I nodded. "Sweetheart, I've learned to never ignore those feelings you get. You *are* psychic, babe. You should probably pay attention to this."

I gave him a half smile and nodded. We went back to watching the news. During the sports report I decided to ask him more about his dad. "Jack, are you going to see him again? I mean, to really talk to him?"

He exhaled loudly. "I don't know. I don't want to. I don't want anything to do with him, but he is Megan's father. I need to figure out if he's sincere about being a part of her life. I don't want her to have to go through any more pain."

"Like you did?"

He pulled me closer. "Yeah. God, Ally. I don't know if I can forgive him. I'm so fucking mad at him."

I sat up and kissed him. "I love you. And I'm here for you, okay?"

"I know."

***

The car slowed and came to a halt on what sounded and felt like a dirt road. I had been bounced around in the back for at least fifteen minutes, but it was impossible to tell how long we had traveled before I woke up. I was more terrified than I had ever been in my entire life and my heart was pounding out of my chest. I heard the driver get out and then the back passenger door opened. I was grabbed by my hair and my neck and pulled violently out of the car. I tried to scream around the duct tape. "Shut up, bitch, or I will kill you." The voice was gravelly and low. I was nearly certain he was going to kill me anyway, so I kept trying to scream. I collapsed onto the dirt, but he yanked me up painfully and turned me around to face him. I didn't recognize his face, but I did recognize the face reflected back at me in his sunglasses. It wasn't my face. The blonde girl in the reflection met my eyes. It was the girl from the news, Ashley Hayes. "Help me, Ally!" she screamed in my head.

I woke up with a gasp, sitting up in bed, my heart pounding. I reached to turn on my bedside lamp, fumbling in my haste and knocking over the stack of books on my nightstand. I managed to get the light on and sat there, breathing hard and trying to fully wake from the nightmare. It had never gone this far and the ending had really spooked me. What was that? Why would my imagination dredge up something so awful? I got up to get a drink from the bathroom and splash cold water on my face. As I got back in bed, I bent down to pick up the books I had knocked over. The one I was currently reading, *A Ring of Endless Light*, had fallen open to the inscription and book plate inside the front cover:

Merry Christmas, Ashley 1983 Love, Mom and Dad. This Book Belongs to Ashley Hayes.

Ashley Hayes. No wonder the name seemed familiar to me. I was reading her book.

***

Okay. So I had a book that used to belong to a dead girl. A dead girl whose remains had been recently discovered by a hiker and his dog. And I was having nightmares about this girl being kidnapped. The problem was I didn't know if the nightmares really were about her or if they were simply a product of my overactive imagination. I mean, I didn't see her face in the dream until I had seen it on television. So, these dreams might be psychic, but they also might be the product of my stress and anxiety. At least I knew why her name had seemed so familiar to me: I had seen it the first night I started reading the book in my hotel room in Galway, unable to go back to sleep after having a nightmare. Wait…that was the first night I had the nightmare. And it was the first night I started reading Ashley's book. Well, crap. It looked like this might be psychic after all, and there was very likely a connection between the book and the nightmares. I really needed to talk to Tara. Jack was going through too much right now with his dad, so I didn't want to burden him with this new development and Cassie was still out of town, so Tara would have to be my confidante. I wasn't sure if I wanted to tell Cassie about my possibly psychic dreams anyway; it would certainly be added to the list of Why Ally is Probably the Next Oracle.

***

We were standing around in the quad at school the next morning, chatting before first period, and I was trying to pull Tara aside for a minute so I could arrange an after school get-together to tell her about my late-night revelations regarding my nightmares.

"Ah, *bonjour mes amis*," Rémy approached our group and began kissing everyone on both cheeks, like I had seen in movies. The rest of my friends seemed to be eating it up, especially Dustin. I could definitely see him trying to bring it into fashion here. Was I the only one who saw how ridiculous and cheesy this guy was?

When he came to me, I raised my eyebrows and gave him a look which clearly said 'hell, no.' He flashed his damn smirk and winked at me.

Jack arrived and elbowed Rémy out of the way. "Dude, do not try to kiss my girlfriend. I will have to hurt you." He pulled me to him for a rare public kiss.

Although I always enjoy his kisses, this one annoyed me slightly because I felt like he was marking his territory more than he wanted to kiss me. It annoyed me even more that Rémy seemed amused by it.

"Jack, do not be upset." Rémy laughed. "I mean nothing by it. This is how we greet one another in France."

"Yeah, well we're not in France, Rémy," he ground out through clenched teeth. "In America, we shake hands."

"Ah, but the exquisite Ally does not seem to want me to touch her at all. I wonder why?" he mused. "You have nothing to fear from me, chérie."

Yeah, right, I thought. I rolled my eyes at both Jack and Rémy. I pulled Tara aside. "Hey, can you come over after school? I really need to talk to you about something," I whispered.

"Sure. Is everything okay?" She looked across at Jack.

"Yeah. It's not about him. It's something else." I didn't want to go into any of it here. She seemed to get the message and nodded.

***

At lunch Jack was moody and distant, finally packing up his trash, saying, "I'll see you in English, okay? I need to go to the library."

"Do you want me to go with you?" I asked, concerned. He wasn't himself today.

"No." He shook his head. "I'm not good company right now. Sorry." He walked away, leaving me to stare after him.

Rémy plopped down next to me. "He is still angry with me, chérie?"

I sighed. "No. I don't think it's you, Rémy. He's going through some stuff right now."

"Well, he shouldn't leave a beautiful woman alone. I certainly never would."

"No, I'm sure you wouldn't. What do you want, Rémy?"

"Me? I do not want anything, chérie, except to be your friend," he said, shrugging.

"Really?" I asked sarcastically. He smirked. "Well, if you really want to be my friend, you need to stop pissing off the guy I'm in love with."

"Love," he scoffed. "You Americans don't know anything about love. I could show you…"

"And for God's sake, stop coming on to me in your smarmy French way. My name is Ally, not chérie!" I was completely out of patience with him. "I thought you were into Tara?"

"Ah, there are so many beautiful girls here. How can I decide?" He laughed.

"Yeah, I can see what a huge burden it is for you." The bell rang and I gladly got up, gathering my trash. I noticed Rémy quietly took Veronica's, giving her a sweet smile so different from the stupid smirk I was usually favored with. Just when I wanted to hate him, he goes and does something nice for one of my friends. I couldn't figure him out.

***

"So, what's up with Jack?" Tara was sitting on my bed, using my laptop to research Ashley Hayes. "He was really pissy today. Are you guys fighting?"

"No." I threw myself down beside her on the bed. "His dad showed up yesterday. He's moving here to Albuquerque and wants to spend time with Jack and Megan."

"Wow." She stopped and looked at me. "Jack's not handling it very well? He wasn't happy to see his dad?"

"Not really. His dad left Jack and Megan to deal with their mom's death all alone. He turned into a depressed drunk. That's when Jack started getting into trouble. I don't know if he's going to be able to forgive him."

"That sucks. I feel bad for him." We were both quiet for several minutes as she researched. I hadn't told her anything yet except I needed her to help me research the case my mom's boyfriend was investigating. "All right, here's what the APD website says about the Ashley Hayes cold case: 18 year old Ashley Hayes disappeared from Oso Grande High School on Tuesday, January 17, 1984. She was seen leaving the campus, but never arrived home. She was never heard from again and no body was ever found. Police suspected she was a runaway, but her family and friends maintain she was happy and would never leave home voluntarily. Listen to this: Ashley was pregnant at the time of her disappearance."

I sat up and looked over her shoulder at the screen. "Does it say anything about her family? Any names or anything?"

"Um, let's see…her mother is mentioned somewhere. Yeah, here it is: Angela Hayes is her name. Why?"

"Can you find an online white pages or something? I want to see if we can find out where she lives."

Tara clicked away to another site. "There are four Angela Hayes in Albuquerque. Are you going to try to call her or something?"

I again ignored her question. "How many in the 87110 zip code?"

"Just one, on Utah St., NE. Ally, answer me," she demanded. "Why do you want to know? This is more than idle curiosity, isn't it?"

It was time to fill her in. I knew I could rely on her to help me sort through things rationally. "I think you were right, Tara. I think these nightmares are psychic. Last night, I saw Ashley's face in the dream and she called out to me for help. I think I'm supposed to help her. Either that or I've completely lost my mind."

"Okay, tell me everything. I'll be the judge of whether this is psychic or insanity. Honestly, I'm pulling for insanity because the last time you tried to help someone it nearly got you killed."

I winced; she was right about that. Then I rehashed the whole thing for her: the nightmares starting the night I began reading Ashley's book, Brian telling us he was lead detective on the murder investigation, Ashley's face in the reflection of the kidnapper's sunglasses, and finally, Ashley crying out to me inside my head to help her. I told her how I was confused in the nightmare about whether it was me being kidnapped or Ashley and how I knew she was pregnant. I told her about crying for someone named Scott. I had told her before briefly about the nightmares, but certainly hadn't gone into any great detail.

"Holy shit, Ally! Where have I been? I didn't know any of this! Why didn't you tell me?" Tara stood and stared down at me sitting on the bed.

"I'm sorry! Don't be mad. I didn't want to talk about it with anyone. I thought the nightmares were because I was still stressed out. I didn't put any of this together until last night. You're the first one I've told." I looked up at her with pleading eyes.

"So, you haven't told Jack any of this?" I shook my head. "Well, fine then. So, what do you want to do?"

"I want to go talk to her mother. It sounds like she never moved; her house is close to the school."

"And exactly what are you going to say to her mother? 'Hi, I'm Ally. I'm a psychic who is having nightmares about your daughter getting kidnapped?' That's gonna go over real well."

"No. I'm going to say, 'Hi, I'm Ally. I have your daughter's book.' I think it will get me a short conversation at least."

"For what purpose? Ally, she's dead. They found the body. The police will try to find the killer. What can you do?"

"I don't know, Tara. All I know is she asked for my help. I have to try."

"Can't you talk to your mom's new boyfriend? You can tell him…"

I looked at her, eyebrows raised when she let the sentence fall. "Yeah, what exactly could I tell him? 'Hey, Brian. So, I've been having some pretty freaky psychic nightmares about one of your murder investigations.' I really don't think my mom is ready for him to know about our little family gift.

It would scare him off for sure."

She laughed, "Yeah, probably. So, she really likes this guy, huh?"

"Did I tell you I caught them making out in the kitchen? He had his tongue in her mouth and his hands all over her ass. I never wanted to see something like that. I wanted to scrub my eyeballs. And Jack just laughed and said, 'way to go, Brian.' Ugh!"

"Typical guy response. At least you didn't walk in on them having sex," she said.

"Thanks for the visual. I was really trying not to go there."

She laughed. "Okay, back to the topic at hand. So, you are going to start your own little investigation of Ashley Hayes? Well, I'll help you with my mad research skills and I won't rat you out on one condition: I go with you to talk to her mother." She stood and looked at me, hands on hips, a no-nonsense look on her face.

"Fine. I didn't really want to go by myself, anyway," I said, relieved.

"Are you going to fill Jack in on all of this? He's going to freak if he finds out later."

"Not yet. He's got a lot to deal with right now. It probably won't go anywhere, so I'll wait a while before I add this to his plate. Come on. Let's go find her house now, before I can talk myself out of it."

CHAPTER EIGHT

"Striving to better, oft we mar what's well."
–Shakespeare –King Lear (1.4.346)

Tara drove because I was too nervous. For all my big talk, I didn't have any confidence I could pull this off, and was truly expecting to have a door slammed in my face shortly. We found the house easily, thanks to Google Maps, and I grabbed Ashley's book and headed up the walk, feeling a little bit like I was selling Girl Scout cookies. Or salvation.

An elderly woman answered when Tara rang the doorbell. "Yes, may I help you?" she asked.

"Mrs. Hayes?" I asked. "Are you Ashley Hayes' mother?"

"Yes," she sounded cautious and confused. "Who are you?"

"Ma'am, my name is Ally Moran. This is Tara Scott. We go to Oso Grande High School, like Ashley did. I, um, I think I have a book that belonged to her and I thought you might want it back." I produced the book and offered it to her. She took it from my hands hesitantly. "Here," I gently opened it to the inside cover and showed her the inscription and bookplate.

"Oh," she breathed, running her fingers over the words. "I remember giving her this for Christmas. But how on earth did you get it?"

"I don't know." I shrugged. "I took it from a shelf in my English class. When I heard on the news Ashley had been found, I—well, I thought you should have it back."

She ran her fingers over the words for a moment more, tears threatening to overrun her eyes, before closing the book, sniffing, and saying, "Thank you. This means more than you know. Would you girls like to come in for a few minutes? I would like to hear more about how you got this." I looked at Tara and nodded. We followed Mrs. Hayes inside. She led us into her kitchen, saying, "Let me make some tea or coffee or something. Maybe I have some hot chocolate around here."

"Tea is fine, thanks," I said as we sat down at her kitchen table. She busied herself heating water and pulling mugs and teabags out of cabinets. Tara and I kept quiet as she worked; it appeared she was trying to pull her emotions together.

"So," she said, setting a mug of steaming tea in front of each of us. "Tell me more about how you found Ashley's book."

"Well, I saw it on the shelf at school in my English class and thought the title sounded poetic. I took it before Christmas, to read on a trip I was taking over the holidays."

"I wonder why it's still there after thirty years?" she mused. "Her English teacher that last year was Mrs. Gordon. She couldn't still be there, could she?"

"No, I don't think so. My teacher's name is Ms. Gonzalez. Maybe Mrs. Gordon left her books when she retired?"

Mrs. Hayes nodded. "Maybe. Ashley loved this book, loved all of Madeleine L'Engle's books. Did you read it?"

"Yes. It was a really great book. It was sad, but beautiful. It kind of helped me with some stuff I was going through." I looked into her face and we shared a small smile, like there was something we had in common now, something in common with Ashley.

"One of the last things I remember talking about with Ashley was how she was going to loan this book to Mrs. Gordon. She loved to talk about books with anyone who would sit still long enough. She was planning to go to the university to study English. She wanted to be a teacher." She seemed inclined to reminisce, which is what I had hoped, so Tara and I sipped our tea and let her talk. "I knew she didn't run away. I told the police, all those years ago, something bad had happened to her. They said she must have been upset and scared because of the pregnancy and so she ran away. But they didn't understand how it was. She was so happy, both she and Scott. Oh, I know we were all a bit shocked when we found out she was pregnant, but not really, you know. Those two were so in love, it didn't surprise me terribly to find out a baby was on the way. I guess that's not the way a mother should feel about her teenage daughter, but she was eighteen. Scott wanted marry her right away, but she wanted to wait until after graduation. He insisted she was still going to college and they would work it out. He was so good to her. It destroyed him when she disappeared. The police questioned him endlessly. They suspected he had done something to her, but they could never find any evidence. I knew she was dead, but I couldn't move away, just in case. I needed her to be able to find me, just in case." She faded out at the end and picked up her mug, her hands shaking so much I thought tea would slop out. I had figured Scott was the name of her boyfriend; now I needed to find out his last name.

"Do you think it could have been Scott? Now that they've found her…" I almost said 'body,' but realized at the last second it was insensitive.

She set her mug down, hard. "Absolutely not. It's the one thing in all of this I'm sure of. That sweet boy did not hurt Ashley. He loved her," she said with finality.

I sensed this was the end of her sharing, so I finished my tea and stood up. "Thanks for the tea, Mrs. Hayes. We need to go. I thought you should have Ashley's book."

She surprised me by pulling me into a hug. "Bless you, dear, for bringing this to me. It's a bright spot in the middle of all this mess."

We left her waving at us as we drove away. "Tara," I said, "I need you to find out Scott's last name and where he is now. I need to talk to him." She nodded in resignation.

"Fine. But remember our deal: no investigating without me. Your research source dries up if I find out you're lone-wolfing it, baby."

"Deal." I chuckled.

***

Tara had to go home, but promised she would start looking online to find out the last name of Ashley's boyfriend and where he was now. Meanwhile, I had other issues claiming my time: Cassie had returned from Ireland and wanted to meet to continue our training. She was eager to keep pushing me to find out whether or not I was the Oracle. Yikes. I had managed to push the word out of my head for a few brief weeks, but now it came clamoring back. I was scheduled to see her in her downtown office the next afternoon. The only good thing, psychically speaking, was the nightmares had stopped ever since I gave Ashley's book back to her mother. At least I was getting some sleep.

Unfortunately, I had plenty of opportunities for meeting with Cassie since Jack wasn't taking up much of my time. We saw each other at school, where he continued to be somewhat withdrawn and moody, but he maintained near radio silence in the afternoons and evenings. My texts were answered with curt replies, which did not encourage a return text. I tried not to let it hurt my feelings; I knew he was going through hell right now. But I wanted so much to help him or maybe simply hold him. He seemed to want to handle it on his own. I knew this wasn't right. This wasn't how couples that loved each other should act, but I didn't know how to reach him. It was forcing me to do some serious soul-searching in regard to our relationship. I needed someone to talk to, but my list of friends and relatives with the right kind of experience was pretty short. In fact, there was only one name on the list: Adele Moran. Grams. She was the only one I knew well enough to talk to who had a successful, long-term relationship in her past. It was a testimony to my level of desperation that I was willing to talk to my grandmother about my relationship with my boyfriend.

After finishing up some homework for physics and Spanish—I really could have used Jack's help on both—I decided to see if my grandmother was available for some girl talk. I finally hunted her down in the kitchen, where she was sitting at the table, going over some case files. "Hey, Grams. Do you have a few minutes?" My mom was out with Brian, so this seemed like a good time for an uninterrupted conversation.

"Of course, Ally." She pushed her reading glasses to the top of her head and cleared a space at the table for me. "What, no Jack tonight? I can hardly believe it."

"No." I flopped down in the chair across from her. "He's meeting with his dad tonight."

She smiled at me sympathetically. "Well, your mother is out with Brian, so it's a perfect time for us to catch up. I feel like we haven't had a chance to talk lately."

"So, what do you think of him? Brian, I mean. Did you like him?" Now that I had her attention, I felt strangely awkward about discussing my own love life. Or lack thereof.

She raised an eyebrow, seeming to understand. "Well, I liked him fine. He has a good job, is well spoken and nice-looking. What did you think of him?"

"Same. She has good taste. Runs in the family, of course."

Grams laughed. "Yes, of course. After all these years, he's the first man she's ever brought around to meet us. Are we ready for what this means?"

"You think they'll get married?" I asked.

"Yes." She nodded. "I think it's very likely. Does it bother you, Ally?"

"No, of course not. I want her to be happy, Grams."

She nodded. "As do I. Do you know the thing I liked best about him? The way he looked at her, the way he touched her. The man adores her." When I scoffed slightly, she raised her eyebrows questioningly. "What? You didn't see it?"

"Oh, I saw it all right. I walked in on them kissing in the kitchen. I saw a bit too much of him touching her, if you know what I mean."

She laughed delightedly. "Well, good for him. Just what your mother needs."

"That's almost exactly what Jack said."

"Speaking of Jack, what did you really want to talk about? Is everything okay with you two?"

"I don't know, Grams. He's distant and moody. I feel like he's pulling away from me. I know it's this stuff with his dad, but why won't he let me help? He won't even talk to me." I couldn't stop the tears building up in my eyes, threatening to spill over.

"Oh, sweetie. I can't even begin to understand what he's going through right now. From what you've told me, his father basically deserted him during a crucial time in his life. They have a lot to work through if they're ever going to have a relationship."

"Jack doesn't know if he can forgive him. If it wasn't for Megan, I think he would tell him to go jump in a lake," I said.

"Oh, I'm sure Jack would find a much stronger phrase, don't you think?" she asked, smiling.

I laughed mirthlessly. "Yeah, he would. Grams, why is he shutting me out? He said he loves me, but he barely talks to me lately. I know, you probably think it's ridiculous."

"What's ridiculous? That he loves you? That you love him? Why would I think it's ridiculous?"

"Oh, the normal reasons: we're too young, we haven't known each other long enough, yada yada." I laid my head on my arms on the table.

"So, because I'm, shall we say, 'seasoned,' I automatically think young people don't know what they're feeling? It may surprise you to know I don't feel that way at all. I absolutely believe you and Jack are very much in love with each other. Love has very little to do with age or time. You and Jack are both old souls."

I sat up. "Really, Grams?"

"Yes, sweetheart. I've watched the two of you together; the way he looks at you, especially when you're not looking, the way he touches you, all tells me he is deeply in love with you."

"Why do I feel a 'but' coming?"

"Because you're as clever as your grandmother. *But* there is a difference between being *in love* and *loving* someone. The two don't necessarily follow each other. Falling in love and being in love is wonderful and easy. Actually loving someone, especially for the long haul, is much more difficult and takes a much greater depth of commitment. It appears as if you and Jack need to decide if you are going to be able to really love each other through all the craziness in your lives. Can he love you through all this psychic mess in your life? Can you love him as he learns to deal with his past?"

"Grams, I hope so. I want to love him, to show him love right now, but how do I do that if he won't let me in?"

"I don't know, Ally. It's different for everyone. I think you need to be there for him, give him the time he needs. And you need to know when it's time to take matters into your own hands and push. Loving someone is hard work. I wish I could tell you more."

"Yeah, me too. It all sounds pretty vague—no offense."

"None taken. Come here." She pulled me into a hug, smoothing my hair as she held me. My tears finally spilled over. "I know you love him, sweetie. You'll figure this out. He's special. You are special together."

"Thanks, Grams. I can't tell you what it means to have you believe in me, in us."

"I do believe in you and Jack. However, I also believe you are too young and you haven't known each other very long, so don't go doing anything stupid, like getting pregnant or married. Do you still have those condoms I gave you? Are you two being careful?"

Well, that certainly dried up my tears fast. Good ol' Grams. I rolled my eyes as I stepped out of her arms. "Yes, I still have the condoms. I carry them at all times, in case I actually manage to convince Jack to ever make mad, passionate love to me. That's right," I said at her surprised look. "Not every teenager in the world is having crazy monkey sex. If it's up to Jack, I will probably be a virgin until I'm thirty."

She laughed. "Oh, I doubt he'll last that long. Like I said, I've seen the way he looks at you. Well, I'm glad he's showing some restraint. I certainly hope you aren't torturing him, trying to push him into something he's not ready for." At my shamefaced look, she continued, "Oh, Ally. That's cruel. Do you have any idea how difficult it is for young men his age to not think about and want sex? Please assure me you will cease and desist at once."

I nodded. "Well, it certainly hasn't been a problem lately."

"Give him time, Ally. Let him know you're there for him."

***

Cassie was waiting for me when I arrived at her office and greeted me with a hug. "How are you, Ally? How have you been since you got back?"

"I'm good, Cassie. When did you get back?"

"A few days ago. My fiancé flew out and joined me after you left."

"Hmm. Well, that sounds fun," I said with a grin.

She laughed. "Yes. It was. That's all I'm saying. Now, let's get to work, okay?"

"I guess. I've been enjoying being normal for a few weeks. I'm not sure I'm too eager to jump back into the psychic freak show."

"I completely understand, Ally, but we don't have the luxury of letting everything play out naturally. If you are the next Oracle, we need to be prepared."

"Prepared for what?" I asked suspiciously.

"Where do I begin? Being the Oracle isn't like being a normal Seer. You will have responsibilities and many people will want to consult you. Ally, the Oracle is the leader of our people."

"What? Leader? No, no, I don't want to be a leader! I didn't sign on for that!" I yelled.

"Ally, calm down. We don't know anything for sure, but I want you to be prepared."

"Cassie, I don't want this." I was whispering now, my voice refusing to cooperate as I went into full panic mode. I started hyperventilating, my vision beginning to blur.

"Okay, whoa." Cassie led me over to the sofa. "Sit down and put your head between your knees. I'll get you some water." I felt a cold, wet object pushed into my hands. "Here, take a sip. That's good. Feel any better?"

I nodded. "Sorry for the full-on freak out. I wasn't expecting this, Cassie. I really, really don't have any interest in being a leader. You guys should look for someone else. Seriously."

"Sorry, sweetie. It doesn't work like that. If you are the Oracle, well, it's all part of the package, I'm afraid."

"Well, the package sucks. Is this why those devious little old ladies are so hot and bothered to get me back to Ireland?" I was getting angry now.

"Ally, there's no need to get yourself so worked up," Cassie placated. "At this point it doesn't even matter whether or not you're the Oracle. You are still a Seer, and as such, you need to learn to control your powers. Agreed?"

"Fine. Agreed," I said sulkily. She had a point, but I didn't like it.

We worked for the next hour to learn to see when I touched another Seer and to control how much I could see. I had previously only been able to see when I touched an object, but we soon discovered I had Cassie's gift as well, which was considered one of the most powerful gifts in the Seer world. She also taught me how to block another Seer from seeing anything I didn't want them to see. I paid attention and worked hard, in spite of my previous irritation, because both of these skills appealed to my need for some kind of control in my life. Turns out when I'm interested, I can really rock the whole Seer thing. I might not have much control over the visions I had, but it made me happy I could control whether or not someone got inside my head.

"Wow, Ally. This is very impressive," Cassie gushed when I was able to completely keep her out of my head after only a few tries. She had her gorgeous assistant brew us a pot of tea as we relaxed after our session. She insisted I put two spoonfuls of sugar in my tea and eat several cookies. "You've expended quite a bit of psychic energy today and you need to replenish. I'm not letting you drive home until I'm sure you won't pass out." I nodded and obediently reached for another cookie. "Now, tell me how you've been doing with your visions. Is there anything new I should know about?"

"Well, no new visions, really, but maybe something else."

"Well, this sounds interesting," Cassie said, sitting up straight.

"I don't know for sure if it's anything, but there's been this kind of weird thing happening." I told her about the book and the dreams and the police identifying Ashley's body. I didn't tell her about cyber-stalking Ashley's mother and taking the book back to her in a thinly veiled attempt to pump her for information. That tidbit was better kept between Tara and me for now. "Cassie, I don't know what's psychic and what's my imagination getting the best of me. Is it possible these dreams are part of some new power I'm getting?"

"I think it's very probable, although I haven't heard of anyone having prophetic dreams in many decades. It's more evidence you may very well be the next Oracle. Sorry," she finished when she saw my crestfallen look.

"Yeah, well, this has been great, Cassie. Really," I said sarcastically and rose to leave.

She laughed ruefully and gave me a hug. "Don't

worry so much. Why don't you go on home and talk to that good-looking boyfriend of yours? It'll cheer you up."

"Yeah, it definitely would," I said wistfully.

She must have caught the negative tone. "Are you guys fighting?"

I shook my head. "No. He's going through some stuff with his family. It doesn't leave a lot of time for me."

"I'm sorry, sweetheart. Hang in there. I think he's worth it."

I nodded slowly and left.

CHAPTER NINE

*"Maybe you have to know the darkness before
you begin to appreciate the light."*
–Madeleine L'Engle

"Mom? Grams?" I called out as I entered the house after my session with Cassie.

"Shh." Grams came hustling out of the kitchen, wiping her hands on a towel. "Your mom is taking a nap."

I had never known my mother to nap. "Is she sick?"

"I don't know. She came home earlier than usual and said she was going to take a short nap. That was two hours ago."

"That's weird, huh?" I felt my cell phone vibrating in my back pocket and hoped it was Jack calling, so I hurried to my room. No such luck. It was Tara.

"Hey, girl. I thought you should know I found out Ashley's boyfriend was named Scott Alder and he still lives here. And before you ask, yes, of course I have his address."

"Cool. Is it close? Can we go tomorrow afternoon?" I asked.

"It's in Rio Rancho, so no, it's not close. But we can still go tomorrow, as long as you let me drive."

"Is that a slam towards my car?"

"Yeah, a little bit. If we have to take a thirty-minute road trip, I'd rather do it in the comfort of my Cherokee. No offense."

"Tons taken. I love my car," I said crankily.

"Whatever. You love the guy who gave it to you. It's my car or no deal, babe."

"Fine. Be that way."

Tara laughed. "I'll pick you up in the morning like old times and we can head out right after cheerleading practice, okay?"

***

Tara had called ahead and managed to arrange to meet Scott Alder at a Starbucks. She had told him we were from the school newspaper and were doing a piece revisiting the Ashley Hayes case because of the recent discovery of her remains. He was reluctant to talk, but had agreed to a brief conversation as long as it wasn't at his home. He said he didn't want his family to have to be burdened with any part of it. When we got to the coffee shop, I wondered if we would be able to recognize him, but it wasn't crowded at that time of day and he was easy to spot as the only person sitting by himself.

"Mr. Alder?" Tara asked. At his nod, we both sat

down at the table with him. "I'm Tara Scott and this is my friend, Ally Moran. Thanks for agreeing to see us."

"No problem. I don't know what I can tell you, though," he said.

"Well, Mr. Alder…" I began.

"Please, call me Scott," he interrupted.

"Okay, Scott." I smiled. "We attend the same high school you and Ashley attended, and the school newspaper is doing a piece in honor of the thirty year anniversary of her disappearance, especially since the, uh, her body was found."

A look of pain crossed his face. "I knew she was dead," he said quietly. "She never would have run away. Never."

"How do you know that, Scott?" Tara followed up.

He looked up sharply, almost angrily. "I knew her better than anyone. We were in love. I guess it sounds pretty stupid, huh?" He laughed ruefully. "We were just dumb kids, and I had knocked her up, right? That's what the cops kept saying, when they were trying to get me to confess to hurting her or something. Well, they didn't know. What we had was real, and it doesn't matter how young we were. I wanted to marry her right then, as soon as we found out about the baby, but Ashley wanted to graduate first. She said she'd marry me right after graduation. We had a plan. We would have been so happy." He stopped to take a sip of coffee and collect himself. "Sorry. It really destroyed me, you know? Not only was she gone, but everyone thought I had something to do with it. I dropped out of school. I couldn't handle it without her. I eventually got my GED, but it took me years to move on."

"Did you think she might come back? You know, just show up one day out of the blue?" Tara asked.

He shook his head. "No, that was her mom. She never could leave that house because she kept hoping, dreaming Ashley would show up one day with our child and some good reason why she left. But I knew better. She never would have done that to me. She never would have taken my child away from me. Not in a million years. I know that for a fact." He said this last statement looking directly into my eyes.

I believed him. I could see the pain and sorrow etched into his features and I knew he was telling the truth. "Scott, do you have any idea who could have done it?"

Again he shook his head. "Everyone loved her, and I'm not just saying that. She was such a nice person. She was popular at school and she treated all the kids really well. She wasn't one to lord her popularity over anyone. I think it had to be some random guy who picked her up on the way home."

"So, you're positive she left school that day?" Tara asked.

"Yeah. I walked her to her locker after school and kissed her goodbye. I had basketball practice and she said she'd meet me at her house later. She said the walk would be good for the baby. It was when I showed up a few hours later everyone realized she was missing."

Tara and I looked at each other. There didn't seem to be any more information we were going to be able to get out of him at this time. It was time to go. "Scott, thanks for meeting us. Here's our card. If you think of anything else, please give one of us a call."

Scott looked at the business card Tara handed him for a moment before pocketing it. "Sure. I don't mind talking to you girls. I like to think I'm helping out my alma mater. I appreciate you being willing to meet me here. I know the cops are going to start showing up at my house soon to question me, but I want to minimize what my family is going to have to go through."

"Do you have kids? Are you married?" I asked.

He smiled. "Yes to both. About ten years ago I met someone who finally helped me move on from Ashley. We have two kids, a boy, 8, and a girl, 4. They're my world."

"I'm glad," I said and stood to shake his hand.

***

"Since when do we have business cards?" I asked as we got into Tara's car. "We're not really even on the school newspaper."

"Since sixth period computer apps. I made some and printed them on card stock. I thought it was important we look legit, you know?"

"Your deviousness never ceases to amaze me," I shook my head at her. "Well, what did you think of him? Do you believe him?"

"Yeah, I do. But you're the psychic. I think it's

119

more important you believe him. Could you tell anything when you shook his hand?"

"He seems to be telling the truth. I mean, I'm not experienced at reading non-Seer people when I touch them, but you would think I could tell if someone had been feeding me a whole pack of lies, don't you? I only got general feelings from him, but nothing seemed off."

"Definitely. And you don't have to be psychic to be able to tell he really loved her. It's so romantic that he waited twenty years before getting married to someone else, huh?"

It was romantic, and I appreciated what he had to say about being in love at a young age, as well. I know a lot of people think it's crazy to believe you could find 'the one' in high school, but I needed to know at least some people felt as I did. I wondered if Jack still felt the same.

***

I was sitting on the couch, channel surfing, avoiding homework, and brooding when the doorbell rang.

"Ally, can you let Brian in, please? Tell him I'll be down in a few minutes. I can't decide what to wear," my mom called from upstairs.

This guy really had her wound tightly. First naps and now she was indecisive about her wardrobe? This was not like the confident, calm woman I knew as my mother. "Come in, Brian," I said as I opened the door for him. "Mom will be down in a few. Have a seat. You want anything? Water? A Coke?"

"No thanks, Ally. Actually, I'm glad to get a chance to talk to you privately."

Uh oh. Was this about to get awkward? Was he going to try to bond or ask for her hand or something? I motioned for him to sit down on the couch as I sat in the nearby chair.

"Yeah, so I was doing some follow-up work on the Ashley Hayes case today and your name came up." Apparently I had it all wrong. This wasn't about Mom. It was about me, and it wasn't going to be a heart-warming moment. He took his phone out and pulled up a picture of the business card Tara had given Scott. Busted. "Imagine my surprise when I'm questioning a former suspect in the Ashley Hayes disappearance, now the Ashley Hayes murder, and I find out a couple of teenage girls, from a high school newspaper no less, beat me to it. Imagine my further surprise when I find out one of them is the daughter of my girlfriend."

I said nothing. I simply looked down at my slippers.

"Are you even on the school newspaper? Jennifer has never mentioned it, and she talks about you all the time."

Well, that was sweet. And frightening to think my mom had nothing better to talk about on her dates than her kid. "Well, I'm not exactly on the newspaper, but I thought it would be um, interesting to maybe do a paper or something on the case. I mean, since it happened in my school and all." I was making this up on the fly.

"Ally, you and your friend are absolutely not to interfere with a police investigation. Do I make myself clear?" he said sternly.

"Crystal. I'm sorry. We didn't mean to interfere. I'm really interested in um, law enforcement, and I was hoping maybe you could be a sort of um, mentor, since you're getting to know my mom so well. It would be great if you and I could get to know each other, you know?"

I have absolutely no doubt Brian saw through this piece of complete bullshit and recognized it for the veiled threat it was: play nice and I will put in a good word for you with Mommy. Be difficult and the darling, adored daughter will be sure to put a few roadblocks up. We simply stared, daring the other to be the first to flinch. I chose to take it as testimony to his love for my mother that he was the first to blink.

"Mentor, huh? You're interested in law enforcement? Well, fine. I guess I can arrange for you to do a few ride alongs. It's this case, specifically, you're interested in?"

I nodded. "Thanks, Brian. I bet my mom is gonna think it's sooo sweet of you."

He chuckled and shook his head. I liked to think he would not underestimate me again. I felt pretty badass at the moment. He brought me back to earth pretty quickly. "Your little private investigation is over as of this minute, however. If I find out you're doing any snooping behind my back, this arrangement is over. Got it?"

"Yep. Got it. I better see what's keeping my mom." I scooted up the stairs, but not before I glimpsed a grudging half-smile from Brian. I found my mom lying on her bed in tears. "Mom? What's wrong? Are you okay? Brian is downstairs waiting."

She sniffed. "I don't have anything to wear. Go tell him to go home."

"What? Mom, you have tons of cute outfits. Don't you want to go out? Are you guys fighting or something?"

"No. I don't know what's wrong with me, Ally. I can't pull it together tonight." She reached for a tissue and dabbed her eyes.

"Here, let me help. Let's find you something to wear, okay?" I went to her closet and found a newish dress Grams had given her for Christmas. "Put this on. It makes your boobs look great. Brian will love it." She laughed, as I had intended, but she complied and put on the dress. It did make her boobs look good, a lot better than I remembered. It gave me a momentary hope someday I wouldn't be completely flat. "Yowzer. Brian may like this too much. Can I borrow it for my date with Jack tomorrow? It does great things for your rack, Mom."

She laughed again. "Thanks, sweetie. Help me fix my face? I don't want to look like I've been crying. I don't know what's wrong with me. You must think I'm crazy."

"Yeah, a little bit, but hey, love makes us crazy, huh? You love this guy?" I used what I learned from Sephora to apply eye shadow to her lids, giving her a smoky-eye look, then finished with some dramatic eyeliner.

She sighed. "Yeah, I really do. Are you good with that? Do you like him?" she asked worriedly.

"Yeah, he's great." I wouldn't let her know about our 'understanding.' It could be our little secret. "Go for it, Mom. You should be happy." She hugged me and I heard another sniff. "No more tears! I just repaired your face. Now get out of here and go meet your boyfriend." I almost choked on the last word. Am I the only one who thinks there should be another word for people over thirty? Gross. I watched from the top of the stairs as Brian pulled my mother into his arms and kissed her. It was the kind of kiss that made my stomach flip; it was so sweet. He pulled back and put his hand on her face, tracing the tears, which were making another appearance.

"Hey, what's wrong, sweetheart?"

She shook her head and hugged him. "It's nothing. I had a rough day, that's all. I'm fine."

"Okay. Hey, I love you." He kissed her again.

Well, I better get to know him. It looked like he was going to be around for a while.

***

Unfortunately, Jack remained distant. Oh, on the surface everything seemed fine, but the change was there. He came over to do homework, but there was no cuddling and talking afterward; he simply packed up and left. At school, he still held my hand in the hall and sat with us at lunch, but more often than not he would leave early. I was trying to be understanding and let him know I was there for him, but I was starting to lose patience. I had no idea what the status of his relationship with his dad was because he wouldn't talk about it. It would be a whole lot easier if I didn't care so much, and I got the distinct feeling it was exactly what he was hoping for: that I would stop caring and pushing and simply give up. If I truly felt like that's what he wanted I would do it, but Tara and Grams assured me he still looked at me like he loved me. They both said they could see so much pain in his eyes; so could I.

Valentine's Day was around the corner and I figured this could be a perfect time to rekindle the romance with Jack and do some of the pushing Grams had talked about. I had Tara help me devise a plan that was sure to put any thought of his father out of his mind, at least for one night. We were on the way to Manny's shop so I could tell him about our upcoming date, since he wasn't answering my calls lately.

"Now, get in there, tell him about the date, and don't take no for an answer. Got it? I'll distract Mat for you."

"Wow. Way to take one for the team," I replied. I was strangely nervous; this was Jack, the guy I was in love with, but he had been so distant lately. I didn't know how much more of the brush-off I could take before I ran away with my tail between my legs.

We arrived at the shop way too soon and Shelly waved us to the back. Mat saw us as soon as we stepped in, coming over to greet us.

"Now this is exactly what I needed this afternoon: two beautiful girls to liven up this boring shop." At his words, Jack turned around, smiling when he saw me. His smile still took my breath away, but it faded too soon. I walked over to him, leaving Tara to occupy Mat.

"Ally, what's up?" I couldn't help but notice he didn't try to kiss me. Crap. This was more serious than I thought. Now I was scared. Was he really trying to pull away? Was I simply too dense to see he wanted out of this relationship?

"Oh, I wanted to stop by and talk about our plans for this Friday and I've had a hard time getting you on your cell lately." I looked into his face for some sign, anything, that would tell me he wasn't pulling away.

"Friday? Um, I don't think I'll be able to do anything." He wouldn't even meet my gaze.

"Jack, it's Valentine's Day," I whispered. "Please."

"Oh. Yeah, okay. Sorry, I forgot. I'm sorry, Ally," he whispered back.

"So, can you go?"

He swallowed. "Yeah, sure. Of course."

I didn't say anything; I threw myself into his arms and kissed him. I didn't give him a chance to say no. He kissed me back, a little desperately it seemed, clutching the back of my shirt. I put everything I had into the kiss and I didn't care who was watching. I felt like I was fighting for everything we had together. Too soon he pulled away, resting his forehead against mine, swallowing hard again. "I love you, Jack." I wasn't going to make this easy for him; this was worth fighting for, damn it! Why couldn't he see it?

He nodded, but he didn't say it back. My heart

was breaking into small pieces. "Just text me the details, okay?" he said as he pulled away.

I nodded, trying not to cry. "Tara, you ready?"

"Yeah, let's go," she called as she pulled her hands out of Mat's.

"So, I'll pick you up at seven, Tara. We'll have a great time!" Mat called as we left.

"Did you actually agree to go out with Mat?" I asked as we got into her Jeep.

"Yes, and I can't begin to tell you how much you owe me for that," she spat at me. "Talk about taking one for the team! It's the only way I could get him to leave you and Jack alone. Tell me it was worth it."

"I'm not sure. He did agree to go out on Friday, but he didn't seem really thrilled about it. Tara, I think I'm losing him," I cried.

"Hey, I saw the way he was kissing you. It didn't look like you were losing anything. It was hot, let me tell you." She fanned her face.

"Yeah, but it felt like a goodbye." My voice trembled as I spoke.

"Hey, no way! Don't think like that. You have a great date planned for Friday. And if it doesn't work, we'll take the more direct route," she promised.

"Such as?"

"Direct confrontation, calling him on all this bullshit. You will demand answers."

"I hope it doesn't come to that," I said, looking out the window. I wanted to go back to the time before his dad came back into his life. We had been so happy and I wanted it back. I was willing to do whatever it took, but I wasn't sure what that was. "So, where is Mat taking you? I can't believe you agreed to go out with him just for me."

She looked, I don't know, guilty? "Oh, well, yeah. Of course. I would do anything for you."

Hmmm. I got the distinct feeling she wasn't as upset about this date as she should have been. This could be interesting. "I want to hear all about it tomorrow."

"Of course. It won't amount to much. I'll let him down easy," she assured me.

Uh huh. Sure she would.

***

I could hardly wait to pump her for info about her date with Mat the next day at lunch. I made a beeline to our table and sat down next to her while Jack headed off to buy lunch, something he had started doing since his dad showed up. "So, how was it?"

"How was what?" It was Rémy, of course, butting his way into the conversation as usual.

"Tara had a date last night," I delightedly informed him.

"But how is that possible since I was busy elsewhere?" He appeared outraged, but I could tell it was an act. He took Tara's hand and kissed it. "I am desolate, chérie." He looked at me and winked.

"She had a date with Jack's cousin, Mat. You remember him from the night at the movies?" I asked.

"But of course. He was with the lovely Lynette,

128

no?" Amazing that Rémy got her name right.

"Yeah, how was the big date?" Jack asked as he sat down with his lunch. "Mat hogged the bathroom all evening. I couldn't even get a shower. I hope the aftershave he slathered on wore off before he picked you up."

Tara looked a little bit like a deer in the headlights as we all stared at her, waiting for her to respond. "Um, it was fine, actually. Mat was really nice and he, uh, he smelled fine." She winced as she said this last bit as Jack and Rémy both laughed. I gave her a sympathetic look and mouthed 'later.' She nodded gratefully.

***

I finally got more of the story that night on the phone. I lay sprawled across my bed and got her on FaceTime. "So, spill. I've been waiting all day to hear about it."

"It wasn't terrible. He was pretty nice. We went to dinner and then he took me bowling."

"Bowling?" It was hard to imagine my stylish best friend doing something as mundane as bowling.

"Yeah." She laughed. "It was quirky and kind of fun. I haven't been for years. He was terrible, but he was really good about laughing at himself. It was a lot of fun."

"Wow," I said. "It sounds great. So, did he kiss you?"

"No. It wasn't that great."

"Well, are you going to go out again? Did he

ask?"

"Um, we left it kind of open, actually. Oh, I don't know, Ally. He's not what I expected, you know? I thought it would be miserable and we wouldn't have anything to talk about, but it was actually kind of fun. He's a lot different when he's by himself. He was really easy to talk to," she admitted.

"Well, I think it's great, Tara. I'm not even going to tease you about it. He's a really nice guy and he's been good for Jack."

"Thanks, Ally. It's kind of embarrassing, you know? I mean, after I made such a big deal about not liking him."

"Hey, what are best friends for?" The thought of us dating cousins was amazing. Now, I had to convince Jack to get back with the program.

***

I had prepared for Friday, Valentine's Day, all week. I planned to have him pick me up after work and then we would have dinner at El Patron, where we had first danced together. Then we would take the tram up to Sandia Peak and enjoy the romantic view. I hoped to remind him of all the best things about our relationship.

Of course, it didn't work out like I had planned. The stars seemed to be aligned against me from the get-go. First, he was more than a half hour late picking me up so we missed our reservation. When we got to the restaurant, the wait was nearly an hour. We sat in stony silence for the most part, every conversational volley on my part met with monosyllabic answers on his. Then, he picked a fight. He said we shouldn't have even tried to go out on Valentine's Day because it was sure to be crowded everywhere. We were finally seated, but so far away from the dance area it didn't begin to resemble the time we had been there with Megan. Everything was falling apart, and I couldn't manage to keep my temper any longer. "Fine, Jack. I get it, okay? Let's just finish dinner and then you can take me home."

He pulled up in front of my house and turned the car off. Normally, this would be the time for heated kisses, trying not to let ourselves go too far. Tonight, it was the time for cold silence in the car. "Jack, what's happening to us?" I whispered in the dark.

"I don't know. I'm sorry. I need some time, Ally. I think we should take a break. I can't deal with everything right now."

"What?" I cried. "What does that mean? What kind of break? Why?"

He rubbed his hands over his face in frustration. "I don't know, Ally. I just can't handle everything right now. I think... I need to be by myself for a while."

"But...I love you, Jack. I thought you loved me. People in love are supposed to help each other deal with the crappy stuff in their lives. You don't...you don't love me anymore? You don't want me?"

"God, Ally. I don't know what I want right now. Everything feels so out of control right now. I'm so messed up and I don't know what I'm feeling." I could see his eyes shining and his lips starting to tremble. "I can't do this anymore."

So this was it. He was breaking up with me. He didn't want me anymore. Oh, God. I needed to get out of the car. Right. Now. I couldn't breathe, I couldn't think. I fumbled for the door handle, desperate to get out. He followed me to the front door.

"Ally, I'm sorry. I—"

"I have to go, Jack." I tried to hold back my tears. "Please let me go," I begged, squeezing my eyes shut.

He nodded, motioning for me to go in. As I closed the door, I got a last glimpse of his face. It was no consolation, but he looked as miserable as I felt.

Can I just say that Valentine's Day *sucks*?

I made it inside and raced to the downstairs bathroom to throw up the little bit of food I had been able to eat at dinner. I curled up on the floor by the toilet and cried hysterically, making myself sick again. That's how Grams found me when she came in from the senior citizen's Valentine's mixer she had been attending. She managed to get me to the couch and held me while I cried some more. I wasn't coherent enough to talk, but she figured out the gist of what had happened. I finally cried myself to sleep and woke up Saturday morning to a quiet house and a hollow chest.

CHAPTER TEN

"Thou art a soul in bliss; but I am bound
Upon a wheel of fire, that mine own tears
Do scald like molten lead."
–Shakespeare –King Lear (4.7.46)

The next few days were a blur. I spent Saturday and Sunday in my room, lying on my bed, staring at the ceiling. I only came out for meals so Grams and Mom wouldn't come in to get me, but I merely pushed the food around on my plate. I cried myself to sleep each night and was late getting up Monday morning. The worst part of the day was physics, where Jack and I were lab partners. We couldn't get out of it, so we worked together with as little communication as possible. It was awful. Lunch was terrible. I hadn't told anyone, not even Tara, that Jack and I had broken up. She was shocked when I showed up at the lunch table by myself.

"Oh, sweetie," she said as she hugged me.

I hugged her back briefly before pulling away. I needed to keep it together at school. I could lose it again after school. "Please don't ask. I don't want to talk about it right now." Or ever, I thought.

Rémy was surprisingly gentle about it, making me like him more. "He is the loser, chérie. I can't believe he let you slip through his fingers. What a fool! I will be happy to take over."

I couldn't even laugh. "Thanks, Rémy. I'll take a raincheck, okay?" I still felt the need to shy away from him when he tried to touch me. I caught a surprisingly frustrated look on his face when I did this.

"I know," he announced. "It is time for us to, what is it you Americans say? 'Hang out' tonight. That's it. No, no arguments," he said as I began to object. "I am not letting you sit and wallow in your misery tonight! We will go out and have fun. You'll see. I can take your mind off of this ridiculous boy, you know. I will pick you up at six o'clock."

"How do you have a driver's license? I didn't think they gave those to exchange students. And how do you know where I live?"

"Ah, ma belle, there are so many things about me you do not yet know. Tonight, we will begin to repair this, no?" He was such a flirt and said the cheesiest things; I had a hard time figuring out when he was serious. But he was really trying to cheer me up, so I was willing to overlook it. And he was so ridiculously good-looking it was easy. Not that I was contemplating dating him or anything, but he was easy on the eyes. And I couldn't help wondering what Jack would think of me going out so soon after we broke up if he heard about it. Would it even bother him? I realize how shallow it sounds, but I hope I can be forgiven.

Rémy picked me up promptly at six, coming in to charm my mom and my grandmother. Both had raised their eyebrows when I informed them I was going out with another guy, but thankfully they withheld the commentary. We drove to a nightclub, Graham Central Station, which Rémy informed me was having a teen night. I had never even thought about going to a teen club as it was so far out of my range of experience. We met Travis and Dustin out front. Rémy told me Tara and Mat would be joining us shortly. Well, Jack would be sure to hear about my date if Mat was here. I wondered if he would care.

I would never have believed it, but I had a really nice time. Three nights after I broke up with the love of my life, I was out dancing and having fun. I didn't want to think about what it said about me, but it was sure better than eating a pint of Ben and Jerry's and crying myself to sleep. Rémy didn't let me sit out a single dance and it was a festive atmosphere; none of the dances were slow. People were here to party, not get romantic. It was exactly what I needed. I even managed to keep from touching Rémy during the evening. Tara and Mat looked like they were having a great time, but I could see she was still trying to maintain some distance.

Rémy dropped me off and didn't try to get creepy, which I was truly grateful for. I thought I might be able to be friends with him, but that was definitely it. I had no romantic aspirations toward him whatsoever and I didn't get the feeling he was losing sleep over me, either. "Thanks, for tonight. I guess I really needed to get out."

"Of course you did, chérie. I'm glad you had a good time. We should do it again next week, no?"

"Sure," I said. "Good night, Rémy."

I still cried myself to sleep.

***

I waited for Jack to ask me about the date, but he didn't. All through physics the next day he worked stoically beside me, handing me items when I asked, asking for items in return. His jaw was flexing throughout class, but he never asked. It was depressing, to say the least. Did he not care? Was I so easy to get over?

I had arranged to meet Brian at his office after cheerleading practice so we could go over a few of the case files before heading out to interview the people who still lived in the neighborhood, including Ashley's mother. I had confessed to Brian I had already met her, telling him about the book, which was ostensibly the reason for my intense interest in the case. I didn't want any awkward moments when we met her later. We found in the case files that not only her mother, but the next door neighbor, and the neighbors across the street were still living where they had thirty years before. Brian planned for us to talk to each of them this afternoon. It was good to have something to take my mind off of Jack for a little while.

"Ally, is your mom okay? She's been acting kind of strange lately," Brian asked as we drove to

Ashley's neighborhood.

"Um, well she has been a little off. I was thinking she doesn't feel very well. Maybe she's sick or something." I wasn't entirely comfortable talking about my mom to her boyfriend, but he was concerned and I felt bad for him.

"She seems a little distant. Has she said anything? Is she mad at me or anything?"

"Brian, I'm not the expert on that. Seriously, dude," I said.

"Sorry. Jennifer told me you broke up with your boyfriend. I'm sorry. Is there anything I can do?"

"You could arrest him," I mused. Brian chuckled. "No, but thanks. Hey, I'll keep an eye on Mom, okay? I'm sure she'll snap out of it."

We pulled up to Mrs. Hayes' house. She was every bit as nice as she had been the last time, but didn't have any more information than I had received previously. It was interesting to watch Brian question her; he was subtler than Tara and I had been. After talking to her for about a half-hour, we headed next door. David Moore was puttering around in his rose garden in front of his house and invited us in for coffee. He was somewhere near 60, balding on top, with a paunch.

"No, thank you, Mr. Moore. We do have a few questions. We won't take up more than a few minutes of your time. I understand Ashley Hayes babysat for you." Brian had pulled out a small notebook, just like on TV. Cool.

"Oh, yes. She was our regular babysitter. My girls loved when Ashley came over. It's so sad, what happened to her. The girls were devastated when she disappeared." He clipped a few dead heads off a rose bush.

"Did you know Ashley's boyfriend, Scott Alder?"

"Well, I'd seen him a few times, but I don't believe I ever spoke to him. I remember he was a suspect, wasn't he?"

"Mr. Moore, is your wife still living? May we speak to her?" Brian asked briskly.

"We divorced years ago. She took the girls with her. They moved to California."

"I see. Well, I'm going to need her contact information, if you don't mind."

"Of course. I'll be right back." He put down his clippers and went inside the house.

"Anything interesting yet?" I asked Brian.

He shook his head. "Nah. It's pretty routine so far. Most police work is boring follow-up like this. It's nothing like you see on television."

Mr. Moore brought the contact information and we headed across the street. Stella and Don Graves had lived in the house directly across from the Hayes' house for 35 years. They were both retired and greeted us warmly, insisting we come inside for coffee.

"Oh, I was so upset to hear about poor little Ashley," Mrs. Graves said as she bustled around preparing coffee. "She was such a sweet girl. I never understood why she would run away. Now we know, I guess. It's so hard to believe she was murdered!" Mr. Graves said nothing, but patted her hand as she sat down.

"So, did either of you see anything that day? Did

you see Ashley? Did she arrive home?" Brian had his notebook out again.

Mrs. Graves shook her head. "Well, we were both at work. It was when we got home that we saw the police cars across the street and went over to see what had happened."

"What about your children? Were any of them home? Did they see anything?"

"Let's see, Mark would have been twelve. He wasn't home until after baseball practice, which was after we got home. Darrell was only eight at the time. I picked him up from his after-school sitter on the way home," Mrs. Graves replied.

"Did you know Scott Alder, Ashley's boyfriend?"

"I met him," said Mrs. Graves. "I was visiting with Angela one afternoon when they both came in. Ashley introduced him. He seemed like such a nice young man."

"Were you aware Ashley was pregnant?" Brian asked.

Mrs. Graves looked uncomfortable for a moment. "Well, yes. Angela confided it to me. We were close friends, you see. She was understandably upset about it, especially at first. But after a few weeks she seemed to accept it. Ashley and Scott were both 18, after all. They were planning a wedding right after graduation. Angela was looking forward to having a grandchild, even if it was a bit sooner than expected."

"Well, thank you both for your time. Here's my card, if you remember anything else."

"And here's mine, in case you can't get hold of

Detective Keller," I inserted as I handed Mr. Graves one of the cards Tara had made.

At the car, Brian let me have it. "Ally, no more handing out your cards. I have voicemail, you know. They can leave a message."

"Yes, sir," I replied meekly. "I just wanted them to have options." Brian rolled his eyes. "So, what's our next step?"

"I'll try to track down Mr. Moore's ex-wife. And we wait on the autopsy results, which will give us more information, hopefully, about the manner of her death."

"How long will that take? I would have thought they would have finished it already," I said.

"It's not like it is on TV, Ally, I told you that. Autopsies take a lot longer than one episode of CSI. It could be months before we hear anything."

"I like TV better," I muttered.

***

Over the next few weeks, Brian and I continued to research the case. He let me look at the case files while I was at the police station only, so I spent quite a bit of time there after school. He had tried to contact David Moore's ex-wife, but so far none of his messages had been returned. Although I was miserable about Jack, having an outside interest helped. This way I only cried at night instead of all afternoon as well. The only consolation was Jack looked as miserable as I felt. He had dark circles under his eyes—mine had finally gone away since I wasn't having nightmares any more, only to return

140

when Jack dumped me—and he looked like he had lost weight. I didn't know if it was from missing me or from dealing with his dad. We didn't talk. I know my mom and Grams were worried about me, so I tried really hard to keep it together in front of them. I spent a lot of time with my head in my pillow, trying to muffle the sobs. Tara had given up trying to get me to care about what I looked like; I had gone back to my slovenly jeans and sweatshirts habit. I couldn't begin to work up the energy to care about what I wore. I didn't bother to wear makeup, either. Rémy took me out several evenings each week, most often to a place where we could dance or enjoy music. I looked forward to these outings because I could forget for a few hours how my heart had been ripped out. I know, dramatic much?

My mom was another source of worry. She had several more crying incidents and was still sneaking home to nap a couple times a week. Brian was really worried about her and pestered me for information any chance he got. One Saturday morning in early March, I was on my way downstairs for cereal when I passed by my mom's room and heard what sounded like her barfing into the toilet. I ran in and held her hair back for her while she finished. I handed her a warm washcloth and helped her back to her bed.

"Mom, what's wrong? Is it the stomach flu?"

She sat on the bed, her arms on her knees, hunched over in misery. She shook her head.

I sat next to her, rubbing small circles on her back. I thought back over the last month and a half, with Mom sleeping so much, her crying jags, her enhanced bust line, and now her vomiting. It finally clicked. "Mom, are you pregnant?" I whispered.

She nodded miserably and said, "I think so." Then she started crying.

I pulled her into my arms and stroked her hair. I must say I was floored, yet grateful we were talking about her being pregnant and not me. It was rather ironic, the teenage daughter comforting her mother about an unplanned pregnancy. "Hey, it's going to be okay. It is Brian, right?"

She laughed slightly at my lame attempt at humor. "Yes, of course."

"Have you told him yet?"

She shook her head. "No. I don't know how to tell him. He's going to think I'm trying to trap him or something."

"What? That's crazy! He's not going to think that. He's in love with you. He's going to be excited. He's been so worried about you, Mom. You need to tell him. Now."

She nodded. "I know. I just need to think."

"Mom, you don't need to think. You need to call your boyfriend and tell him he's going to be a dad. Mom, this is good news, you know? I'm going to be a big sister."

"How can you think so, Ally? How could I have done this again? What kind of person gets pregnant out of wedlock twice? I'm a terrible role model! How many times did I preach safe sex to you?" She wailed, now beginning to sob.

"Well, it was more Grams than you, actually. Maybe she should have bought you some condoms, huh?"

"Oh, Ally! How can you not hate me? Aren't you disappointed in me?"

"Disappointed? Not even a little bit. Mom, I'm happy for you. It's not like you're a 15-year-old who's going to have to drop out of high school and live on welfare. Is it that you don't love Brian? You don't want to be with him?"

"No! I love him. I want to marry him. But now he'll feel trapped. How am I going to tell him?"

"Mom, that's crap. Don't do this to yourself. Call him." But I couldn't get through to her, at least not right then. I kissed her hair and left her curled up on her bed, and went to find Grams. Mom had given me permission to tell her the news.

Grams wasn't terribly surprised. She had been putting two and two together as well. She advised giving my mom some time to let it sink in before we started worrying about her.

It was much later that it finally sunk in for me: I was going to have a sibling. Finally, I would have a little brother or sister, and even though it wasn't the ideal set of circumstances, I couldn't help being excited. It was nice to have some good news for a change.

CHAPTER ELEVEN

"How can anyone bear the light? It burns, burns."
–Madeleine L'Engle

I was sitting with Brian in his office on Monday afternoon, updating the case file—so much of this investigation consisted of grueling paperwork—when his phone rang. He motioned to get my attention and put it on speaker.

"Thanks for getting back to me, Mrs. Moore. I was beginning to wonder if I had the right number," Brian said.

"It's Ms. Davis. I don't go by Moore. Call me Shannon, please. What did you want to talk about, Detective Keller?"

"I need to ask a few questions about the time you lived here in Albuquerque with your ex-husband, David Moore. It pertains to the Ashley Hayes case. Were you aware her body was found?"

"Yes. That even made the news here. I don't know what I can tell you. I didn't know anything at the time and I don't know anything now."

"What was your relationship with Ashley Hayes?" Brian asked.

"She was our babysitter. That's it."

"How often did she babysit for you?" Brian continued.

"Oh, at least once a week. Sometimes so I could get the shopping done, sometimes so David and I could go out."

"When was the last time she babysat for you before her disappearance?"

"Oh, Detective, that was so long ago, I don't remember," she sighed.

"Please try, Ms. Davis. It could be important. She disappeared on a Tuesday."

"Um, let's see…I think she might have babysat for us on Saturday night. I can't be positive."

"Ms. Davis, did you know about Ashley's pregnancy?"

"No. Oh my goodness, that poor girl," she breathed.

"When was the last time you saw her?" Brian asked as I pushed a note toward him. He looked at it and nodded.

"I don't really remember. It must have been the day before. I seem to remember seeing her as she came home from school."

"Do you remember what time that was?" he pressed.

"Well, it must have been the usual time, around three o'clock."

"But you didn't see her arrive home at that time the next afternoon?"

"No. I had taken the girls to visit their

grandparents in Las Cruces. We stayed overnight. I remember hearing about Ashley's disappearance the next evening, when we got back."

"One more thing, Ms. Davis," Brian took the note I had written. "Did you know her boyfriend, Scott Alder?"

"Well, I didn't know him, but I had met him briefly and I saw him bring her home quite often," she replied.

"What did you think of him?"

"Oh, well, I guess I thought he was a nice boy. I don't know, I never really thought about him that much."

"Well, thank you for your time, Ms. Davis." Brian hung up. "What do you think?" he addressed me.

"I don't know. There's something she's not telling us. My Spidey-sense is going off," I said.

He laughed. "Yeah, mine too. We usually call it a hunch around here. I really want to talk to her in person. I may need to take a little trip out to sunny California." He was quiet for a moment. "Ally, can I talk to you about something else?"

"Sure," I said it more as a question than a statement.

"I know this is awkward, but I'm getting desperate. Ally, your mom won't talk to me. She ignores my phone calls and messages, and when I stopped by her school to see her, she had the secretary tell me she was in a meeting and couldn't see me. She's never done that. She used to sneak out of meetings to see me. Has she said anything? Is she seeing someone else?"

All right, so maybe what I did next was wrong. Maybe it betrayed a confidence, but I couldn't sit by and let my mom make the biggest mistake of her life. Maybe I simply had a pathological need for somebody's love story to end well, I don't know. I leaned forward to get right in his face. "Brian, she's not seeing anyone else. She has been really emotional lately, is constantly tired, her boobs have gotten bigger, and she barfs regularly in the morning. Now, why don't you use your mad detective skills to put it all together? Or you could Google the symptoms."

His reaction was almost comical. He thought about it for a minute, then sat back in his chair. "Oh, shit. She's pregnant," he breathed.

"Got it in one, Sherlock. Now, what are you going to do about it?"

"Why didn't she tell me?" He sank his head into his hands and groaned.

"I don't know, Brian. She's afraid, I think. She thinks you'll think she's trying to trap you or something crazy like that. But you're not gonna think that, are you, Detective Keller?" If that last bit came out sounding a little bit like a threat, well, that's how I intended it to sound.

"God, no. Look, Ally. I'm sorry about this. This is really awkward. I didn't mean for you to know."

"To know what? That you and my mother are having sex? Or were, rather." I crossed my arms and stared at him.

"Ouch," he said, putting his face back into his hands. "What do I do?"

"Well, Brian. I think you man up. You're going

to have a kid. You had better not leave her to deal with it on her own, like my dad did."

He reached into his desk drawer and pulled out a small black jewelry box and handed it to me. I opened it to find a decent-sized diamond engagement ring. "I've had that for weeks, trying to work up the guts to ask her. I want to marry her, Ally."

"Why are you so scared to ask her?" I stood up to pace in front of his desk.

"I'm forty-two years old, I work as a low-paid civil servant, your mom is the first woman I've dated in over five years, and she is so independent. Why would she want to marry me?"

"Because she loves you, you big dope. God, and I thought teenagers had issues. Brian, take this ring and go hunt my mother down. She should be at school right now, so go find her. Don't let her send you away. Barge into her office if you have to, get down on one knee, and beg." I handed the ring back and he took it, put it into his pocket and stood to leave.

"Thanks, Ally. I owe you one."

***

Mom came home later that evening—much later. I guess they had some making up to do. Eww. Gross. Not thinking about it. She was wearing the engagement ring and a huge smile. I didn't know if I would be in the doghouse for spilling the beans, but she gave me a huge hug and whispered 'thanks' in my ear.

148

"So, for obvious reasons," she said as she rubbed her still-flat tummy, "We are not going to have a long engagement. We're thinking early June, as soon as school's out, for the wedding."

"Since I'm getting all my romance vicariously these days, I want to hear how he proposed. I think I deserve to hear the whole story because if it wasn't for me butting my nose in, there would be no engagement," I said.

Mom gave me a sympathetic look and said, "Well, it was quite the movie moment, let me tell you. He burst into my office with my secretary chasing after him. He pulled me out from behind my desk, kissed me thoroughly, and then went down on one knee and proposed."

"What did he say?" I pressed.

"He said, 'Jennifer Moran, I love you and have been carrying this ring around for weeks trying to get up the nerve to ask you to marry me. Please do me the honor of becoming my wife. Oh, and I know about the baby and I don't feel the slightest bit trapped, so don't even go there.' Thankfully, my secretary had backed out of my office and closed the door while he was kissing me. That's not the way I want to inform my co-workers about my pregnancy."

Grams and I both laughed and hugged her. "Oh, Jen, I'm so happy for you," cried Grams.

"Yeah, Mom, me too. I'm really trying hard to hold back on the 'I told you so,'" I said.

"I can see that," Mom said wryly. "But I will give credit where it is due: you were right, Ally. I was wrong. And I was a basket case. Can we please chalk that up to raging pregnancy hormones and forget it?"

"Forget what?" I said as I hugged her again.

***

With Brian in California to interview David Moore's ex-wife in person, I had a lot more time on my hands. Luckily, Rémy was only too happy to fill in the gaps. He took me to a concert at the Launchpad, a venue in downtown Albuquerque, and somehow managed to get us into the 21-and-over area. I don't even want to know how he did it. He took me back to teen night at Graham Central Station, the dance club we had enjoyed before. I really appreciated his efforts to keep me cheered up because I was still having such a hard time getting over Jack. It was so damn difficult to see him at school every day and not be with him, talk to him, touch him. I tried several times to get him to talk to me, but he always managed to make an excuse and slip away. I would feel like I was starting to get over him and then something would happen to remind me that my heart was still ripped into shreds inside my chest.

I was coming out of the library Tuesday after school, having asked the librarian to help me locate some scholarly critiques of *King Lear*, which we were still reading in my English 1102 class at CNM. I was starting to seriously hate that play. All the characters in it let horrible things happen to them, as if they had no control whatsoever over their own destiny. Maybe it hit a little too close to home for me. Anyway, I wasn't looking where I was going and bumped into a hard, solid someone who was turning into the library. Of course, with my luck, it was Jack. He grabbed my upper arms to steady me.

"Are you okay?" he asked, looking hard into my face.

I couldn't form words. I looked up into his handsome, yet weary face and bit my bottom lip.

"Ally," he shook me slightly. "*Shit,*" he breathed.

I looked down at his hands gripping my arms. He wasn't wearing the Claddagh ring any more. That hurt. I had been keeping a glimmer of hope alive as long as he continued to wear the ring I gave him for his birthday, but he had finally removed it, along with the last hope I had for our relationship. I brushed his hands away, finally recovering my wits. "I'm fine. Sorry. I didn't mean to bother you." I walked away, my stomach twisting in pain.

"Ally, wait," he called after me.

I stopped but didn't turn around.

"I'm sorry," he said after long minutes.

"Me too," I whispered and jogged away before I cried in front of him.

***

On Thursday afternoon, Rémy met me at my house so we could watch movies and order pizza. He was turning out to be a fun guy to hang out with, but I hoped he wouldn't get any romantic notions about me. I needed a friend, not a new love interest, and I was still very hesitant to touch him or let him touch me. We were about halfway through *Olympus Has Fallen*—Rémy loved American action movies—and I had paused it to get a refill of Coke from the kitchen. I didn't realize he had followed me until I turned around, literally into him. He caught me by the upper arms and stared hard at me for a moment before swooping in suddenly to kiss me. It wasn't a very romantic or sweet kiss, just a hard pressing of his lips against mine, and it made me furious. I tried to pull away, but he held me in his iron grip, his lips pressed tight to mine, not moving. Suddenly, my mind felt invaded and I realized I was able to see into his mind as well. I saw him walking along a river, I assumed in France, and I saw him arriving in Albuquerque, meeting so many new people, but looking for me. I saw the day we met in the counselor's office through his eyes; his shock at finding me so soon after his arrival. It was startling to see it through his viewpoint, to see his preoccupation with getting to know me. A word appeared in my mind: *Jessamine*. I had no idea what or who it was, but I had never felt anything so strongly and knew it was important. I thought about how much Rémy had been lying to me all these months and immediately I was incredibly angry and felt it burst out of me.

"Ow!" Rémy pushed me away, his hand going to his lips. "What did you do? It felt like you shocked me! Did you do that?"

"Ugh! What the hell? You bastard! You're a goddamn Seer!" My anger had physically shocked him, which I found oddly satisfying, although I had no earthly idea how I had done it. I had felt intense anger and then I had given Rémy an electric shock.

"Oui. And so are you," he accused, chest heaving.

I was so mad I couldn't even think what to say next. So, I punched him in the face, my fist hitting him right in the jaw. The pain was intense and radiated up my arm. I said a very bad word.

"*Merde!*" cursed Rémy, holding his jaw. "What was that for?"

"For lying to me all this time. For kissing me without my permission. And for generally being a jerk," I yelled, cradling my hand against my body.

"Well, I wouldn't have had to lie to you if you hadn't been so afraid to be touched. I've never met a girl as skittish as you before. You've sensed from the beginning I was psychic, haven't you?"

I shrugged. "Maybe. I don't know what I sensed. Mostly not to trust you, which was clearly accurate. God, my hand hurts."

"Let me see," he ordered, motioning to my hand.

"No!" I turned away from him. "I'm mad at you!"

"Yes, I got that. Punching me was a big hint. Now stop acting like a spoiled child and let me see your hand. We have much to discuss." He took my hand in his. "Where do you keep your antiseptic? You've split the skin. We need to clean this up so it doesn't get infected."

While he administered first aid to my hand, I calmed down enough to ask him what was going on. He said he was in Albuquerque for the sole purpose of finding me. I finally put it together that France equals Gaul and Rémy was from the other group of

Seers that developed in ancient Gaul, now France. Sheesh, I could have saved myself so much trouble if I had Googled the word 'Gaul' when I first heard it. In his group or clan, boys *and* girls could be born with powers, but it was very random. Many were born with no powers whatsoever. He had been sent by the Oracle to find me.

"You've met the Oracle?" I asked. "Ouch!" I hissed as he poured antiseptic on my split skin.

"Don't be such a baby," he reprimanded. "You didn't have to hit me, you know. Yes, I know the Oracle. She is my grandmother."

"What? She got married? But you guys stole her or kidnapped her or something, right?"

"Don't believe everything you hear, chérie. The real story is she ran away with her lover so they could be together. Her clan was trying to keep them apart. There was no kidnapping. She has lived in France voluntarily with my grandfather for many years. She wants to meet you." He finished bandaging my hand.

"Oh, great. Does she think I'm the next Oracle, too?" I asked as I got a bag of frozen vegetables out of the freezer for his face.

"Thank you," he said as I handed him the makeshift icepack. "So you know about that, eh? Well, good. It saves time. I don't know exactly what she thinks, but she received a prophecy and it led to you. You were not too difficult to track down, but it did take a while to get all the paperwork and identification I needed to become a high school-aged exchange student."

"Wait. You're not really in high school? How

old are you?" I demanded.

"I'm 22," he admitted quietly.

"What? Oh my God, everything about you is a lie!" I fumed, walking away from him to sit back on the couch in the living room. Well, at least it explained how he was able to get into the 21-and-over area at the Launchpad. I had to assume he used some other type of persuasive powers or something to get me in without an ID.

"It was necessary, chérie. Things are happening which are very concerning to us. My grandmother may not be with us much longer, and she needs to see you before she passes. It is urgent, Ally. You must come back to France with me."

"You have got to be kidding me!" I was still yelling. "I can't just pack up and leave! I'm supposed to be going to Ireland soon. The Seer Council wants me to go to Ireland over spring break and are insisting I spend time there this summer."

"Well, we'll have to start planning how to get you to France instead. Don't worry. I can be very resourceful."

I had calmed down quite a bit by now and realized he was in as much of an awkward position as me. "So, are you going to stick around? Will you finish the school year? I mean, you're actually a grown-up and you're stuck in high school. God, that's miserable."

"It's not so bad. Of course I'll stay. I still need to figure out how to get you to France. Besides, I like it here. I like my friends." He said this last bit with a pointed look at me.

I smiled at him. "I'm sorry I punched you,

Rémy. You didn't deserve that. Is your face okay?"

"It's fine. Probably better than your hand. I'm sorry I kissed you, but I was desperate. I dread what Jack will do to me when he finds out." He laughed ruefully.

"Jack? He doesn't care anymore. I can kiss whoever I want to kiss," I blustered.

Rémy laughed. "I am not blind, chérie. He still cares, believe me. Can we talk about what happened when I kissed you?"

"You mean the shock I gave you?" I asked.

"Yes, that, but also the word you saw: Jessamine. What is that?"

"I have no idea. You've never heard it before?" He shook his head. "It sounds like a name or a place, don't you think?"

"Perhaps. I will have to look into it," he said.

"I'll get Tara to research it. She's really good at finding—"

"I would rather we kept this between ourselves," he interrupted. "Please, Ally. I know you tell her everything, but this needs to be our secret."

I looked into his gorgeous face and saw nothing but sincerity. "Okay," I said reluctantly. "But I don't like all these secrets. You mentioned a prophecy earlier. Can you tell me what it was?"

"Of course, since it involves both of us. My grandmother saw a vision of you, here in Albuquerque, which is why I came here to find you. Then she heard these words:

The time for unification of the clans is at hand. One Oracle shall arise as another fades away. One will unify and be the heart of the Oracle. One will protect and be the strength of many. A new day for Seers is dawning.

That was the prophecy my grandmother received," he finished.

"Um, what? What the crap is all that supposed to mean?" I made him repeat it until I had it memorized. "Okay, so let me get this straight: Everyone thinks I'm this Oracle that will arise as another fades away, huh?"

"Everything does seem to be pointing to you at this point." He nodded his assent.

"So, then who is this 'one who will unify'? Is that supposed to be you since you came to find me?" He shrugged. "And if it is you, what is that part about being 'the heart of the Oracle'? Please don't tell me your grandmother is trying to play matchmaker with the two of us." He wouldn't meet my eyes, so I figured this was exactly what his grandmother was trying to do. "Okay, let's forget about that for now. What about that last part, about 'one who will protect and be the strength of many'? Is there supposed to be a third person in all of this? And now we have this word, Jessamine, to figure out. Ugh! This is all so vague and cryptic! I hate this!" I fumed.

"I know. Prophecies are always vague, and my grandmother delights in appearing mysterious. Let's try not to worry about it all right now. Let's be glad we finally know the truth about each other and move forward from this point, all right?" I nodded reluctantly. What else could we do? "Now, let's finish this movie, shall we? Gerard Butler is my idol." He put his arm around me and pulled my head down on his shoulder. I fought it for a moment, sitting up, but then gave in and voluntarily put my head on his shoulder. He had been nothing but nice to me lately, helping me have some fun after Jack dumped me. Besides, it was comforting. Now that I knew what was going on with him, I felt like I could relax. So he was a Seer? So his grandmother and my own Seer Council thought I was the next Oracle? So there was some funky prophecy that might imply Rémy and I were supposed to be together? Big deal. I couldn't wrap my mind around it all right now.

"So, you're 22? And hanging around with 17-year-olds? That's kinda creepy. What do you do back in France? Do you work?" I asked, needing a subject change.

"It's not 'creepy.' You Americans have such a preoccupation with age. Back in France I am a student at the L'Universite de Rouen, where I live. I'm studying business. I've had to do online classes this semester so I don't fall behind. It's been difficult with all the high school homework."

"Hmm. Being psychic will probably give you some unfair advantages in the business world, don't you think?"

He laughed and smirked. Strangely, the smirk didn't bother me as much anymore. "So, you are not angry at me anymore? Can we be friends again?" he asked, looking down at me.

I pulled away to look him in the face. His incredibly handsome face. Too bad my heart still belonged to someone else. "Yeah, we can be friends. But no more kissing, okay? I'm not ready for that, and I don't care if your grandmother thinks we should be together."

"I know. You are still in love with Jack. I understand. He is a fool for letting you go, but he is still in love with you too. Maybe he will come to his senses, no? Besides, I don't have romantic feelings for you. I like you, but my heart also belongs to someone else," he admitted.

"This is interesting. Anyone I know? It's not Tara, is it?" I sat up excitedly.

"Ah, no. She is quite beautiful, of course, but a bit too, um, *strong,* for my taste."

I laughed. "Yeah, I can see that. And I think she and Mat might finally make a go of it. So, who holds the elusive key to your heart?"

"I don't think I'm ready to disclose that yet. I have no idea if my feelings are reciprocated. But, ma belle, what about this separation between you and Jack? I don't really like him very much, but I can see it is hurting both of you to be apart. Have you talked to him?"

I curled up against him again and he put his arm around me. "I've tried, so many times. He won't talk to me. I think it's really over."

"Don't be so sure or so pessimistic," he said. "Love will find a way. I have to believe that."

"Why? Because you're French?"

"What does being French have to do with it?" He laughed.

"Well, aren't you all supposed to be the experts at romance?"

"Ally, I think people are the same at heart, no matter what their nationality. I choose to believe love will overcome the barriers we put up. What's wrong with that?"

"Nothing, Rémy. Nothing at all."

CHAPTER TWELVE

"Pray you now, forget and forgive."
–Shakespeare –King Lear (4.7.99)

Friday at school was slightly more bearable than it had been in a while. It was a relief to be comfortable around Rémy and not have to hide anything from him anymore. We had talked a lot about our powers the night before and he was impressed and in awe of the range of my developing powers. His were more limited, but better developed than mine, perhaps because of his advanced age, which I enjoyed teasing him about. He was gifted in the area of persuasion—not surprising—and in locating people and things, much like my mother, but far more powerful.

Sitting next to Jack in physics was still awful, but I was starting to get used to it. I could tell he wanted to ask me about the bandage on my hand, but since I didn't want to tell him, I didn't give him any sort of opening. I kept busy with the notes we were taking for an upcoming lab, trying not to let on that writing really hurt my hand. I guess I didn't do a great job of that because about ten minutes into the lecture, Jack reached over and gently stilled my wrist.

"I'll give you a copy of mine later, okay? I can tell it hurts," he whispered. I looked over at him, surprised. These were the first real words he had spoken to me in nearly a month. I nodded and put my pen down in relief. I tried to pay attention to the rest of the lecture, but not having to write left my mind too free. I kept sneaking glances at Jack, watching his head bent over his spiral notebook. He must have felt me looking because he caught me several times. As soon as the bell rang, I packed up quickly and left without saying a word to him.

During lunch, I noticed him sitting by himself at a table not too far from ours and I'm pretty sure he was glaring at Rémy and me. And I'm pretty sure Rémy was well aware and enjoying it, taking the opportunity to touch me frequently and making me laugh. If I didn't know better, I would say Jack was jealous, but that was ridiculous. He broke up with me. Why was he glaring at Rémy and me like he cared? Where did he get off? He didn't want me, but no one else could have me, either? I made sure Jack could see I was enjoying Rémy's attention. How was it possible I could be so angry with a person and yet still love him so much? Maybe if I didn't have to see him every day and sit by him in two classes I could get over him.

I was emotionally exhausted by the end of the day and told Rémy I needed to be alone tonight. I had some serious wallowing to engage in. I sped home and immediately changed into my comfy *Teenage Mutant Ninja Turtles* pajama pants, a cami—sans bra because it was sadly unnecessary—and a truly disgusting old sweatshirt with the neck raggedly cut out. I scraped my hair up into messy pigtails and I was ready for an evening of abject self-pity and chick flicks. Mom and Grams were out checking on wedding venues, so I had the house all to myself. The only hitch in my plans came when I checked the freezer and realized we were out of ice cream. Unacceptable. No pity-party would be complete without several pints, so I did what any self-respecting, recently dumped girl would do: I drove to Walmart in my pajamas to buy some damn ice cream. Classy, I know. I was in the freezer aisle, three pints already in my cart, trying to decide between Chunky Monkey and Cherry Garcia for my final pint, when I heard a squeal and was attacked from behind.

"Ally!" It was Megan, hugging my legs. Trina was right behind her. Oh, God, this was going to be awful. I turned around and squatted down to hug Megan back.

"Hey, munchkin. Hi," I choked out.

"Ally! I miss you! Why don't you come over anymore? Jack is so sad. Don't you love him?" she cried.

"Oh, sweetie. I'm so sorry. I miss you, too." I really did miss her. When I fell in love with Jack, I also fell in love with his family. He had taken so much away from me. I was incredibly pissed at him. "Of course I still love your brother. I still love you too. Jack needs to be by himself for now." I couldn't go on; the tears were coming no matter how hard I tried to hold them back.

"Megan, sweetheart, let her go." Trina pried her off me and pulled me into her arms. "Come here, mija. I'm so sorry, Ally."

I nodded and continued to cry, right there in the middle of the frozen food aisle. "I miss him so much, Trina," I whispered.

"I know. He misses you too. Have you talked to him?"

I shook my head. "He won't talk to me. He doesn't want me," I cried into her neck.

"I know that's not true. He's miserable without you. He's just going through a lot right now." She pulled back to look into my face. "He still loves you, you know."

I shook my head again, sadly. "I don't think so, Trina. I've got to go before my ice cream melts." I knelt down to hug Megan again briefly. "You both take care, okay?"

I cried all the way home. I crammed the ice cream in the freezer and fell onto the couch to continue my cry in peace.

I fell asleep and didn't wake up until it was starting to get dark outside. Mom and Grams were still gone, so I grabbed a pint of ice cream and a spoon and settled down for dinner and a movie with the two most important men in my life: Ben and Jerry. I was about halfway through my Chunky Monkey and *While You Were Sleeping* when the doorbell rang. Thinking it was a) Rémy and I would get rid of him or b) the UPS guy needing a signature, I took my ice cream with me to answer the door. I was wrong. It was Jack, looking freshly showered with wet hair and a recent shave, wearing one of my favorite pairs of faded jeans, a dark blue t-shirt, and his leather jacket. I stared like an idiot, ice cream dripping off my spoon.

"Hi," he said quietly.

"Hi," I said stupidly.

"Um, I brought your physics notes."

"Oh." Awkward silence.

"Can I come in?" he asked hesitantly.

I stepped away from the door and walked back into the living room, leaving him to follow or not. I set my ice cream on the coffee table and reached for the remote to pause the movie.

"*While You Were Sleeping,* huh? That's one of your favorites," he offered.

I didn't respond. I didn't want to talk about how he knew what my favorite movies were. I needed him to give me the goddamn physics notes and leave. Now. My stomach was starting to hurt and he needed to go before I got sick. I had wanted desperately to talk to him, but now that he was here, I couldn't handle it. I turned the TV off and took my ice cream back to the freezer. When I turned around, he was there, sitting at the kitchen table.

"So, you and Rémy, huh?" he asked.

I shrugged. I didn't feel like going into this with him, either.

"Shit," I heard him mutter under his breath.

"What do you want, Jack?" I cried. I couldn't take much more of this. My heart felt like it was being re-shredded and I was on the verge of throwing up.

"Trina and Megan said they saw you at Walmart today. I had to come over."

Could this day get any worse? I couldn't find my voice, so I shook my head, reaching up to wipe away the tears that were spilling over. "Why?" I finally forced myself to ask. "Why did you have to come over?"

"Is it true, Ally? Is what they told me true? Do you still love me? Even after everything I did?" he whispered hoarsely.

I gave a sob and wrapped my arms around my stomach, trying not to vomit. He got up and walked over to me, hesitantly putting his arms around me. I stayed like I was for an endless moment before giving up and wrapping my arms around him, sobbing violently into his chest.

He pulled me tightly against him, his head resting on mine. "God, Ally. I'm so sorry. I was such a fool. Is there any way you can forgive me?"

I pulled back to look into his eyes. Was this a cruel dream or could it possibly be true? "Jack?" I hiccoughed through my sobs.

He took my face in his hands and leaned in to kiss me. It was the softest of kisses, but it felt like coming home. He pulled away. "Ally, querida," he breathed against my lips. "God, I love you. I never stopped loving you. I'm so sorry I hurt you."

"You broke my heart, Jack," I sobbed.

"I know. I'm so sorry. I broke mine, too. I'm miserable without you. Please, Ally," he was literally begging, tears beginning to escape his eyes. "If you still love me even a little bit, please give me another chance."

I had thought it would make me feel better to hear him grovel, but it didn't. I had thought I would revel in him crawling back to me and begging me to take him back. Anything that hurt him, hurt me too. I was so tired of all of it: tired of both of us being miserable, tired of being apart. I needed to forgive him so we could move on with our lives, together this time. Here in his arms was where I belonged. I leaned back into him. "I love you too, Jack. I never stopped." I pulled away and cupped my palm on his jaw. "I tried to get over you. I really did, but I couldn't."

He put his hand over mine and brought it up to his lips, kissing the ring I had never removed. "You never took it off." I shook my head, hurt he had taken his off. He reached into his shirt and pulled out a chain with the Claddagh ring hanging from it. "I tried. I wanted you to think I had so you would move on, but I couldn't." He pulled the chain over his head, undid the clasp, and put his ring in my palm.

My heart twisted with painful joy, knowing he hadn't been able to put the ring away and forget it, forget me, forget us. I slid it back onto the ring finger of his right hand, the heart facing toward him, where it belonged, signifying he was mine.

Then he was kissing me again, kissing me as if his life depended on it, which maybe it did; I know mine did. I realized while I could live without him, it was a life devoid of full joy. So I kissed him back, investing every ounce of myself. For once, he didn't hold back and it intensified quickly. His mouth opened mine and his tongue stroked inside. He reached down, grabbed my rear end, and pulled me tight against him. I wound my legs around his waist as he placed me on the counter and set about devouring my mouth in the best way possible. I had missed this so incredibly much. As we kissed, I felt my soul and heart being healed. Suffice it to say that by the time he pulled away, both of us were panting and he had discovered I wasn't wearing a bra. And I knew exactly how much he wanted me. Yeah.

"Jesus, Ally. I'm sorry. That got out of hand," he breathed, resting his forehead against mine. "I have missed you so damned much."

I put my fingers against his lips, shushing him. "Don't ever apologize for this, Jack. Please."

"Okay, I'll try." He smiled. "But I don't want our first time to be on your grandmother's kitchen counter. For God's sake, I don't even know if she or your mom is home. What was I thinking?"

"I don't really think you were. At least not with this brain," I said as I tapped his head. He looked at me, slightly shocked, and then we were both laughing and kissing some more, but lighter and not nearly as intense.

"Tell me what happened, querida," he insisted as he took my injured hand gently in his. Oh, how I had missed hearing his pet name for me.

"I kind of punched Rémy in the face," I admitted.

"Why would you do that? It looked like you two were getting along just fine today," he said, sounding miffed.

"Jealous?" I asked, amused.

"You're goddamn right I'm jealous. I don't care if I had no right to be. I wanted to kill him today, watching him touch you and make you laugh. Are you and he…?"

"No! God, Jack! Do you think I would be kissing you like this if I were with someone else? You had better say no," I warned.

"Of course not. It's only my insane jealousy talking. Sorry," he said quickly.

"We're just friends. He really helped me cope this last month. I haven't been doing very well without you."

"Yeah, me neither. God, Ally, life sucked without you." That called for more kissing. "So why did you punch him?" he asked against my lips.

"Because he kissed me," I said, going back in for another kiss.

"What?" Jack pulled back, holding my arms. "Why the hell was he kissing you? You said you were just friends. I am going to kill him!"

"Calm down," I said, running my fingers through his hair, which was still damp from his shower. He smelled incredible and tasted even better. I kissed him and said, "Rémy kissed me and I punched him."

"He's that bad of a kisser, huh?"

I laughed. "Oh, he wasn't really putting much effort into it. He was fed up with trying to touch me, so he grabbed me and kissed me." At Jack's growl I continued, "He's a Seer, Jack. He touched me to read my mind and see if I was one, too. That's why he's here in Albuquerque. He came to find me."

"Son of a bitch," was his response.

'Yep." I filled him in on the rest of the story between kisses, trying to make up for a month without any.

"So, let me get this straight: that little douche-bag came here to find you because his grandmother is the Oracle. And she got some kind of prophecy and sent Rémy over here to convince you to go to France with him. And he's really 22 years old and not a high school student. Am I missing anything?" he said through clenched teeth.

"Nope, that sounds like the gist of it," I said breezily. I didn't fill him in on the part about Rémy being the heart of the Oracle. I figured that could wait.

"Let me see your hand," he said as he gently unwrapped the bandage. I winced as he pulled it away. "Please let me kick his ass." He kissed all around the injured area.

I leaned forward and kissed his hair. "No. I need you to get along with him, okay? He's been a really good friend. And I punched him of my own free will."

"Fine. For you, I won't kill him." He nodded reluctantly as he re-wrapped my hand.

"Jack," I said, getting serious for a moment. "I need you to promise me something."

"Anything."

"No more pulling away. I can't take it. Being apart from you nearly destroyed me. Your past is part of you and I love you. All of you. You have to let me in. I know you're going through a tough time with your dad, but please let me help. "

"Okay," he said, kissing me. "If you promise in

return not to try to hold back or withdraw because of your psychic oracle-ness. It's part of you and I love you. All of you," he repeated. After another lengthy kiss, he lifted me off the counter. "As much as I love this outfit, it's giving me way too many ideas. Why don't you go put on something a little more, uh, inaccessible, and I'll take you out for a tofu burger or something and we can talk. I'm nearly certain you only had ice cream for dinner."

I laughed and told him to give me fifteen minutes. When I reappeared at the top of the stairs he was sitting on the couch, petting Wicky. As I walked down the stairs, his eyes got big, and he set the cat away from him and rose to meet me.

"Holy mother of God." I had gone all out, donning a tight blue sheath dress with a plunging neckline, courtesy of Tara, and high heels. "I think this is going to take more than a tofu burger."

"I want to make sure you understand what you've been missing," I said in what I hoped was a seductive voice. I prayed I wouldn't ruin the effect by tripping on the ridiculously high heels. I had a sudden flashback—not psychic—to the night we started dating, right after his probation hearing, when I had come down the stairs wearing another of Tara's choice of dresses. Note to self: Jack appreciates a sexy dress. Good to know.

"Oh. My. God," he said as he pulled me into his arms.

Of course, this was the scene Grams and my mom walked in on: Jack and I kissing insanely, my hands in his hair, his on my rear end. "Ally, is that Jack's car outsi—apparently so," finished Grams wryly. "Hello, Jack."

I wasn't about to jump apart guiltily. I had nothing to be ashamed of by kissing my newly-restored boyfriend. He did, however, remove his hands and put one arm around my waist. "Hi, Mrs. Moran, Ms. Moran. How have you been?"

"Oh, *we've* been fine, Jack. I can't say the same for Ally, but she appears to be doing well now. How have you been?" Grams asked pointedly.

"Not good, actually. I came over to beg Ally to take me back. I was stupid and let go of the most important thing in my life."

Grams seemed to approve of his honesty. "Well, you're back now. I certainly hope there was groveling involved. And call me Adele. Are you two going out?"

"Yes, Grams. Jack is taking me to dinner because he apparently doesn't approve of my ice cream-only diet. And, yes, there was some groveling. Don't wait up." I took his hand to lead him outside.

"What a lovely dress, Ally, what there is of it," murmured my mother.

"Rather ironic, don't you think, Mom? See you later." I gave her a hug and kissed her on the cheek. "Get some rest, okay?"

***

"What was that about with your mom?" Jack asked. "What am I missing?"

So I filled him in on the big news. "And if you say, 'way to go, Brian', I will have to hurt you."

He laughed. "Okay, I'll save the high-fives for when I see him in person. Are you all right with this? With your mom getting married? With her having a baby?"

"Yeah, I am. I'm really happy for her and Brian. I'm going to be a big sister, Jack!"

"You're going to be great big sister. Now, where should we go to celebrate us being us again? You look amazing, so let's not let that go to waste."

After some discussion, we finally decided to go to the Cooperage, a fairly expensive steakhouse with an enormous chuckwagon salad bar. I'm not even kidding about the name. I didn't want him to spend so much on me, but he argued our getting back together was a worthy occasion. He also said they had a band playing on Friday nights and he wanted an excuse to dance with me and show me off. "Come on, querida. My cousin, Kenny, is the bass player and he's been bugging me to go hear him. You know I'm going to win, so let's save time. Give in now." He said this last part while kissing my neck and jaw, which, as always, rendered me nearly incoherent.

"You don't play fair," I sighed. "Fine. We can go."

***

Tara was beside herself when I texted her late Friday night to tell her Jack and I were back together.

Tara: OMG! Want 2 hear all about it! Coming over 2morrow.

Me: OK. Can't wait to tell you. So happy!

Tara: So happy 4 U!

***

"Oh, God, Ally! That's so romantic! I wish I had that kind of romance in my life." She was sprawled across my bed early Saturday morning. She had actually shown up before I was even awake, my late night with Jack having caused me to sleep in later than usual.

After a month-long separation, we couldn't stand to say goodnight and stayed at Village Inn, a 24-hour coffee shop, until close to 3 a.m. We talked and drank decaf, holding hands the entire time. He told me he was trying to find a way to build some sort of relationship with his dad, mostly for Megan's sake. He said the main reason he had told me he needed time apart was because he was feeling so much hate in his heart toward his father he couldn't reconcile the love he was feeling toward me. He had felt like he was being torn apart from the inside. He had actually started counseling in the last few weeks and felt like it was helping. His counselor was helping him understand and accept that he, himself, bore some of the responsibility for the damaged relationship; he couldn't chalk it all up to fate or bad luck. He planned to keep seeing his counselor for the foreseeable future, which I thought was a great idea. He promised to talk to me from now on about what he was feeling and not pull away.

"From what I've seen," I said to Tara, "you've got some romance going on. What is up with you and Mat, anyway?"

"I'm not really sure, actually. We've gone out a couple times, but after coming on so strong, he's really taking it slow. He hasn't even tried to kiss me! I don't know, maybe he's not as impressed as he thought he would be." She tried for a nonchalant tone that didn't fool me in the slightest.

"I'm positive that's not what the problem is, Tara. The guy has been crazy about you for months. Could it have anything to do with the fact that he's 20 and you're only 17?" I rooted through my drawers for something to wear, finally settling on my favorite jeans and a t-shirt.

"Maybe. Manny and Trina sure raised those boys with a strong sense of right and wrong, huh? Is that the best you can do?" she gestured to my clothing choice.

I shrugged and motioned for her to take over. "Well, they got Jack kind of late, but yeah. I agree with you. Jack has such iron control," I mused.

"Ooh, this sounds interesting. Do tell," she pounced while handing me a denim skirt and chiffon blouse. I laughed. "Oh, no you don't! We are not going down that path again. Suffice it to say my V-card is a bit more tattered than in the past, yet still intact."

"Hot," she said.

"Yeah, it was." We both laughed. "So, what do

you think about a double date sometime soon?"

"Yes! I was so bummed that right as I started dating Mat, you broke up with his best friend. Do you realize how cool it is that we're dating cousins/best friends? God, we could be related someday, Ally."

"Let's not get ahead of ourselves," I warned.

"Oh, please. You and Jack are totally destined for wedded bliss." She rolled her eyes.

"Oh, are you getting visions of the future now?" I asked, archly.

"I don't need no stinkin' crystal ball to tell me you and Jack are the real thing, sweetie."

"Yeah, well the last month gave me some serious doubts about that."

"Hey." She came around the bed to hug me. "You've had a really tough time, but it all worked out. Jack's had some major suckage in his life in the last few years. He's so lucky to have found you, and if he doesn't appreciate it from now on, I will have some interesting words for him."

I laughed ruefully and hugged her back. "Thanks, Tara. I need a fan in my life."

"Well, I'm your biggest. Don't forget it."

***

Rémy was also happy for me when he heard Jack and I were back together, although he couldn't resist teasing me. "Ah, ma belle, and right as I was about to make my move. How shall I go on? All my hopes are dead!" he said this as he kissed both my cheeks Monday morning at school.

176

"Oh, whatever, you big tease." I hugged him in return. "Thanks," I whispered as I kissed his cheek.

"Yeah, Rémy, thanks," Jack said, a bit grudgingly, while offering his hand. "Wow, that bruise looks like it hurts." He gestured to where I had punched him.

Rémy shook Jack's hand, smirked, and said, "It was worth it." They stared at each other for a moment, obviously exchanging some mysterious bro-code, then both slowly smiled and nodded.

***

Brian returned from California and arranged to meet me after school. "Congratulations, *Dad*," I said and hugged him in greeting. "You did good. Mom is about ready to burst from all the happiness."

He laughed. "Thanks, Ally. I really do owe you one. Hey, I'm sorry about, you know—"

"Knocking up my mom?"

"No, I'm not sorry about that," he said. "But it's a bit awkward talking about it with your future stepdaughter. I hope it doesn't embarrass you."

"Nah. I'm a big girl. And I'm ridiculously excited about having a sister or brother. Are you ready for all these wedding plans Mom and Grams are getting into?"

He blew out a breath. "I don't know. I'm hoping I can simply write the checks and show up when and where they tell me."

I laughed. "That's probably a good plan. Let them have their way."

"Well, your mom has never had a wedding, and this will be her only one if I have anything to say about it. I want to her have her dream wedding," he said quietly.

"You're a nice guy, Brian Keller." I punched him lightly on the arm.

"Even though I knocked up your mom?" he asked wryly.

"Hey, you have great taste. So, tell me how things went with the ex-Mrs. Moore in California."

"It was pretty much a wasted trip. She didn't have anything useful to add, but I still get the feeling she's holding back for some reason. I did get contact information for her two daughters and will be trying to get in touch with them this week."

"So, what's our next step?"

"I want to talk to Scott Alder again," he stated.

"Why? The guy is innocent." I couldn't tell Brian how I knew this, but I needed to make him understand this was a dead end. Mom and Grams wanted to wait to tell Brian about our 'family gift.' They didn't think it would be a deal-breaker, but wanted to save the drama for later.

"Ally, I hate to tell you this, but in cases like this, nine times out of ten it is the husband or boyfriend that did it. They're the ones with the motive." He got out the file on Scott and opened it.

"Not this time. He loved her. Her disappearance destroyed him, Brian."

"Maybe the guilt destroyed him, Ally. I have to follow up on this."

"Fine, but I want to go with you." I was adamant. I hoped to be able to ask questions that would show Brian that Scott had nothing to do with Ashley's disappearance.

"Fine. Let's go. He's expecting us in about 20 minutes."

***

This time we questioned Scott in his home. His wife, Anna, served us coffee and then sat beside Scott, scooting her chair possessively closer.

"I really don't know what else I can tell you, Detective Keller. I told you everything I remember the last time you were here."

"I need to go over it again, Mr. Alder. Why don't you start at the beginning and tell us about your relationship with Ashley." Brian took out his notebook.

Scott sighed and began. "Ashley and I met at the beginning of our sophomore year when she moved here to Albuquerque. She was so beautiful." He stared down at the table, lost in his memories. Anna reached her hand over and placed it on top of his. He looked up and gave her a weak smile. "I was just a little punk-ass kid, but we became friends. I finally worked up the nerve to ask her out at the beginning of our junior year. I was shocked when she said yes. We were inseparable after that. And then she got pregnant." He looked up at Anna and mouthed 'sorry.' Anna put her other hand on top of Scott's and shook her head. "I wanted to get married right away. I was going to drop out and get a job, but she was adamant we both finish high school. She was never ashamed. I remember telling her parents. We stood before them, holding hands, and she said, 'Mom, Dad, we're going to have a baby. We love each other and we're getting married right after graduation. Please try to be happy for us.' Well, after a while they were. They were going to help us out so we could both go to college, at least part-time. We had it all planned out."

"Tell me about that last day, the day Ashley disappeared," Brian said when Scott paused.

Scott put his head in his hands, running them through his hair. "After school, I walked her to her locker and kissed her goodbye. She was going to walk home, like usual, because I had basketball practice. That was the last time I saw her. When I went by her house later to pick her up, she wasn't there. Her mom had thought she was with me."

"When did her mother call the police?"

"I think it was pretty soon after I got there, maybe within a half-hour or so."

"And did you actually see her leave school that afternoon?" Brian followed up.

He shook his head. "No. I left her at her locker."

I nudged Brian under the table and raised my eyebrows, silently asking if I could ask a question. Brian looked at me for a moment before nodding. "Scott, what about any ex-boyfriends of Ashley's? Who did she date before you?"

"She went out a few times with a guy named Barry during her sophomore year. I don't remember his last name. I hated that guy."

"Why?" I asked.

"Because he was going out with the girl I wanted," Scott said as if I should understand something so obvious.

"Well, how did he treat her?" I pushed. Brian gave me an exasperated look.

"I don't know. He kind of showed her off, I guess. I thought it was messed up and I knew he wasn't good enough for her."

"How did they break up? Who did the dumping?" I pushed.

"She did. They didn't go out very long. She got tired of it and broke it off."

"How did Barry respond?" I leaned forward, looking at Brian to make sure he was getting this down in his notebook. He rolled his eyes and started writing.

"I don't know. I wasn't there. He had moved on to another girl by the next day, though."

"So, he wasn't jealous or anything?"

"It didn't seem like it," Scott replied.

"Okay," Brian took over. "Mr. Alder, the problem is we only have your word for it Ashley left school by herself that day. Nobody saw her leave school. Nobody saw her walking home. Nobody saw her arrive home."

Scott looked up, straight into Brian's eyes. "I did not kill Ashley. I loved her. I was going to marry her," he said fiercely.

"Don't leave town, Mr. Alder. We'll see ourselves out," Brian said as we rose to leave.

***

As we drove away, I turned to Brian. "Listen. He didn't do it. I know that for a fact. You are barking

181

up the wrong tree. The real killer is still out there."

"Ally, I know you like him, but he's our best suspect. He's the only one with any kind of motive."

"What's his motive? He was in love with Ashley!" I argued.

"It's a heck of a way to get out of becoming a teen father," Brian responded.

"He had no reason to want to get out of it! He was excited about the baby! He was still going to be able to go to college! Brian, there is no way he wanted to get rid of Ashley! Why can't you see that?" I was exasperated.

"Ally, I'm sorry." He shook his head. "We're going to have to agree to disagree about this. Scott Alder continues to be our leading suspect."

"Well, I guess I'm going to have to prove you wrong." I crossed my arms and narrowed my eyes at him.

"I guess so. God, you're a lot like your mom, you know that? But remember: you are absolutely NOT to question anyone without me, got that?"

"Yes, sir, Detective Keller, sir." I saluted him.

"Smart ass," he muttered.

CHAPTER THIRTEEN

*"Only darkness, and darkness is cold. And maybe
it's better than the burning of the light."*
–Madeleine L'Engle

Tara wasted no time in planning a double date.
So, Friday night Jack and I dutifully met her and
Mat at the movie theater. After a fun, but ultimately
forgettable film—at least there was less teen drama
to put up with during this movie—we congregated
at BJ's Brew Pub for a late dinner. Unfortunate
name aside, they served great veggie burgers, onion
rings, and house-brewed cream soda, which we
enjoyed while teasing Tara and Mat about how long
it took her to finally agree to go out with him.

"I think she wanted to make me completely
insane. That's why it took her so long to say yes,"
said Mat, putting his arm around Tara and pulling
her close to kiss her hair. As far as I knew, he
hadn't yet tried to kiss her for real yet, and I knew
this was frustrating Tara no end.

"Yeah, well maybe your insanity is what scared

me off for so long." Tara pushed him away playfully.

"You have no real idea of the depth of his madness," Jack said, trying to sound serious. Mat threw an onion ring at him, which Jack caught and ate.

"No, the truth is you were discriminating against me because I'm not one of those college boys you usually date. You weren't ready for what a real working man can bring you." Mat had finished his EMT training in December and was now working full-time as a paramedic attached to a fire station. He had started a few weeks ago.

"Oh, and what exactly can you bring me?" Tara looked at him, disbelieving.

"I'll tell you later, corazon. Better yet, I'll show you."

"Promises, promises," she taunted. "You're all talk, Jimenez."

Mat got a slightly dangerous look in his eyes and leaned in to whisper something in Tara's ear. Or maybe he was nibbling her earlobe, because she closed her eyes and bit her lip.

"Um, we're still here, you two," I said disgustedly. "Get a room."

"Oh, now don't be like that, Ally. Just because Jack doesn't have my moves doesn't mean you have to hate on me and my girl," answered Mat with a very self-satisfied grin.

"Whatever," said Jack as he leaned over and began to kiss me along my jaw and neck. I had my own moment of eyes closing and lip biting.

"Looks like Jack does okay in the 'moves'

department," Tara said wryly. "I certainly haven't heard any complaints from Ally.

"Yeah, I taught my little cousin everything I know," bragged Mat.

Jack pulled away and I could tell he was about to engage negatively with Mat, so to distract him I grabbed his jacket and pulled him back in for a real kiss. It was lovely and slow and left no room for thinking about anything else.

"Now who needs to get a room?" muttered Mat as we broke apart.

***

I texted Tara later that night.

Me: Call me if you're home. I want to hear about it.

I had barely hit send when she called. "You little hypocrite," she said in greeting. "I'm supposed to kiss and tell, but you can be stingy and keep all the good, juicy details about you and Jack to yourself?"

"Yes. I don't see why you have a problem with that. Now spill!" I ordered.

She laughed. "Fine, but I expect some quid pro quo."

"Okay, smarty pants. I'll see what I can do. Now, did he finally kiss you or what?"

"Yes, he finally did."

"That's it? Seriously? When? Where? How was it?" I screeched.

"What do I get in return?" she taunted.

"Oh my God, Tara! I'm going to reach through this cellphone and strangle you!" There was only expectant silence from her end. "Fine. I will tell you exactly how Jack kissed me goodbye tonight. Deal?"

"Deal. Okay, my first kiss with Mat. Here we go: he pulled up in front of my house, turned off the engine, and turned to face me. He said, 'Tara Scott, I joke around a lot, but I need to be serious for a minute. I'm nuts about you. I'm probably too old for you, but I don't care. I want you to be my girlfriend. I want to be your boyfriend. And I really, really need to kiss you right now.' I stared at him for a second, then I nodded. He took my face in his hands and laid his lips against mine, so gently. Oh, God, Ally! It was amazing. It was the best kiss I've ever had."

"So, you and Mat, huh? I'm really happy for you. He doesn't know how lucky he is."

"I know, right?" We both laughed. "Now it's your turn. You didn't think I'd forget, did you?"

"I was hoping. Fine. Here goes: Mom stayed the night at Brian's and Grams is out with Roger, so Jack came inside, swooped me up into his arms and carried me upstairs to my bedroom, where he made mad, passionate love to me for hours on end. He's still here, sleeping beside me, so I need to be quiet."

There was stunned silence on the other end for a moment. "You are such a bitch and I hate your guts. I'm hanging up now."

"Okay, okay!" I laughed. "I'm sorry! I couldn't resist. I'll tell, I promise."

"I'm waiting," she said coldly.

"Fine. My mom really is at Brian's and Grams was already in bed, so Jack came in and pulled me down onto the couch with him. He pulled onto his lap, tucked my hair behind my ear, which I love, and kissed me, really softly. Then he held me, for like an hour. It was one of the most romantic things he's ever done."

I heard her sigh. "Wow."

"Yeah," I sighed in return.

"Those Jimenez boys have got it going on, girl," she said.

"Tru dat, homie."

"Okay, I'm hanging up now before you get any more gangsta. Goodnight. See you tomorrow. Let's make a pact to go on a double date at least once a month. Okay?"

"Sure. It was a lot of fun. Two sets of best friends going out. What could be better?"

***

I had been racking my brains to find a way to get out of going to Ireland over spring break, especially since Jack and I had only recently gotten back together. I was not eager to be gone from him for an entire week. It turned out I needn't have worried; I was attending a high school that operated on a semester schedule and a community college that operated on a trimester schedule. Short version: I had CNM classes during spring break, so I couldn't go to Ireland. Whew! Dodged a bullet there. Cassie told me she explained it to the council and they understood; we began making plans for me to go in the summer. The plan was for me to fly over by myself a few days after my mom's wedding. Cassie was getting married around the same time and would be on her honeymoon, but I assured her I was fully capable of traveling by myself. I actually preferred it that way.

The Wednesday before spring break, I was sitting on Jack's couch, finishing an economics quiz. Jack had already finished and I was determined not to ask for his help.

"Argh!" I exclaimed, frantically shuffling through my notes.

"What's wrong, babe?" Jack muted the basketball game he was watching and looked up at me from his spot on the floor.

"Nothing. I can't find my notes on demand curve shifts. It's okay."

He smiled and handed me his notebook. "Is that your last question? Here, use my notes. I want you to be done so I can ask you something."

I took his notes gratefully and finished my quiz, gladly closing my laptop for the night. "I'm all yours. What do you want to ask me?"

He turned off the television and looked up at me. "I talked to my dad yesterday. He's settled here in Albuquerque and really likes his new job, so he wants to sell our house in Taos."

I slid behind him, my knees on either side of his shoulders, and began to massage his tight shoulder muscles. "Are you okay with that?"

"Yeah. I get that he needs to move on. What I wanted to ask is if you would be willing to come with me to Taos this weekend? When I moved down here, I left a bunch of my stuff in my old bedroom. Dad said it would be better if I went and packed up anything I still want. When he goes to sell the house, he can just get rid of anything I leave."

"I would love to go with you. It'll be our first road trip. I'll need to be back by Tuesday for my CNM English class, though," I said as I honed in on a particularly tight spot on his left shoulder. "Since I used it as an excuse for not going to Ireland, I better not ditch."

He groaned in appreciation at my massage and tilted his head to give me greater access. "I figured we could leave Friday after I get off work and drive back Monday. We can stay with my cousin, Donny. When I take you home tonight, I'll come in to ask your grandmother and mom, and assure them we will have separate bedrooms."

I laughed and leaned forward to kiss his cheek. "Spoilsport. You're such a good guy, Jack."

He pulled me down onto his lap and began kissing me. "Yeah, well I never said it was easy."

After a short discussion and a phone call to Trina, Grams and Mom were fine with me going and I waited impatiently for Friday to arrive. Trina had loaned Jack her Ford Escape, not wanting us to make the four-hour trip in Jack's forty-nine year old car, so we enjoyed a higher level of comfort than usual. We stopped in Santa Fe for dinner and arrived at his cousin Donny's house late. Donny had waited up for us and showed us to our rooms, telling us we would meet his wife and baby in the morning.

I woke the next morning to the smell of coffee and the sound of an infant crying. I got ready quickly and wandered out to the kitchen to find Jack feeding cereal to a baby and Donny flipping pancakes at the stove. "Good morning," I greeted them both and kissed the top of Jack's head. "Who's your friend?"

Jack chuckled as he loaded another spoonful of grayish goo into the baby's mouth. "This is little Alex."

The baby gave me a mushy smile and banged his hands on the high chair tray, demanding more. "That's my boy," Donny said fondly. "Did you sleep all right, Ally?"

"Great, thanks. Can I help with anything?"

"Nope, I got it. Just help yourself to coffee or orange juice." He turned back to the pancakes as I poured a cup of coffee and sat down next to Jack and Alex.

"Wow, Jack. I had no idea you were so domestic," I said as he continued to feed the baby, looking like he was enjoying himself, making airplane noises as he shoveled the cereal in Alex's greedy little mouth.

"I like kids," he shrugged.

"Good thing," a tall, attractive brunette entered the kitchen. "Because the Jimenez family is certainly fertile. You're feeding a rhythm method baby, you know. Keep that in mind, Ally, if you decide to stick with this one." She hugged Jack from behind. "It's good to see you again, Jack. It's been way too long. Hi, Ally." She gave me a hug. I was getting used to how affectionate Jack's family was. "It's nice to meet you. I've heard lots about you. I'm Audra."

"Thanks. Nice to meet you too."

Donny turned around to greet his wife with a kiss that was a bit more than perfunctory. Jack and I looked at each other with amusement.

"Thanks for letting me sleep in, babe. And for getting breakfast. And for feeding the baby." Audra punctuated each statement with another kiss.

"Hey, *I'm* feeding the baby," Jack argued. She didn't answer him as Donny pulled her back for another long kiss. Jack rolled his eyes at me.

"So, when are you two heading over to pack up your stuff?" Audra asked as she poured herself a cup of coffee.

"Right after breakfast," Jack answered. "I just want to get it over with. I don't think it will take too long and then I can show Ally some of the sights around here. She's never been to Taos."

"Where are you going to take her?" Donny asked.

"I thought we'd take a look at the Gorge Bridge and the pueblo. Maybe stroll around the Plaza. We'll eat dinner somewhere downtown," Jack said.

"That sounds fun. Why don't we meet you at Mosaic this evening? We want to take you out to dinner," Audra offered.

"You guys don't have to do that," Jack began.

"No, no. We want to. Please? We got a babysitter for tonight and could really use some adult time. You'd be doing us a favor," she wheedled. "They have a really great vegetarian selection, Ally. Come on, Jack, please?"

"Give in, Jack," Donny sighed. "She'll get her way. She always does." Audra gave him a dirty look.

"Okay." He laughed. "If Ally's fine with it."

"Of course," I said. "It sounds like fun."

"Oh, good." She clapped her hands in gleeful victory. "Let's meet there around 7, okay?"

"Where is this place?" Jack asked.

"In the Hotel La Fonda, so if you end the day on the Plaza, you'll be right there."

Donny served breakfast, which was delicious: pancakes, bacon, and fresh fruit. He had even prepared some soy bacon for me.

"You have the nicest family," I told Jack as we drove across town a half hour later. "I really like Audra and Donny."

"Yeah, they're great. Donny was away at college during my asshole years. It's nice to have one person in the family who doesn't remember what I was like then. I haven't seen him since their wedding last spring."

"Well, it's really great of them to let us stay with them. So, have you ever heard the Taos Hum?" I referred to the low frequency humming sound some people swore they could hear in this area. It was somewhat famous and had even been mentioned on the X-Files.

He laughed. "No. And I don't know of anyone who has. I don't think it's real, querida. Sorry."

"So, you believe in psychics and what was it? Curanderas? But you don't believe in the Taos Hum? Seriously? I'm so disappointed, Jack. This could be a deal-breaker." I tried to look serious.

He chuckled and reached for my hand. "Yeah, well, I personally know several psychics and at least one curandera. I might believe in the Hum if I actually heard it."

"Well, I guess we can still be together. You are a pretty good kisser, after all."

"Pretty good? I can see that you need a reminder in the very near future." He rubbed his thumb over the back of my hand. "If you think I'm only pretty good, you should have an opportunity to reevaluate." He pulled into the driveway of a fairly large adobe-style house.

"Hmm. You could be right."

He blew out his breath. "Well, here we are." He turned to look at me, taking both my hands in his. "Thank you for coming with me, Ally. This is going to kind of suck. Thanks for being here."

My heart melted at his vulnerability. "Of course, Jack. I love you, you know?"

"I know." He smiled and leaned over to kiss me.

We walked up the driveway and Jack used his key to open the door. The house was cool inside and Jack turned lights on as we went. I withheld comment on the bare walls and boxes stacked everywhere; Marcos had apparently done some packing before moving to Albuquerque. I followed Jack down a hallway to a bedroom with a blue wooden J on the door. Inside, although it smelled musty, it looked as though the boy who had lived there had just stepped out; the bed was unmade and dirty clothes were piled on the floor.

"Jesus, it looks just like I left it," he breathed. He walked over and toed the pile of clothes. "That's what I wore the day before I got arrested."

"You haven't been back since?" I whispered.

He shook his head. "No. I went straight to juvenile detention and from there, straight to Manny and Trina's. They packed up some clothes and books for me. Okay, first things first." He went to the closet, kneeled down, pulled back a piece of loose paneling, and retrieved a metal lockbox, which he set on the bed.

"What's that?" I asked.

He sighed heavily. "My stash. I'm really embarrassed about this, Ally. It's one of the reasons I wanted to come in person and pack up my room, rather than letting my dad handle it. He probably wouldn't have found it, and I couldn't leave it here for the next owners. What if some kid found it?"

"God, Jack. Don't be embarrassed. Not with me." I reached out to touch his arm. "What are you going to do with it?"

"Burn it. Come on." I followed him out of his room to the kitchen, where he stopped to find some matches. He led me through the glass doors onto the back patio, where he set the box on a table and bent down to turn the dials on the combination lock. It opened after a few tries to reveal baggies full of pills and marijuana, a small bong, and several dirty magazines. "Yeah, I was a real prize, huh?" he asked, running his hands through his hair. He emptied the box into the kiva fireplace at the corner of the patio and dropped a lit match on top of the pile. The magazines caught fire quickly, spreading it to the rest of the drugs and paraphernalia. He found a piece of wood and smashed the bowl of the bong while everything burned. I stepped close to him, put my arm around his waist, and leaned against him. He pulled me close as we watched the vestiges of his misspent youth smoke and smolder. When the flames had burned themselves out and all that remained of his drug/porn stash was cinder and glass fragments, we turned and walked back inside the house to his bedroom.

I started pulling books off the shelf, sorting them into piles while Jack went out to the SUV to get the boxes we had brought. Jack had said he only wanted his books, CDs, and a few other assorted items; he had grown so much in the past few years he had no need for the clothes that were left. "So, do you want to keep all your Captain Underpants books? It looks like you had the complete series," I asked as he returned.

He laughed, coming over to look at the books I had set aside. "Yeah, I was a big fan back in the day. Let's bring them for Megan." We finished packing the few things from his childhood he wanted to keep in less than an hour. I was distracted by the box of school pictures we found, enjoying seeing Jack from kindergarten through early high school.

"Oh, my gosh, you were an adorable little boy, Jack."

He came to look over my shoulder. "I want to see your school pictures when we get back to Albuquerque. It's only fair, querida. All right, I think we're done here. Let's load these boxes in the SUV." It took only a few minutes and then Jack locked the house back up. He pocketed the key and stood staring at the door for a few seconds.

"Are you okay?" I asked quietly.

"Yeah." He nodded. "It was actually not as bad as I was expecting, but it wasn't my favorite thing, either." He pulled me close. "Thank you for helping me do this, Ally. It means a lot to me." Then he kissed me, a bit fiercely, showing me exactly how much he appreciated my help. "All right," he said as he pulled away. "What do you say we see some of the sights Taos has to offer?"

We spent a glorious, relaxed afternoon sightseeing, driving ten miles north to see the Taos Gorge Bridge, a 564-foot-high suspension bridge spanning the Rio Grande River. We then turned back toward town to visit the Taos pueblo, a thousand-year-old adobe dwelling where people still lived. We returned to town to wander around the plaza until it was time to meet Audra and Donny for dinner. Jack seemed lighter and so relieved to have the unpleasant chore of revisiting his childhood out of the way; I hadn't seen him this carefree for a long time. Or maybe ever.

We had an enjoyable evening with Donny and Audra as they treated us to dinner at the elegant Mosaic restaurant. I went with them to Mass the next morning and we spent the rest of the day relaxing around the house.

As we drove back to Albuquerque on Monday, I thought about how much I enjoyed traveling with Jack; this trip had cemented our relationship in a new way I was having a hard time understanding. It was different being so alone with him for such an extended time. I may not have understood it, but I liked it an awful lot.

***

The wedding plans overshadowed everything around the Moran household. Mom and Grams dragged me to a winery in the north valley they had fallen in love with for the ceremony and reception. I gave my stamp of approval, of course, and they seemed happy to include me. I went with them to pick out a dress for my mother and for Grams and myself. Grams was going to give her away and Mom had asked me to be the maid of honor. I will admit to getting a bit teary-eyed when she asked. I got even more teary-eyed, and not in a good way, when I saw some of the choices for bridesmaid dresses.

"As God is my witness, Mom, I cannot wear something like this," I held up a turtle-poop green, off-the-shoulder monstrosity.

She laughed and rifled through another rack. "I was thinking of something a little more like this." She held up a royal blue dress that was sleek and sophisticated. I fell in love on the spot.

"Yes. That one. Please, Mommy," I whimpered.

She laughed and handed it to me to try on. When I modeled it for her and Grams, they both said it was the one. At our third stop, Mom tried on a gown that was perfect: it was ivory and flowed from her shoulders in a Grecian style that flattered her and wouldn't highlight the baby bump that was sure to be visible by June.

Although the wedding was definitely top priority

around our house, Brian and I still had a murder to solve. Sunday afternoon, during a marathon session to pick out invitations, I took pity on Brian, who was overwhelmed by all the wedding plans, and took him out for coffee so we could discuss the case. Mom sputtered a bit about him leaving, but he assured her he would love whatever invitations she picked out.

"So where are we, Brian? I know you like Scott as a suspect, but do you have any evidence against him?" I asked after we settled in a booth and the waitress had left a pot of coffee.

"Not yet. This case is going to be very difficult to prove because of the time span. I think Scott did it, but I have no way to disprove his alibi. The autopsy came back." He paused to take a sip of his coffee.

"And?"

"Patience, Grasshopper," he said, shuffling papers within the file, finally finding the one he was looking for. "Ashley died from blunt force trauma to the head. Her killer struck her multiple times on the back of the head with some sort of weapon."

I was lost in thought for a moment as I tried to think back to the last dream I had of her, the one in which I saw her reflection in the lens of the sunglasses sitting on her killer's face. Why hadn't I paid attention to the man in the sunglasses? Oh, yeah, because I had been so shocked to see a face other than my own in the reflection. I remember now. It was such a relief to be done with the nightmares; I hadn't had a single one since I gave the book back to Ashley's mom. "Was she raped?"

"There's no way to tell after this amount of time. There was no soft tissue, only skeletal remains, so only injuries that involved bone are left. A fetal skeleton was detected." He hesitated. "I'm sorry, Ally, if this is too much for you. I don't need to share the autopsy results with you," he apologized, mistaking my silence for disgust.

"No, I'm fine." I shook my head. "I can handle it. I feel like I need to, for Ashley. She had to go through it, and she wasn't much older than me."

"Okay. Well, we need to review all the alibis again to see if we can spot any discrepancies. I've gone over them several times, but I could use a fresh pair of eyes. I don't have enough time to devote to this case," he groused. "I'm swamped with more current cases that have better chances of being solved."

"Okay, well, let's hear the alibis."

He opened his notes and walked me through the alibis of everyone connected to the case, starting with Ashley's parents. Both were at work at the time of her disappearance, verified back in 1984. David Moore was also at work, again verified. His wife, Shannon, was in Las Cruces with their two children. The Graves, across the street, were at work, Mrs. Graves arriving home at approximately five-thirty with her youngest son. The oldest son, 12 year old Mark, was at baseball practice until six-o'clock, but unfortunately was not questioned at the time.

"Why didn't they question him?" I asked.

"I have no idea." He threw his hands up. "That's not the first example of shoddy police work I've found in this case. The lack of follow-up on Scott Alder's whereabouts is also very disappointing, and is proving impossible to find thirty years later. He was allegedly at basketball practice, and didn't leave school until at least five o'clock, but we have only his word on that."

"What about other, random people? Weren't there ever any other suspects?"

He handed me another, thicker file folder. "These are all the tips that came in from the tip line set up after Ashley's disappearance."

I flipped through a few pages. "Brian, there must be hundreds of them."

"Yeah, and that represents thousands of hours of police follow-up work, looking into any leads that looked even slightly promising."

"Did anything come from it?" I asked hopefully.

"Not a thing. Sorry, Ally. Scott is really the only viable suspect at this point."

"Just because you don't have a better suspect doesn't mean it's him. I'm telling you, he's innocent," I insisted.

Brian looked at me sternly. "Ally, I wish I could believe that, I really do. I know you like him."

"Please don't arrest him without telling me first, okay? Give us a chance to figure out who really did it. Please, Brian." I wasn't above begging.

He nodded briefly. "I'll try. That's all I can promise. Now, I really need to speak with Mark Graves. I've left messages, but he seems reluctant to get in touch with me for some reason."

"Does he live here in Albuquerque?"

"No. He lives in El Paso. I really don't need

another road trip right now," he groaned. "I'm trying to support your mother with all this wedding stuff, and I don't relish another melt-down." We had all been subject to my mother's recent hormone-induced emotional explosions in the last few weeks.

"Definitely not for the faint-hearted," I agreed. "And what about David Moore's kids? Have you managed to track them down, yet?"

"I did speak to his youngest daughter, Karen, a few days ago. She said they moved to California when she was seven, about a year after the disappearance. I haven't talked to the older girl yet."

"Okay, what's our next step?" I asked.

"I'm going to try to get the Graves to contact their son. I'll let you know when I have something."

"What's in the last folder?" I asked as Brian tried to slip it under another.

"Autopsy photos. Personal effects. Nothing you need to see."

I tended to agree with him, but something stopped me. "I think I do, Brian," I said quietly.

"You sure?" I nodded and he silently handed the folder over to me.

The first set of photographs was of the skeletal remains. It wasn't disgusting, like a recent dead body would be, but the starkness of what was left, nothing more than a collection of dark brownish bones, arranged into the semblance of a body, with a skull at the top, was incredibly sad. This collection of discarded bones was all that was left of a once-vibrant 18-year-old with her whole life ahead of her. The skull showed the damage that had caused her death. To the side of the body was another tiny collection of bones: Ashley and Scott's baby. I had expected to be unable to hold back tears when I saw it, but was surprised by the intense anger burning inside my body. Somebody had cut short these two precious lives before they even had a chance to live. I made a silent vow, right there at the table: *'I will find out who killed you and your baby, Ashley. I know it wasn't Scott. I will find out who did this, so you can rest. I swear it.'* I know she heard me. She was there with us, just like I dreamed she had been with me ever since I opened her book in the hotel in Galway. I turned to the last set of photographs, her personal effects. The tattered remains of her shoes and clothing were lying beside a crusted pendant on a chain. I had to look closely to be able to tell what it was: a small, silver dolphin. Of course. She had loved the Madeleine L'Engle novel, *A Ring of Endless Light*. It was all about dolphins.

"Brian, where is this necklace now?"

"In evidence. Why?" he asked.

"Is there any way we could take it to Mrs. Hayes? Could we give it back to her?"

He looked at me with his head tilted for a second. "Yeah, I think we could do that. What's going on in that head of yours?"

I flipped through the pictures again and shook my head. "It's not here. Is this everything that was found near the body?"

"Yes. Why? What are you not seeing?" He reached to take the pictures and look at them.

"Well, it's just that if she disappeared between school and home, she would have had school books and probably a backpack or bag of some kind. She would have a purse or something. Girls always have all sorts of crap with them. Where is Ashley's crap? Why didn't she have anything with her? Or if she did, where is it?"

Brian looked back and forth between me and the photos before nodding. "Shit. I can't believe no one thought of that. Good catch, kid. You think her mom will have some information about what Ashley usually carried." He said this last bit as a statement. "I'll find out about the necklace and then we'll go talk to Mrs. Hayes, okay?"

I nodded.

"Let's get back to your mom. I probably need to approve of some wedding invitations and taste cake or something. I'm starting to wish I had insisted on eloping to Vegas," he grumbled.

*****

Now that Tara was with Mat, I was curious to find out who Rémy had his eye on. That's the problem with friends pairing up: you want to see everyone happily settled in a couple. I watched him closely, but he didn't seem to be flirting with anyone in particular. Knowing Rémy, if he wanted a girl, all he would have to do is crook his finger and one would come running, at least at this school. So, being the intrepid investigator I clearly was, I decided to take things up a notch.

"Rémy, Tara and I are hosting a little party this

Friday and we want you to come," I said as we met before school.

"Of course, chérie. Tell me when and where. I would not miss it for the world," he said this while kissing my cheeks in greeting, which still made Jack growl. I'm 99.9% sure that's why Rémy continued to do it.

"Well, feel free to bring a date," I suggested.

He smirked knowingly. "Well, I'll see what I can do. Do you have any suggestions?"

"No. Isn't there anyone you want to bring? I could, you know, invite her."

"No, mais no. Don't go to any trouble for me." He laughed. "I'll probably come alone."

I looked to Jack for help. He shrugged. "I got Mat and Tara together. You're on your own for this."

"You are seriously taking credit for that? Unbelievable!" He laughed. "Rémy, who is it? Come on, tell me," I wheedled. "I could help."

"Do you honestly think a Frenchman needs an American girl's help in getting a date?" he asked, appalled. "No. How about you are surprised on Friday?"

"Fine. If you don't want my help..." I tried to sound offended.

"I really don't, chérie."

***

I had another appointment to meet with Cassie that afternoon. She was trying to help me work on my communication methods, specifically my ability to mentally talk with other Seers without touching them. I was now fairly adept at reading what someone was thinking about if I touched them, frequently practicing on Mom and Grams. Jack and Tara were frequent volunteers, as well, but I hesitated to use them because they had no ability to see anything I was thinking. It made me feel weird to use them like that. Plus, the impressions I got from non-psychic-type people were really fuzzy. The person I had the greatest success with was Rémy. He and I seemed to have a strong psychic connection, a fact I didn't stress too much as it irritated Jack. Rémy was far better at it than I was, perhaps because he was *so* much older, something I delighted in teasing him about. He was also very good at blocking me out, which annoyed me and kept me from finding out which girl he was interested in. I was currently bugging him about teaching me how to do it better; I still had to concentrate so hard to keep anyone blocked.

Rémy had been adamant I not tell anyone besides Jack he was a Seer. He relented and let me tell Tara, but refused to countenance the idea of Grams, Mom, and Cassie knowing about him. We both had great hopes the two Seer clans could be unified someday, but he wasn't ready to expose himself right now. Our clan believed his clan had kidnapped and stolen the Oracle, which, according to Rémy was not true. He said she had run away with her lover, a member of the Gaulish clan. He should know, as the Oracle was his grandmother. He felt it was imperative we keep between ourselves for now the fact the clans had connected. I wasn't sure this was the best idea and thought perhaps Rémy was letting his love for spy thrillers interfere with real life.

"All right, Ally, let's get started," Cassie began briskly, bringing me back to what I was supposed to be doing. "We'll get warmed up by doing some readings with you touching me. Then we'll move apart slowly." Cassie was also very good at blocking out what she didn't want me to see or what she considered inappropriate, so all I got were some scenes of her shopping and planning for her own wedding, which was coming up about the same time as my mother's. I'd had all I could take of nuptial preparation, so I focused on other, more interesting things in her mind, managing to get through some of her blocking attempts to see her and Gregory, her fiancé, kissing. "Okay, that's enough of that. You've obviously been practicing," she said in an irritated manner.

"Sorry. This mind-reading stuff crosses some serious personal boundaries. I'll try to be more careful," I said contritely.

"That's good. Why don't we move on to the next step?" she replied a bit coolly.

"Yeah. Good idea."

She moved across the room and sat down on the sofa. "You stay there and concentrate on what I'm thinking—only on what I'm thinking."

"Okay, okay," I muttered. Jeez, I said I was sorry. I closed my eyes, focused intently, and heard…nothing. Absolutely nothing. I opened my eyes and peeked at Cassie. She met my gaze with raised eyebrows. I closed mine again, clearing my throat. "I feel ridiculous."

"Concentrate, Ally. This is really important. You must learn to develop your powers if you are to take your place as the next Oracle."

"Well, maybe I'm not the next Oracle. Maybe you and the council are wrong, did you ever think of that?" I sounded petulant, but I couldn't help it.

"Do you believe that, Ally?"

"I don't know what I believe," I whispered.

"I know," said Cassie sympathetically. "For now, let's try this."

I tried again. I concentrated, fiercely, trying to see into Cassie's mind while sitting across the room from her. For the longest time I saw nothing, no matter how hard I tried. Then, finally, I got the slightest glimmer of a thought from her. She was thinking about balancing her checkbook and cleaning her toilets. I opened one eye and peered at her. "Seriously? I said I was sorry."

"Yes, well, I don't want to parade my love life around for your vicarious pleasure."

"Ouch." Sensitive much?

"Okay, why don't we call it a night? I think you've made great progress, Ally. Keep practicing."

CHAPTER FOURTEEN

"The weight of this sad time we must obey;
Speak what we feel, not what we ought to say.
The oldest hath borne most: we that are young
Shall never see so much, nor live so long."
–Shakespeare –King Lear (5.3.325)

Brian and I had an appointment to see Mrs. Hayes early in the week. He picked me up after cheerleading practice and we drove over together.

"Are you as sick of all these wedding plans as I am?" I asked as we pulled away from the curb in front of the high school. On days like these, when I had something to do after school, Jack or Tara would pick me up in the mornings so I wouldn't have to take my car back home before heading out with Brian.

"Yeah, but do not repeat that to your mother, okay? I want her to have the wedding of her dreams, and I know it's stressful planning one so quickly."

"I've said it before, but you're a good guy, Brian

Keller, you know that?" I said, somewhat grudgingly.

"Why do you have to sound so surprised by that?" he asked.

"Don't take it personally, Brian. The teenage daughter is supposed to give the new guy in her mom's life a hard time. It's in the script."

He laughed. "Oh, sorry. I didn't get the memo. So, what are your goals for this afternoon in questioning Mrs. Hayes?"

"I get to question her?" He nodded. "Wow. Okay. Well, I guess I'm hoping she remembers what Ashley carried around with her—you know, a purse, a backpack, or whatever. I think we need to know what happened to her stuff. It might tell us something about where she was that last afternoon before she was killed."

"You've got the makings of a pretty good detective, Ally."

"Thanks," I said, a bit surprised. I never expected to get along with him so well. Am I supposed to like the guy who knocked up my mom? Oh, well, water under the bridge, I guess.

"So, what are your plans for the future? Career-wise, I mean," he asked.

"You know, I'm not absolutely set on anything yet. It sounds kind of lame, but I might be interested in teaching."

"Why is that lame? Your mother is in education," he said.

"I don't know. It doesn't seem ambitious enough, somehow."

"I don't know about that. It seems like a great

career choice to me," he argued.

"So says another under-paid civil servant," I pointed out, reminding him how he had once described himself.

He chuckled. "Yeah, very true. But life's not all about money. I make enough to get by. I guess it comes down to what is really important to you."

"Hmm." We arrived at the Hayes' residence and were invited in by Ashley's mother. Once we had tea in front of us, I took the dolphin necklace out of my bag and handed it to Mrs. Hayes.

She took it with a confused look. "What…how did you get this?" she whispered.

Brian chimed in. "It was found with Ashley's remains, ma'am. We thought you should have it."

I reached out to lay my hand on her arm, unintentionally picking up waves of sadness rolling off her. "Mrs. Hayes, we don't want to upset you, but we were wondering if you remember what else Ashley would have carried with her on a regular school day. Did she take a purse or a book bag of some sort?"

She continued to stare at the dolphin pendant, oblivious to my question. Tears were streaking down her cheeks. "Scott gave this to her for Christmas. He knew she loved dolphins." She set it down on the table and reached for a tissue. "I'm sorry. This brings back so many memories. What was your question?"

"What kind of purse or bag did Ashley carry with her to school? Do you remember anything about that?" I repeated gently.

"Well, I don't remember much about her purse

although she always carried one, but I do remember her backpack because it was so silly," she said, laughing slightly as she wiped her eyes.

"Silly?"

"Yes. She insisted on carrying what was really a child's backpack, plastic, with bright colored dolphins all over it. She loved it. I guess it was in style, I don't know."

"Ally?" Brian asked, clearly at a loss.

I finished Googling dolphin backpacks on my phone and showed the picture I thought most likely to Mrs. Hayes. "Does this look familiar?"

She gasped. "Yes, it looked exactly like that! How did you find it?"

"It's a Lisa Frank design," I said as I clicked on the image and read. "It was a company that was popular in the 80s and 90s. It's still kind of popular, mostly with young girls." I showed the picture and brief article to Brian. "Mrs. Hayes, where is her backpack and purse? Neither was found with Ashley."

She shook her head. "I don't know."

"You never found them here at the house?"

"No. She left with them that morning."

We thanked Mrs. Hayes and left her with Ashley's necklace and more sadness than a mother should have to bear.

"Brian, this means she never got home that afternoon, that she was taken somewhere between school and home, doesn't it?" I was excited by our discovery.

"Hold on. It certainly looks like it, but I need to do some more checking. We have photographs of

Ashley's room in evidence. I need to go over them carefully to make sure Mrs. Hayes is remembering accurately," Brian cautioned. "I'll let you know, okay?"

***

On Wednesday evening, Jack picked me up after he got off work to take me to dinner. It was so good to be with him again and I was thankful there was very little awkwardness since our breakup, although he was being overly nice, bringing me frequent presents, which needed to stop. For the most part, it was as if we had never broken up.

"Jack, you don't have to bring me a present every time you pick me up for a date," I objected as he presented me with a small gift bag.

"Shh," he said as he kissed me. "It's more for me than you."

"Ooh, you bought me lingerie?" I asked hopefully.

He laughed. "No, little smart ass. I meant it makes me feel better."

I opened the package to find a small bag of my favorite gummy bears, the good kind from Germany. "Mmm, you do know my weaknesses." I set the gift on the entry table and took his hands, leading him to sit with me on the couch. "All right. Jack, you don't need to apologize any more. Let's move past our breakup, okay? I know why you needed time. I never stopped loving you, you never stopped loving me, so let's forget it. I want to move on. Please?"

He looked deeply into my eyes. "Fine. Let me say it one last time and then I swear I'll never mention it again. Alethiea Grace Moran, I am so sorry I broke up with you. It was the stupidest thing I've ever done. I will never pull away from you like that again. You are the most important thing in my life." He leaned forward and kissed me deeply before pulling back. We had both agreed to cool it with our physical relationship since the night we got back together and came way too close to having sex on my grandmother's kitchen counter. Neither one of us was ready for that and wanted to concentrate on strengthening our relationship for now. I think Jack still felt guilty about that episode. When we let our kisses get out of control, we tended to forget all about why it was a good idea to refrain from going too far. At least I did; Jack was usually better at calling a halt, except when he wasn't. That night in my kitchen gave me a small glimpse into the passion he kept bottled up inside. I was looking forward to the day when we didn't have to hold back anymore.

We went to a casual deli in the uptown area for dinner and then walked around the shopping center, holding hands and window-shopping. The weather had turned mild, making it a perfect night for strolling and enjoying time together. We stopped in at Lush, a wonderful place that specialized in vegan bath and body products and I stocked up on my favorite body cream, then headed in the direction of Frost for some gelato. The only hitch in these lovely plans came when I realized I was not feeling well. At all.

"Can we sit for a minute, Jack?" I asked, already heading for a nearby bench.

"Sure. What's up? Hey, are you okay, sweetheart?" he asked in concern as I leaned forward, putting my head between my knees. "Are you having a vision?" he whispered.

"Nope," I choked out. "I think I'm sick. I need to go home. I'm sorry."

"Don't be sorry. It's not your fault. Come on, let's get you home."

I had to sit down twice on the way to the car, trying desperately not to throw up in front of my boyfriend. Finally, Jack swung me up into his strong arms and carried me the rest of the way to his car, strapping me into the passenger seat. I was feeling too wretched to object.

We didn't make it far before I cried, "Oh, God. Pull over, Jack!" I barely made it out of the car before barfing epically into some nearby bushes. Jack put the car into park and came over to hold my hair back. He handed me some napkins so I could wipe my mouth. "Jack, wait for me by the car. You don't need to see this." I was barfing again.

"Shh. Don't waste your energy talking. I'm not going anywhere. Let's get you home, querida," he said as he scooped me up again and gently placed me in the passenger seat.

"Ohhh," I groaned. I didn't remember ever feeling this horrible and that includes how I felt after getting my head slammed into a trophy case. We made it home without any more vomit stops, thankfully. Jack found my keys in my purse and opened the door for us as I pushed him out of the way, running for the downstairs bathroom, barely making it to the toilet. He followed me, wetting a washcloth and wiping my face as I leaned helplessly against the shower stall. "Just let me die," I cried.

"I don't think so, babe. I think you've got food poisoning. You're in for a really rough night. Where's your mom and grandma?"

"I don't know. I can't think right now, sorry." I fell over and curled up in the fetal position on the bath mat. "You can go, Jack. I'll be fine." He ignored me and began groping around in my pockets. "I'm really not in the mood, honey," I groaned.

"Hilarious. Where's your phone?" I rolled over and presented him with my backside. He took my phone out of my back pocket and began searching my contacts. "Adele? Yeah, it's Jack. Ally's sick, I think with food poisoning. No, we're at your house. Of course. I'm not going anywhere. Yeah. See you soon." He clicked off and pocketed my phone. "She'll be home soon. Let's get you up to bed." He picked me up and carried me upstairs.

"Someday, I really hope I'm not sick or half-dead when you carry me to bed," I said against his chest. I felt it rumble as he chuckled.

"How can you joke when you feel so awful?"

"Just gifted, I guess." I tried to object when he began undressing me and helping me put on my pajamas. "I thought it would be a lot sexier when I finally got you to take my clothes off."

"Yeah, me too." He tucked me under my comforter, kissed my forehead, and went to scavenge some 7-Up or ginger ale. He brought back

7-Up and a large bowl in case I couldn't make it to the bathroom. He sat on my bed, wiping my face with a cool washcloth, and then simply holding my hand.

"This is way above the call of duty for boyfriends, Jack. I'm so sorry. You shouldn't have to do this."

"Hey." He brushed my hair back. "It's all part of the package, querida. I love you and will absolutely take care of you when you get sick. You would do the same for me. Now try to get some sleep, okay? I'll stay until your grandma gets home." I smiled and fell asleep, feeling extremely loved and coddled.

I spent one of the worst nights of my entire life, mostly hugging the toilet after a short nap. The next day I couldn't begin to go to school and spent the day lying feebly on the couch, watching daytime television. I hope I never see Drew Carey and *The Price Is Right* again. I finally quit barfing around 2:00 a.m. when there was nothing more to heave. My super-awesome boyfriend stopped by on his way to school, bringing me purple Gatorade, my favorite. He must file away every random bit of crap I say, ready to produce the necessary info when the need arose. I sure as heck couldn't tell you his favorite flavor, or if he even liked Gatorade. I needed to be a better girlfriend, clearly. I would get right on that as soon as I could keep some dry toast down.

"Now, I'm not going to text you today because I don't want to risk waking you up, but you can text me anytime and I promise I will text back, no matter whose class I'm in." He made sure my Gatorade was close at hand and I had my fluffy blanket from my bed. "I will come by tonight after I get off work and bring your homework." He kissed the top of my head—I wasn't about to offer my lips after a night of projectile vomiting—and left.

I slept until lunchtime and then sent a text to Jack. He FaceTimed me, saying everyone at lunch wanted to talk to me.

"Ally, how are you feeling? I miss you so much!" exclaimed Tara. She got really close to the screen and whispered, "You look terrible. Take a shower and put some makeup on before Jack gets there. Seriously."

Dustin and Travis both crammed their faces into the screen. "Hey, Ally! Get better, okay? We miss you!"

Rémy appeared next. "Ah, chérie, it is so boring here without you! Hurry back, won't you? Jack is so irritable when you are not here." I could hear Rémy laughing as Jack ripped the phone away from him with a muffled 'dickhead.'

"All right, sweetheart. Enough of this. You get back to sleep. I love you, you know?" I could see he had turned away from the rest of the group.

"Yeah, I do know. I love you too."

"And you are absolutely not to shower and put makeup on for me. Just rest. Got it?"

"Yes, sir. Bossy much?"

"Only with girls I love."

***

Food poisoning sucks. I have never been so sick in my entire life. I don't even eat meat, so how the heck did I get food poisoning? What, did I get bad tofu or something? I couldn't believe how sweet Jack was during my exorcist impression. I'm sure that would have been a deal-breaker for many guys. Actually, it didn't surprise me in the least he was so awesome while I was sick, because that's the kind of guy he is. I am so damn lucky to have him.

Friday morning I was determined to go to school. I had managed to keep a piece of dry toast down yesterday, but was still incredibly weak as I got ready for school. I needed to go today, not so much for school itself—which I would have happily skipped—but for cheerleading practice after school. We were getting ready for the state competition in a few weeks and I really needed to be there.

The other reason I was pushing myself to go to school was the party at Tara's house tonight I was co-hosting. Mom would never let me go if I stayed home from school. It wasn't going to be a Veronica Albluth-style party, mind you. We had only invited a few of our good friends, like Travis and Dustin, some of Tara's orchestra friends, and Jack and Mat, of course. Party might be over-stating it, actually; it was more of a small-group gathering, I guess. We had also invited Rémy, who was supposed to be bringing the mystery girl he'd been crushing on for months. I was a little obsessed with finding out who she was.

"Ally, are you ready? Tara's honking in the driveway," Mom stopped in the door of my room to find me curled up on my bed. "Oh, sweetie, stay home another day. I'll call the school."

"No, no," I said, wrenching myself into a sitting position. "I'll be fine, really. I have to go." Tara was picking me up so we could get in some last minute planning for tonight. My barf-fest had put a serious crimp in our party planning.

"I like it better when Jack picks you up. He at least comes to the door instead of honking for you and irritating all the neighbors," she complained.

"Yeah, well he's trying to impress you. Tara's not. Bye Mom, love you," I said as I kissed her on the cheek and left.

"Well, it's not Marla Garcia," Tara said in greeting as I got in her SUV. I knew she was referring to Rémy's date for the evening; she was as obsessed as I was. "I heard some rumors, but it turned out to be wishful thinking on Marla's part."

"You mean, with your vast network of informants, you can't find out who Rémy asked to the party? I'm starting to doubt your super-sleuthing skills, Nancy," I teased.

"Oh, ha, ha. Please—Nancy Drew my ass. I'm much more of a Veronica Mars. Rémy is being hyper-sneaky just to piss us off, you know. He's enjoying this game."

"Yeah, I know. He drives me crazy. I'm so glad you didn't date him for very long."

"Me, too. He was a great kisser, though," she sighed.

"I wasn't impressed. Is he better than Mat?" I asked in disbelief.

"No one's better than Mat. Rémy was a close second, however." She drove in silence for a few minutes. "Hey, are you sure you're up to this party tonight? You're still pale, sweetie. I mean, more than your normal pasty, white color."

"Thanks," I said as I flashed her a dirty look. "I'll be fine. I need to be at cheer practice today, anyway. You'll pick me up afterward, right?"

"Yes. We'll head to the grocery store for a few last minute items and then over to my house for final prep."

Jack was waiting for us in the parking lot, leaning against his car. He straightened up as we pulled into the spot beside his and opened my door for me, pulling me into his arms for a kiss. I sighed in pleasure and locked my arms around his neck, pushing my hands into his thick, black hair as he insinuated his tongue between my lips.

"Get a room. Seriously," said Tara in mock disgust.

Jack laughed against my lips. "Sorry. It's been more than 24 hours since I kissed this girl and I was having withdrawal."

"She's just jealous. Come back here." I pulled him back where he belonged.

"Leaving now," Tara announced and waved as she walked away.

Jack looked into my face, pushing my hair out of the way. "How are you feeling, querida? Have you eaten anything today?"

I smiled weakly. "I had some toast."

"This morning?" he prodded.

"Last night," I admitted. "I didn't feel like eating this morning."

"Hang on," he turned back to his car and leaned

in. "Here. You are going to eat this granola bar while we walk to class. I have a bottle of water for you, too."

I reached up and pulled him down for another kiss. "Thanks for taking care of me, bossy." The last part earned me a light swat on the rear as we walked to class.

I barely made it through the day. I guess I should have stayed home, after all. Jack tried to talk me into letting him drive me home at lunch, but I was determined. I guess I can be a bit stubborn at times, but I choose to look at it as a positive character trait. By the time cheerleading practice started, I was done in. My coach benched me and I was much relieved to sit on the bleachers while my team practiced. The rest was good for me, and after about a half-hour, I was feeling somewhat better. When my cellphone rang, I didn't recognize the number and took it out into the hall.

"Hello," I said in greeting.

"Oh, hello, dear. Is this Ally? This is Stella Graves. You know, I live across the street from Angela Hayes?"

"Oh, yes. I remember. How can I help you, Mrs. Graves?"

"Well, I tried to contact that nice Detective Keller, but I had to leave a message. I thought I'd see if I could get hold of you, since you left that cute little business card."

I cringed at that comment. "What can I do for you?"

"Well, dear, my son, Mark is in town, but only for the evening. I know you and the detective wanted to ask him some questions, so I thought this would a good time."

"And Brian didn't answer his phone?"

"No, he didn't. Mark can't stay very long. Do you think you could come over and talk to him right now? He's being rather difficult and will only talk to you or Detective Keller in person."

I thought furiously for a moment. The Graves lived about three blocks from the school, and I certainly wasn't contributing much to cheerleading today so I could easily walk over. I was feeling better and maybe the fresh air would be good for me. I was fairly sure I could talk to Mark Graves and still be back in time for Tara to pick me up, or I could call her from there. "Sure, Mrs. Graves. I can be there in about ten minutes, okay?"

"Oh, that would be wonderful, dear. I think Mark has remembered something important, but he refuses to talk to us about it. I'm sure he'll talk to you." Mrs. Graves hung up.

I grabbed my stuff and headed out, not bothering to tell anyone where I was going. I know: dumb. Really dumb. You would think I'd have learned. As I walked, I called Brian, but also got his voicemail. I left him a message telling him what I was doing and asking him to meet me at the Graves' house if he got the message in time.

Two blocks into my little jaunt, I realized I was still far from my normal, perky self, but it was further to go back than forward. I felt dizzy and weak and was seriously questioning my decision to walk over to the Graves' home. As I rounded the corner onto Ashley's street, I saw Mr. Moore in front of his house, working at his roses. I really needed to sit down for a few minutes before I passed out. I sank down to the curb, dropped my head to my knees, and hoped I wouldn't fall into the street. When I could focus, I would think about who I could call to come get me.

"What are you doing? Why are sitting on the curb?" I heard a cranky voice above me.

"Hi, Mr. Moore. Do you remember me?" I asked weakly.

He squinted at me, pruning shears still in his hand. "You're the girl that was with the detective, aren't you?" He still sounded a bit cranky, but I was getting desperate.

"Yeah, I am."

"Why are you sitting in the street? You're going to get hit by a car if you're not careful," he warned.

"Well," I strove for a patient tone. "I've been sick and I'm afraid I was about to pass out."

"Hmmp," he groused. "Well, come into the house for a minute." He motioned for me to follow him in the house, which I did. I sank gratefully on his couch. "Do you want some water, girl?"

"Yes, please. That would be great." I leaned my head against the back of the couch and closed my eyes. Oh, man, I did not feel well at all. I hadn't been able to eat very much at lunch and I had no energy in reserve. I would rest here for a few minutes and then walk over across the street to the Graves' house. Maybe splashing some water on my face would help.

"Mr. Moore," I called. "Can I use your bathroom, please?"

"It's down the hall!" he yelled, still sounding cranky. I could hear him opening cabinets in the kitchen and I sat up with a sigh. I heaved myself off the couch with difficulty and wandered down his hall, opening the first door I encountered. It was a bedroom, probably a guest room, and I was backing out when I noticed a dusty cardboard box on the floor. It wasn't the box itself that caught my eye, but what was peeking out the top: something bright-colored and plastic. I looked back to make sure Mr. Moore was still in the kitchen before sneaking in the bedroom to look inside the box. My shock was absolutely complete when I saw a Lisa Frank dolphin backpack, a small, black purse, and several pairs of women's underwear. Why would Mr. Moore have Ashley's school bag? I could think of only one plausible reason. Oh. My. God. I had found the murderer. That was my last thought before my world went black.

CHAPTER FIFTEEN

"It is the stars,
The stars above us, govern our conditions. "
–Shakespeare –King Lear (4.3.34)

Jack

I felt my phone buzz as I was applying Bondo to the rear quarter panel of a Honda Civic. I hoped it was Ally and that she was feeling better after her bout with food poisoning; I hated that she had felt so bad. It was cute she hadn't wanted me to see her throw up, but it didn't bother me. I loved that girl with every fiber of my being, whether she was puking or not. She was, however, more than a bit stubborn and had insisted on going to school today. I had worried about her all day, the worry getting worse as the day went on. In my distraction, I didn't even look at the caller ID. "Hey, babe. I was just thinking about you. Are you feeling any better?"

"Jack, it's Tara. Is Ally with you?"

"No. I thought you were picking her up today."

My gut cramped in apprehension, adding to the worry I had been feeling all day.

"Yeah, I was supposed to, but she's not here. I'm at the school and nobody on the cheerleading squad knows where she is. Jack, she's not answering her phone. It goes straight to voicemail." Tara sounded winded and worried.

"What? How can they not know where she is?" I demanded, throwing my towel on a nearby table.

"A couple of the girls said they saw her leave about an hour ago, but she didn't tell anyone where she was going. Apparently she was sitting out the practice on the bleachers and left without saying anything." She spoke fast, almost yelling.

"Well, where the fuck is she, Tara?" I yelled, running my hands through my hair in frustration. Now I was scared. The last time Ally disappeared without telling anyone, she ended up in the hospital with a concussion and stitches in her head. And today she was still weak from being so sick. God, where could she be?

"I don't know, Jack. I'm really worried."

"Shit!" I began pacing. "I'll meet you at the school. Wait for me. Call Adele and Jen while you're waiting and see if they know anything. If they don't, have Jen call Brian, okay?"

"Yeah, okay," her voice sounded small, like maybe she was crying.

"Tara, we'll find her." I hung up, running toward the office. "Manny! I gotta go, man!" I filled my uncle in about what was going on and left, breaking every speed limit on the way back to the school. *God, please don't let anything have happened to*

Ally, I begged. I broke another law by dialing Mat's number while I drove. I had already tried to call Ally, but only got her voicemail.

"Mat, I need you, man," I spoke quickly in Spanish, my brain switching without conscious thought. "Ally's missing. Meet me at the school, okay? I think it might be a good idea to have a paramedic. I have a bad feeling about this."

He didn't ask questions or argue; he said he'd meet me in a few minutes.

Tara was waiting in front of the school, pacing as she talked on her phone. She hung up as I got out of my car and threw herself at me. "Nobody's seen her, Jack! Where the hell could she be? I'm so scared," I pulled her into my arms as she cried.

"We're going to find her. Tell me what I've missed." I set her away from me so I could look in her eyes.

"Grams and her mom don't know where she is and she didn't call them. Her mom is going to call Brian. She told me to wait here until she calls me back." Her phone rang again. "Hello? Oh, Mr. Keller. Yeah, he is. Here." She handed her phone to me.

"Brian?" I asked. "Have you heard anything from her?"

"Jack, I got a message from her about an hour ago saying Mark Graves, the son of one of Ashley's neighbors, called and wanted to talk to us this afternoon. I was in a meeting and no one could get hold of me, so she walked over to his house and wanted me to meet her there. I'm on my way there now. I'm sure she's fine and simply not answering her phone while she talks to him, but you can meet me there if it makes you feel better. I know you're worried, but try to calm down. You can yell at her in a few minutes." He gave me the address.

Mat pulled into the parking lot and Tara ran to meet him. I jogged over to them and began catching him up.

"Guys! English, please," Tara interrupted.

"Sorry," I apologized. "I was filling him in." I switched to English and finished telling him what was going on. In spite of Brian's assurances, I still had that sinking feeling in my stomach I couldn't dismiss. "Tara, call Rémy. We may need him." She looked hard at me for a moment before nodding. Mat didn't know anything about Ally and Rémy's psychic abilities, but now was definitely not the time to worry about secrets. I would gladly announce it to the world if it meant finding Ally safe and sound. "Tell him where to meet us."

We rode together in my car, pulling in behind Brian's Subaru. He came out of the house followed by an elderly woman. "She never showed up," he said quietly. "I have units on the way."

Oh, my God. It was happening again. Ally was apparently a danger magnet who managed to get herself in the worst situations. How could such a small person get in so much trouble? If anything happened to her, I didn't know what I'd do; she was my life. I started pacing, cursing a blue-streak under my breath.

Adele and Jen pulled in the Graves' driveway. Brian pulled a sobbing Jen into his arms while Adele listened to him rehash the details. Rémy arrived as he was finishing.

"What's he doing here?" Mat asked. He had never liked Rémy, a hatred stemming from when Tara had dated him.

"Cool it, Mat. He might be able to help find her. They have a connection." I didn't have time to go into it with him right now. I pulled Rémy aside. "Can you find her? I know you guys have been working on reading each other without touching."

"Jack, I will try, but we've never had much luck at any kind of distance," he said, frowning.

"Try. We have to find her. I have a really bad feeling, Rémy."

"As do I." He walked away a short distance and sat down, closing his eyes. I watched for a few minutes until he opened his eyes and shook his head.

"Goddammit! Where could she be?" I yelled at Tara and Mat. They both shook their heads. Tara was crying now. I couldn't lose Ally. I just got her back. I felt so helpless and desperate. What could I do? I was willing to do anything to get her back. I turned around when I heard the old lady arguing with a guy who had come out of the house.

"Tell them, Mark! I don't care if you're embarrassed. That little girl's life may be in danger."

The man nodded and began to talk. "I'm sorry. I should have called a long time ago. I was ashamed and I didn't think it was important."

"Mr. Graves, you need to tell us what you know. Now," Brian said firmly. "Did you see anything the day Ashley Hayes disappeared?"

"I was home that afternoon," he admitted quietly. "I skipped baseball practice and came home. I was in my tree house." He pointed to a dilapidated tree house in the side yard that overlooked the street. "I had found a stack of girlie magazines the day before, next to a dumpster, and I hid them in my tree house. I snuck home that day to look at them."

"Did you see Ashley that afternoon?" Brian asked.

Mark nodded. "I saw her walking home. She was really pretty and I had a crush on her. I liked watching her," he admitted.

"Did she go home?"

"No. Mr. Moore was home and he called out to her. That's what caught my attention. She went into his house," he pointed across the street to the house on the corner. "I didn't think anything of it because she babysat for them."

"Did you see anything else?"

"No. After she went into his house, I went back to my magazines. I ended up falling asleep until my parents got home." He looked ashamed.

"Did you hear anything else? Any cars or anything?" He shook his head. "What about when you woke up? Did you notice if Mr. Moore's car was still in the driveway?" Brian pushed.

"I'm sorry. I didn't pay attention."

"Jack!" It was Rémy, jogging over to us. "I finally got through to her."

"What? On her phone?" Jen asked, confused, since there was no phone in his hand.

"Rémy's a Seer." I had no time or patience for secrets right now. "He and Ally have a strong connection." Adele and Jen nodded, shocked. Mat and Brian looked confused.

"Jennifer, what the hell is he talking about?" Brian asked.

"Not now!" she insisted. "Please, believe what he says. I'll tell you everything later." Brian nodded reluctantly and we all looked to Rémy.

"She's nearby, but she's very vague and confused. I think she may be unconscious. She's in pain," he ended softly.

I started across the street to where Mark Graves had pointed, determined to get to her. That must be where she was, for whatever reason. Mat grabbed me, holding me back.

"Jack, no," he shook his head. "Let the police handle this." I shook his hands away, but realized he was right, no matter how badly I wanted to go to her.

"Okay," Brian said briskly. "I think we need to assume Mr. Moore was the last person to see Ashley alive and may very well be the killer. I think it's also very likely Ally, for some reason, may be at his house. I'm calling S.W.A.T." He started dialing his phone.

The S.W.A.T. team arrived within fifteen minutes and the waiting began. I felt like I was going to come out of my skin, not knowing what was happening to Ally. We had only Rémy's assurances she was alive; none of the attempts to contact David Moore by telephone had been successful. The S.W.A.T. team deployed around the house, preparing to breach if they could not contact Moore. I was frantic, pacing back and forth, worrying about what would happen to Ally in the chaos of police bursting through the front door of a killer's house. I felt like I was going to go crazy if something didn't happen soon.

"Rémy, what's going on, man? Please, you've got to tell me something!" I grabbed him and began to shake him.

"She's alive, Jack! Calm down! You're not helping her by losing control like this!" He grabbed my shoulders, trying to push me away.

"Sorry." I removed my hands and ran them through my hair, wanting to pull it out. "What can you hear from her?"

He shook his head. "Nothing. She's not communicating with me. I'm sorry, Jack. I don't know why. I can feel her, but nothing else. I'll keep trying, I swear."

"Aagh!" I yelled, along with a string of curses.

"Jack." It was Tara, coming over to comfort me. "She's going to be okay. You have to believe that. She's strong and she loves you so much. She will find a way to survive. I know she will." She ended on a sob and I pulled her in for a hug. I met Mat's eyes over her shoulder and he came to take her from me.

"We've got movement!" One of the S.W.A.T. members yelled. We all crowded around Brian, who had binoculars trained on the front of the house. "Someone's coming out! Hold your fire!"

The front door opened and there was Ally, running down the path, her hands held together in front of her body, a piece of duct tape across her mouth. Brian grabbed me before I could run for her, holding me back. Behind her, in the doorway, David Moore appeared with a shotgun in his hands.

We both watched, horrified, as Moore raised the gun and toward Ally. "Ally!" I screamed and used all my strength to break away from Brian. No force on earth could keep me from going to her.

She watched me run toward her, saw I was looking behind her, and whipped her head around as the gun went off. Time slowed down as she turned her head back toward me. A blue pulse exploded from her and knocked Moore and me to the ground. I looked up in time to see Ally fall to the concrete path.

***

Ally

I regained consciousness slowly, as if emerging from a thick fog, only to find myself lying on the floor in a completely white room. Hmmm. That was odd, because I clearly remembered being in Mr. Moore's spare bedroom right before the blackness enveloped me. So, where the heck was I and what the heck happened to me? And why did my head hurt so badly?

"He hit you on the back of the head with a lamp." A young, blonde woman walked toward me. I definitely recognized her.

"Ashley?"

"Yes." She nodded. "Hi, Ally. It's good to finally meet you. Sorry it's under these circumstances."

"Yeah, me too. I'm not, uh, dead, am I?" I slowly stood up as I waited for her answer.

"No." She laughed. "That crazy old bastard didn't hit you hard enough to kill you. You're only knocked out. You're actually going to wake up for real in a few minutes, so we need to make this fast."

"O-kay," I drew out the syllables. "What do we need to make fast?"

"Well, how you're going to get out of here, for starters. David Moore is very unstable and you are in grave danger, Ally," Ashley took both of my hands in her own. I could feel them as if she were a real, living person.

"How can I feel you? Aren't you a ghost?"

She chuckled. "Ghost is actually a made-up thing. You can't believe everything you read, Ally."

"Well, what are you?" I asked peevishly.

"I don't really know what to call it. I guess I'm a spirit of some sort. I found you when you started reading my book and I've been able to communicate with you through your dreams. I have waited a long time to see Moore caught. You're the only one I've ever been able to communicate with since I died. I can see the others, my mom and Scott, but they can't see me or sense me. You're becoming very powerful, Ally. I don't really understand it."

"Yeah, me neither. Hey, I knew it wasn't Scott. What happened all those years ago, Ashley? Can you tell me?" I needed to know, needed to see the full picture of what had happened.

"Sure," she sighed. "But I'll make it quick, because we need to get you out of here. So, that

Tuesday, January 17, 1984, I kissed Scott goodbye after school and walked home, like I did every day he had practice. Right as I turned the corner at the Moores' house I noticed Mr. Moore's Jeep in the driveway, which was really unusual for that time of day. As I walked by their house, he called to me from the front porch and asked me to come in to set up a babysitting job. I thought it was a little bit weird, but I went in anyway. You know those little niggling feelings you sometimes get?" I nodded. "Well, don't ever dismiss them. They are really important and might save your life someday. That one I had could have saved mine. He knocked me unconscious, just like he did to you."

"God, Ashley, I'm so sorry. Why did he do it?" I felt bad for making her go through it all. "Listen, you don't have to tell me anymore," I offered, even though I really wanted to know the rest.

"No, it's fine." She motioned for me to sit next to her on a bench I hadn't noticed before. I could have sworn there was nothing in this room a second before. "This next part is really hard to talk about, Ally. Would you mind reading it from my mind? I've watched you do it with that lady, Cassie, and your friend, Rémy."

"Uh, sure, no problem. Will it work? Because you're, you know…"

"Dead?" she said, stating the obvious. "I think it still works. Let's give it a try." She reached out and took my hand, sweeping me into her mind and memories.

She was lying on a big bed, apparently in the Moores' bedroom, her hands and mouth duct-taped.

David Moore was beside her, stroking her face, arms, and body. "Oh, Ashley," he crooned. "We belong together. Why can't you see that? I was going to leave my wife for you, but last night she told me she heard from that bitch across the street you're pregnant." He stood and paced before returning to her. "Slut!" He slapped her hard across the face. Ashley started crying hysterically, choking behind the duct tape. "I thought you were so beautiful and pure! Then I found out you've been screwing that boy! You are mine!" He slapped her and hit her until she fell unconscious again. When she woke again, she was bouncing around in the back of Moore's Jeep. She felt it stop and then rough hands were pulling her out to stand. She could see herself, battered and bruised, in the reflection of David's sunglasses. She looked around and saw he had brought her to a rocky hiking area that looked to be in the foothills of the mountains. There was no sign of another human being anywhere. Her hands and mouth were still taped, but her legs were free. He forced her to walk in front of him and she saw the trailhead sign for the Osha Trail as they passed. After walking for what felt like at least thirty minutes, he forced her off the trail and deep into the brush. They walked for at least fifteen more minutes before she felt a sharp pain in her head.

She took her hand away. "That's it. He hit me with a large rock. The first blow knocked me out, then he continued to bash my head in until I was dead. He buried me in a shallow grave, but it was so far away from the trail nobody found me until recently."

"Oh, Ashley. I'm so sorry." I put my arms around her and hugged her, finding it strange that she felt solid, like a real, live person. "He was obsessed with you? That's awful. I'm so sorry for what happened to you and your baby."

She nodded against my hair and said, "Thanks. He didn't rape me. I know you've been worried about that, Ally. I think since I was pregnant, he felt like I had been ruined. I guess that's why he went crazy and killed me. It's what set him off. He stole so much from me, from my family, and from Scott. He never got to meet his little girl."

"It was a girl?" I whispered.

"Yeah. She's beautiful." At my shocked look, she nodded, saying, "She's here with me. Scott will get to see her someday. I'm so glad he finally found someone else and has a family. He was the best thing that ever happened to me and he deserves to be happy. I loved him so much, Ally. He reminds me of your Jack, actually."

I smiled at her. "So it doesn't bother you to see him with his new wife and family? You aren't jealous?"

"Not at all. It's not like that here. Now that I'm dead and I know I can't be a part of his life anymore, I only want the very best for him. I want him to be happy." She clasped my hand once more, then said, "Okay. Time's up. You're waking up and we need to figure a way to get you out of here. I will not accept that he can do this to two girls. This stops now!" she said fiercely.

"What should I do? Am I tied up? What are my

options?"

"Yes, you're tied up with duct tape, like I was, and you're lying on the bed in his guest room. He didn't tie your feet, so we can work with that. He's sitting at the kitchen table, cleaning his shotgun."

"He has a gun? Shit! I don't want to get shot, Ashley! Why did I come in here?" I moaned.

"Because you felt really, really sick. You should have stayed home today, Ally. You know, Jack is right. You are about the most stubborn person I've ever met. You might want to work on that, sweetie."

"Thanks," I said sarcastically. "I'll get right on that as soon as I get out of here without getting freaking shot."

"You need to get up very quietly, find something to hit him with, maybe the lamp he hit you with, and then sneak up behind him and bash the crap out of him. I think it's your best option."

"I don't know if I can do that. I'm scared, Ashley." I could feel myself beginning to panic.

"Calm down, Ally. You can do this. You have to. Jack, Tara, everyone you love is outside waiting for you. There's a S.W.A.T. team and everything, but you need to get out of this house before David has a chance to use that gun. He is completely unstable and has absolutely nothing to lose at this point. He does not plan to leave this house alive and doesn't mind taking you with him," she warned.

"Jack's outside? And my mom?" I hesitated, feeling something in my mind. "Rémy! He's out there too. I can feel him trying to reach me. Why can't I get through to him?"

"I don't know. I don't understand the connection

you have with him. Maybe you can't reach him because you're unconscious." She looked at me sympathetically. "It's time to go."

"Okay. Will I see you again?"

She shook her head, smiling. "No. There's no reason. You don't need to talk to dead people on a regular basis."

I smiled wryly. "Bye, Ashley."

"Bye, Ally. Thanks for helping me." She began to fade from my vision.

I woke slowly, groggily, but remembered what she had instructed me to do. I sat up as quietly as I possibly could, looking around for the lamp David had used to hit me. It was on the floor by the bed. I grabbed it awkwardly because of the position of my hands, tied together with the tape. I stood for a moment to get my balance and gather my waning courage. My mouth behind the duct tape was bone dry; I couldn't even manage to work up enough saliva to swallow. Okay, I needed to calm down. I could do this. I had to do this. Jack was right outside. My mom and Grams were with him. I crept into the kitchen, praying he wouldn't turn around. He was sitting at the table, re-assembling his shotgun, and mumbling.

"I loved you, Ashley. Why did you cheat on me? How could you do that? I had to do it. I did. I had no choice. We were supposed to be together. It wasn't my fault. I couldn't help it. You should have loved me!" He was sobbing pathetically as he worked. "Now this girl knows! What am I going to do? I can't let her leave! She has to die. It's over, Ashley. It's finally over."

His crazy ramblings caused my blood to freeze in my veins; he might be insane, but he was planning to kill me. I was completely terrified, but knew I had to try to get away. To do nothing was to give in and be killed. I had nothing to lose. I crept toward him as quietly as humanly possible. I managed to get almost close enough when he must have sensed me and began to turn around. I was out of time. I lunged with the lamp, striking him on the side of the head with as much force as I could possibly muster. He fell out of his chair to the ground, but I could see he was only stunned, not knocked out. I turned and literally ran for my life.

I reached the front door and wrenched it open, hoping I wouldn't get shot either from behind or from the S.W.A.T. team out front. I made it as far as the front path when I heard Jack yell my name. I saw him break away from Brian and run toward me. I turned to see what he was looking at behind me and was horrified to see David Moore raise his shotgun. If he didn't hit me, he would hit Jack. Everything within me screamed at the thought of Jack getting shot and I felt a huge energy pulse rocket away from my body right as the gun went off and everything was bathed in blue light. Then the concrete was rushing up to meet me.

CHAPTER SIXTEEN

"I saw eternity the other night,
Like a great ring of pure and endless light."
–Henry Vaughan

I woke to Mat's face right above mine, his hands running over my body, checking for injuries. I tried to sit up, but he pushed me gently back down and removed the duct tape from my hands and mouth as gently as possible. I whimpered as I felt like all the skin on my lips was ripped away.

"Hey, lie still. Were you hit? We have an ambulance on the way," he said.

The last thing I wanted was another hospital visit. I sat up saying, "Mat? What are you doing here? I'm fine. I didn't get shot. I passed out. I've been sick. Ow, my head really hurts." I reached back to feel the lump. "That bastard! He hit me! God, I'm tired of getting hit in the head. Where is Jack?" I finally noticed someone was holding my other hand and turned to see who it was. "Jack!" I threw my arms around his neck, knocking him over.

I didn't care in the least and crushed my mouth against his, even though it really hurt my lips. I remembered then that Ashley had told me everyone was outside waiting for me. Well, they could wait a second longer because I needed to be in Jack's arms.

"Apparently, she's fine," said Mat wryly.

"For God's sake, Ally," Grams broke in. "Let the boy breathe."

I reluctantly broke away as Jack sat us both up, saying, "I can breathe just fine." He kissed me on the forehead before helping me stand. "Let's get her inside, okay?" He kept his arm around me as we followed everyone inside the Graves' house and Jack led me to the sofa. Tara brought me a glass of water, which I gratefully gulped. Mrs. Graves bustled to the kitchen muttering about making tea for everyone. Mom and Grams sat on either side of me, Mom worriedly examining the back of my head. "When the paramedics get here you need to let them do a more thorough examination than Mat was able to do. And if they say you need to go the hospital, there will be no argument from you. Do you understand me?"

"Yes, ma'am," I said and hugged her. "I love you, Mom."

"I love you too, Ally-bear. You have got to stop doing this."

"I'm sorry. I didn't think I was doing anything the least bit dangerous," I defended myself.

"How in the world did you end up in Moore's house?" Brian asked.

"I got a phone call from Mrs. Graves asking me

to come over and talk to her son. None of us could reach you and she said he was leaving soon so I decided to walk over and meet you here. I called you and left a voicemail. I overestimated my recovery from that damned food poisoning and needed to rest. I was right in front of Mr. Moore's house, and I had to sit on the curb to rest. He saw me and invited me in for a drink of water. I didn't think anything of it. Boy, was that ever a mistake." I realized I was rambling and paused to drink more water. I told them how I had gone to the bathroom, opening the wrong door. I had seen the cardboard box sitting on the floor and couldn't resist taking a quick look. When I saw what was inside, I immediately realized David Moore was the killer and I planned to get out of there as fast as humanly possible, but the crazy old coot had bashed me in the head with a lamp. I didn't tell them all about meeting Ashley; that would have to wait until Brian and Mat weren't present, although I figured Mom was going to have to spill the beans to Brian sooner or later. That would be a fun conversation. "Did you arrest him, Brian? You got him, didn't you?"

Brian knelt down in front of me. "He shot himself. He's dead."

The paramedics arrived and I was able to keep my thoughts to myself as I was examined. They looked at the lump on the back of my head and shone a light in my eyes to check my pupils.

"Well, there doesn't seem to be an obvious concussion. You have a couple of options," the paramedic said. "You can let us take you to the ER in the ambulance. You can get someone else to take you, or you can go home and get some rest. Have a family member watch you carefully for a few hours. You need to drink lots of fluids to get yourself rehydrated after being so sick." I had told them the reason I passed out was from the food poisoning. Nobody mentioned the blue energy pulse. I wondered how many had seen it and what in the world they thought it was.

"Please, Mom." I gave her my best sad puppy-dog eyes. "It's Friday. I swear I'll stay home all weekend and rest. I won't budge from the couch. Please don't make me go to the hospital." She and Grams conferred in whispers for a minute.

"All right," Mom finally relented. "But the first sign of any problems and I will drag you to the hospital myself." She looked up at Brian. "Can we take her home now?"

"Yeah, go ahead. I need to stay here for a while, but I'll stop by later to finish questioning her." He looked at me carefully. He had apparently seen the blue pulse and I knew there would be some interesting conversations in our future.

"All right. Come on, Ally. Let's get you home," Grams said. "I assume you're coming, Jack?"

He looked at me for affirmation. "Yeah, of course. I'll meet you at the house, okay? I need to drop Tara and Mat off at the school so they can get their cars." He leaned down and kissed the top of my head. "I'll see you in a few minutes, babe."

As I watched him walk away, I finally noticed one other person who hadn't said a word yet. "Rémy!" He smiled his little smile at me and I remembered feeling him in my thoughts, checking where I was and if I was okay. "Come to the house too. Please?" It was time to let a certain cat out of the bag.

"Of course." He nodded and left, following Jack. I hoped Tara would be smart enough to send Mat home. I really needed to tell Grams, Mom, Jack, Tara, and Rémy about Ashley and everything she had told me. And I knew they wanted to know about the blue pulse. I really didn't want to complicate it with trying to explain the whole crazy psychic thing to Mat and Brian at this point. Grams and Mom looked at me, apparently questioning why I was inviting this boy, but I shook my head at them slightly. They were going to have to learn to trust my judgment.

***

I was upstairs in my bedroom, changing into my sweats/pajamas when I heard a soft knock at my door.

"Ally? Are you decent? Your mom said I could come up and see if you're okay," Jack called softly. I opened my door and pulled him in quickly, shutting the door behind him. I threw myself in his arms for the second time that evening.

"Jack!"

He wrapped his arms around me, pulling me tight against his warm, hard body. "It's okay, querida. I've got you."

"I need you to hold me."

"Always."

We stayed like that for several minutes, simply

holding each other, until I finally let go and led him to sit beside me on my bed. I held his hand tightly. "I was so scared tonight, Jack," I whispered.

He sighed and lifted me onto his lap. "You have no idea." He pulled my head to rest under his chin. "I almost lost my mind tonight when we couldn't find you. You have seriously got to stop rushing off to save the day, babe."

I pulled away to look into his eyes. "Jack, I swear I wasn't trying to do that."

He chuckled ruefully. "I know, I know. But don't plan on me letting you out of my sight for the next several weeks…or decades."

I laughed and pulled him down for a kiss. "I am absolutely fine with that." I went back to kissing him, which he complied with nicely for a few minutes.

"Are you sure you're okay? Maybe you should have gone to the emergency room." He brushed my hair out of my face and looked hard at me.

"I'll be fine, Jack. I simply need to rest. You're my best medicine, you know." I smiled at him and moved back in for another kiss.

"Oh, I am, huh?" he asked. I giggled and nodded, sinking my fingers into his thick hair. "Well, maybe you need a stronger dose." With that he pushed me onto the bed and followed me down, half covering my body with his own, and began really kissing me, opening my mouth with his, stroking his warm tongue against mine. His hand slid down to my thigh, wrapping it around his hips. "Mmmm. I could stay here all night, babe." He kissed me once more and sat up. "But everyone is downstairs waiting for us. Your mom is sure to bust through that door any second, so why don't you put some pants on so we can go downstairs."

"Pants?" I looked down and realized I was in my underwear. "God, Jack," I complained as I reached for my sweatpants. "Why didn't you tell me I was parading around in front of you in my underwear?"

He laughed and rubbed his hands over his face. "Uh, let's see—because you look super hot and sexy? I'm happy to let you parade in front of me in your panties anytime you want."

I threw my stuffed dog at him and laughed. "That's so altruistic of you, Jack. Thanks a lot!" He laughed as well and clasped my hand, entwining our fingers, as he guided me down the stairs.

Grams fussed over me, making sure I was wrapped in a fluffy blanket with a cup of tea. Tara and Rémy arrived at the same time and I had the task of telling everyone why I had invited him.

"Grams, Mom, you've met Rémy before. I told you he's an exchange student this semester from France. At least, that's what he's pretending to be. In reality, he's twenty-two years old and is a Seer. His grandmother is the Oracle." I decided it was better to drop the whole bomb at once.

"Well," said my mom as she sank onto the couch next to me. "Jack said earlier he was a Seer, which both Brian and Mat heard, by the way. But the Oracle…"

"My goodness," said Grams.

"*Bonsoir, mesdames*," Rémy said quietly. "I apologize for keeping so much from you. I can only say I felt it was necessary."

"Rémy," I held my hand out to him, motioning for him to sit by me. "I felt you, in my mind. Thank you."

He smiled tightly. "Of course. I'm glad Jack thought to call me."

"All right, sweetheart. You've gathered us all here. Now, what is it you needed to tell us? Perhaps you should start with the blue light?" Grams asked.

I shook my head. "I have no idea what that was. I saw the gun pointing toward Jack and I don't know. I—I couldn't let Jack get shot. I don't know what happened." They were all staring at me. I shifted uncomfortably. "What?"

Jack knelt in front of me and took my hands in his. "Sweetheart, that blue pulse…exploded from you. It knocked Moore and me down. I've never seen anything like it. It came from you, Ally."

"I didn't want him to shoot you, Jack," I whispered.

"Well, it seems you've developed yet another power," observed Grams. "We'll need to tell Cassie about this."

"There's more," I said. "I saw Ashley tonight. I actually spoke with her." At all the shocked looks, I continued. "After Moore knocked me out, I 'woke up' sort of," I used my fingers to make air quotations, "in a big white room with Ashley walking toward me. She told me what happened to her all those years ago."

"Ally, you don't need to tell us. Let me." Rémy held his hand out towards me. Jack stood to allow Rémy to take his place next to me.

I looked up to see Jack narrow his eyes at the

sight of him holding my hand. I smiled and winked at Jack as I placed my other hand on top of Rémy's. "That would be great, actually. Thanks." I closed my eyes and let him read my memories. I felt him probe into my mind as I went back over the entire episode with Ashley. When we were finished, he sighed, put my hand back in my lap, and patted it as he stood up, gesturing for Jack to take his place. I laid my head down in Jack's lap and he pulled the blanket up around my shoulders, brushing my hair back, as Rémy began to tell my story. I tried to listen, but couldn't keep my eyes open.

I woke as Jack was gently placing me in my bed. "This is getting to be a habit," I murmured. He smiled and tucked the covers up around me.

"I'll come over tomorrow after work, okay?" I nodded sleepily. "I love you, Ally." He kissed me.

"I know," I mumbled. I was asleep again approximately thirty seconds later.

***

Brian showed up bright and early Saturday morning to finish questioning me. Although Grams, Mom, and I would have preferred to wait to tell him about our psychic abilities until after this investigation was over so as to keep it from muddying any of his opinions, I was expecting him to ask about the pulse. There was absolutely no way he would let that go. It wasn't, however, terribly germane to the basic facts of what had happened: I received a call from Mark Graves and decided to meet Brian at the Graves' home. I walked over from school, but felt too weak from my recent food poisoning to continue. I stopped at David Moore's house because he was on the front porch and I asked him if I could have a glass of water and sit for a few minutes. I went to the bathroom and opened the wrong door. I saw the box on the floor of the guest bedroom and looked inside to find Ashley's backpack, her purse, and several pairs of her underwear. Moore found me spying and coshed me on the head with a lamp. When I woke up, my hands and mouth were duct taped, but I was able to stand up, grab the lamp, and sneak into the kitchen. I managed to hit him on the head, and although it didn't knock him out, it did give me time to escape. I ran out the front door and collapsed on the walkway right as he shot at me.

He nodded and finished writing in his notebook. Then, as expected, he looked up and said, "Okay. Now who is going to tell me what the hell that blue pulse-thing was? And what on earth was Jack talking about when he said Rémy is a Seer?" He looked at the three of us, who were looking at each other, not wanting to be the one to tell him.

Finally, Mom sighed and said, "Brian, honey, there's something I need to tell you." She took his hand in hers and proceeded to tell him about our family's little gift that keeps on giving. As he listened, the expression on his face went from incredulous to a kind of horrified acceptance as Mom detailed our powers. I jumped in and told him about the nightmares connected to Ashley's book and how she appeared to me when I was unconscious in David Moore's living room.

"So, you're telling me you are all psychic, right? I am supposed to believe my fiancée, her mother, and her daughter are like, mind readers or something?" he said.

"No, Brian. Grams and Mom can't read minds," I clarified.

"But you can?"

In response, I reached over and placed my hand on his arm and closed my eyes. I concentrated hard; it was crucial I clearly read his thoughts in order to convince him. "You're thinking about how we are probably all crazy, but you're also thinking it explains a lot about what happened, especially how I knew it wasn't Scott who murdered Ashley. You're also hoping the baby won't be like us. Finally, you're still wondering what the hell the blue pulse was about. Well, I'm wondering the same thing, Brian."

"You don't know what it was? How is that possible? It came from you, Ally! I could swear it came from inside you!" he was almost yelling.

"Brian, sweetheart, calm down, please," Mom pleaded.

"She knocked two grown men flat on their asses! That doesn't happen every day, Jennifer!" He stood, running his hand through his hair. "I'm sorry. I shouldn't yell at any of you. I don't understand what's happening here." He pulled my mom into his arms. "I'm sorry, Jen."

Grams and I took the opportunity to escape and let Mom finish talking to Brian, hopefully assuring him his child would not be a complete freak.

They finally called us back into the living room

and Brian asked a few more questions before telling me to get some rest. "I don't know what to think about all this, but I know what I saw in front of Moore's house. I can't explain it and I will certainly not be including it in my report." We all laughed quietly. "I do know I am marrying your mother and you will be part of my family, Ally. You, too, Adele. And I will protect my family. I won't tell anyone about this, I swear."

"I've said it before, but you're a good guy, Brian Keller," I said as I hugged him. "Thanks. And don't worry: your kid won't be a freak."

***

Grams brought me lunch on a tray and otherwise fussed over me for the rest of the day, which was comforting.

Jack came by after work around six o'clock. As I hugged him, breathing in his freshly showered scent, running my fingers through his still-damp hair, I felt a strange lump in his shirt. I backed away, reaching up to feel a soft mound in his shirt. I raised my eyebrows. He chuckled and reached inside the blue chambray button-up he was wearing untucked over a black t-shirt. He had the sleeves rolled up, showcasing his sculpted, brown forearms. I got distracted for a moment, running my fingers over his skin. Sexy, manly arms are really my thing. Mmm.

"Ally?" Jack chuckled. "Am I interrupting?"

I felt my face flush at being caught. "What? Can't I admire your hotness?" I tried to brazen it out.

"Whatever," he said, embarrassed. "Do you want your present or not?"

"Ooh, yes. Definitely! You brought me a present?" I danced up and down a little. He brought out a small, adorable stuffed cat. I squealed and hugged it. "Thank you, Jack."

He smiled. "So, you're not going to complain about me bringing you a present?"

"Not today. You can always bring me presents the day after I almost get shot," I allowed.

"There had better not be any more of those days, Ally. My heart can't take it." He brushed his knuckles over my cheek. "Anyway, I figured you needed a cat to go with the dog you threw at me from your bed."

I gave him an offended look. "Oh, yeah? I don't remember you complaining much last night." I started lightly beating him with the stuffed cat, laughing as he tried to grab it, which he did quickly, holding it high above my head. I was laughing so hard I could barely stand, trying to jump to reach it. He grabbed me before I could fall, pulling me against him and we both suddenly realized a much better use for our time. He lowered his head and laid his warm lips against mine. I clasped my arms around his neck and gave myself over to simply feeling for the moment. We both opened our mouths together and reveled in the closeness as our tongues moved against each other. I could forget the rest of the world when I was kissing Jack; I could feel the delicious shivers all the way to my toes.

"Good gracious, Ally! Every time I turn around

you are mauling that boy. Let him in the door at least," Grams said as she brought in a tea tray.

We broke apart and went to sit together on the couch. "I really don't mind, ma'am."

"I'm sure you don't," she said with a sniff.

We all had tea while Jack told us about his day, regaling us with a story of a customer who showed up to pick up her car, dismayed to discover it was red. She insisted she had ordered a blue paint job and would not be convinced otherwise until Manny showed her the original work order with her own signature on it requesting red. Grams then left us alone to watch a movie Jack had brought, a sci-fi thriller I had wanted to see. She went to her room to watch television. Mom had gone home with Brian and I wondered whether she would be home early or whether she would stay the night like she frequently did on weekends. She hadn't done that until we all found out about the pregnancy, and I don't think she would have done it then if I hadn't pointed out the ridiculousness of the situation.

"Come on, Mom," I said. "It's not like I don't know you two are sleeping together. It's that whole birds and bees thing, you know? Go be with the guy you're in love with. Grams and I are fine here."

"Oh, sweetie, it's just that, well, I don't feel like I'm being a very good role model for you. I certainly don't want you spending the night at your boyfriend's house."

"Yeah, I'm pretty sure Trina and Manny wouldn't be huge fans of that, either. But I think this is a little bit different situation. Nobody's judging you, Mom. Besides, you guys are engaged."

It had apparently made her feel better about staying with him a few nights a week.

"Ally, have you talked with your mom and Adele about your living arrangements after the wedding?" Jack asked during the previews.

"Yeah. Mom is moving in with Brian and Grams and I are staying here."

"You're okay with that? Are you going to miss your mom?" He caressed my neck as he talked.

"Mmm. I'm having a hard time concentrating with you doing that. Don't stop," I said when he halted. "Yeah, I'll miss her, but I think it'll be better for the newlyweds. And I will miss out on all the midnight baby crying this way."

He laughed. "Yeah, I hadn't thought about that. What about next year? Are you going to live here while you go to the university? Or are you and Tara going to move into the dorms?"

"Why? Are you offering something else?" I asked hopefully, thinking back to our conversation during his birthday dinner.

He stopped caressing my neck as I felt him freeze. I sat up and looked him in the eye. "Don't panic. I'm teasing, Jack."

"No, that's not it at all. I got a visual of us living together and I liked it a lot. But as wonderful as it sounds, I can't do it. I guess I'm too old-fashioned to live with someone before marriage."

I leaned in to kiss him sweetly. "Yeah, me too. I think the commitment should be all or nothing." I kissed him for another minute before asking him something I had been wondering about lately. "What about everything else? I mean, you know…"

I was too embarrassed to finish.

"Everything else? Ally, are you asking when we're going to start having sex?" He held my face in his hands, looking very serious. I nodded, unable to meet his gaze. He pulled me in close. "Sweetheart, believe me, I have never wanted anything so badly, but I'm really, really trying to wait until you're at least 18. I think you should be older. And I kind of think we should be at least engaged. I know it's really old-fashioned, but, Ally, sweetheart, you're a white-picket fence kind of girl."

"I am?"

"Definitely. It's a good thing, querida, so don't look so depressed. Are you okay with that?"

I finally looked into his eyes and nodded. "In the cold light of day, yeah, I agree with you. When we're in the middle of making out, not so much. But I know I'm not ready."

He laughed and pulled me back. "I totally get it. We're going to have to show a lot of restraint, babe. We've got at least a year to wait, maybe longer. When we finally do sleep together everyone is going to know, so it needs to be totally above board, sweetheart."

"How is everyone going to know?" I asked, shocked. I'd never heard of *that* before.

He leaned in to kiss me. "Because I'm going to have a ridiculously smug look on my face afterward. And I might need to shout it from the nearest rooftop."

"Oh." I laughed. "I thought maybe there was something I had never heard about that was a giveaway. Whew. That's a relief. Hey, maybe you could just tweet it out," I suggested.

He pretended to ponder this. "That would probably be much more efficient. Good idea, babe. Seriously, Ally, I never want it to be something we have to sneak around for or that we're ashamed of."

I sat up and looked at him seriously. "Jack Ruiz, you are the most amazing guy. How did I get so lucky to get you?"

He smiled my favorite smile. "I'm definitely the lucky one, querida."

CHAPTER SEVENTEEN

"The wheel is come full circle."
–Shakespeare –King Lear (5.3.176)

After the excitement of solving Ashley Hayes' murder, the rest of the semester seemed boring in comparison. My non-school time was taken up with final wedding preparations. I spent countless evenings addressing invitations, cataloguing wedding gifts, and putting table decorations together. I made a mental note to elope to Vegas when I got married. I wondered what Jack would think about that and then was embarrassed to realize I was already planning our wedding. What a girly thing to do! Next thing you know I would be writing 'Mrs. Jack Ruiz' all over my notebooks! Yuck! There was so much to do for this wedding I had to fight for time to spend with Jack, who was leaving for basic training the morning after the wedding for eight long weeks. I was leaving the following day for a month in Ireland, during which I would be working with the Seer Council to try and figure out whether or not I was the up-and-coming Oracle.

Tara's long-delayed party finally took place three weeks after the ill-fated first party date. I was positioned in her front hall, greeting guests, when Rémy arrived with his date, which he had managed to keep under wraps this entire time. I nearly dropped my soda when I saw him walk in with none other than Veronica Albluth on his arm, looking radiant and more alive than I had seen her look for many months.

"Holy crap! I mean, um, wow, Veronica. You look great. I'm really glad you came. Rémy, can I talk to you for a minute?" I turned around and walked toward the kitchen, daring him not to follow.

"What the hell, Rémy?" I demanded when he arrived in the kitchen.

He smirked. "What do you mean? You don't like my date? Are you perhaps jealous?"

I ignored the last part of his comment as unworthy. "I like your date very much. Do you know what she went through last semester? Do you have any idea how fragile she is?"

"Will it surprise you to know she told me everything? Calm down, Ally. I have no intention of hurting Veronica. She's a beautiful girl and I enjoy spending time with her. Besides, I am interested in seeing an American prom and Veronica is willing to go with me. We should all go together."

"You're too old for her," I countered, ignoring his suggestion.

"Oh, that's rich coming from you. How old is

Jack? I forget." He pretended to think.

"Shut up. He's only two years older than me. You're like, four years older than Veronica!"

"She's 18, a legal adult. Calm down. I'm not doing anything. It's only a date. I'll be going home soon, and she's understands this is simply a fun, easy relationship. Neither of us is serious. She's enjoying some positive attention for a change."

I stared him down, hoping to make him squirm. He stared back. Damn him. Jack came in at this point and put his arm around my waist.

"Everything okay in here? I think your date is looking for you, man," he said as he kissed the top of my head. Rémy always brought out the possessive side of Jack, which I usually found somewhat amusing.

"Yes," Rémy replied firmly. "We're done here. I need to get back to my date. Have a wonderful evening. Let me know about the prom." He stalked back to Veronica.

"What was that all about?" Jack asked.

"Oh, nothing, I guess," I sighed. "I'm trying to stick my nose in someone else's business and I'm not very good at it. Come on. Let's not waste one of our last nights together." We went back into the living room and I concentrated on enjoying myself and minding my own business. This was not a typical party like the one Veronica had thrown last semester. We had planned some board games and a movie. There were only a handful of our really close friends and the various dates they brought. There was no alcohol and absolutely no drugs. I preferred to hang out with people who didn't rely on artificial means to have a good time. I watched Veronica all evening and was surprised to find she was enjoying herself like the rest of us. I had become so used to her partaking in the popular kids' idea of fun I was amazed she could get into our kind of party. I was eventually able to relax and enjoy myself.

I was sitting between Jack's legs, leaning against his chest as he leaned against the couch watching the movie when he leaned forward to whisper in my ear. "What did Rémy mean earlier when he said to let him know about the prom?"

I shrugged. "Oh, nothing. He wanted us all to go together to the prom, that's all."

"Are we going to the prom?" Jack asked, surprised.

"No, of course not." I shrugged again. I frowned, wondering why I was feeling unsettled about this. I had never had the slightest desire to go to my prom, but when Rémy mentioned it, I had felt the strangest spark of envy.

"Come on." Jack stood and pulled me up, leading me into Tara's kitchen. He put his hands around my waist, lifted me to sit on the counter, and stepped between my legs to look me in the eyes. "Talk to me," he ordered.

"I don't know, Jack. I've never wanted to go to the prom, but when Rémy said he and Veronica are going, I felt a momentary desire to go. It'll pass, don't worry."

"Why should it pass, sweetheart? I'm sorry I didn't ask you; I honestly didn't think about it. But I'm asking now. Ally, will you please go to the prom with me?"

"Oh, Jack, you don't have to. I know prom is probably the very last thing you want to do. It was super-sweet of you to ask me, though." I leaned forward to kiss him.

He pulled away a moment later with a stubborn look on his face. "Are you turning me down? Are you seriously refusing to go to the prom with me? Because if you are, I need to find another date."

"What? You're not going to ask some skanky girl to the prom! I'm the only one you'll be taking to the prom, mister."

"So you'll go?" he pressed.

I looked at him through slitted eyes. "You tricked me. But yes, I would love to go with you to the prom, if you're sure you don't mind going. I don't know why I want to. I must be crazy."

"Maybe because you're about to graduate from high school and it's one of those things girls are hard-wired to want to do. It's a rite of passage, babe." He leaned in to kiss along my jaw. "I don't want to hear you complaining when we're 80 that I never took you to your prom." I gave him a dirty look. He laughed. "I love it when you get jealous, querida."

"Thank you for asking me to the prom, Jack. I didn't even know I wanted to go. It'll probably be awful, but at least I won't feel left out. You are the sweetest guy I know. I love you an awful lot."

"I know." He leaned back in and took my mouth, framing my face with his hands as he devoured me.

"Well, well, well," Tara interrupted us. "This does look more fun than the lame movie. Don't mind me. I'm just getting more popcorn. Carry on."

I laughed and jumped down from the counter. "Jack and I are going to prom."

"Really?" she squealed. "Yay! Mat and I are, too, and I was going to bully you into it later tonight. Thanks for saving me the trouble." I was staying the night with her after the party. "Let's go shopping for dresses tomorrow. Oh my gosh, this is going to be so much fun!" She pulled me into an enthusiastic hug. I met Jack's amused eyes over her shoulder as he grabbed the popcorn and retreated to the living room. I hugged my best friend back and made plans for prom shopping the next day.

***

Tara, Veronica, and I scoured the mall Saturday for prom dresses and shoes. It was hard to not get excited about the dance in the face of Tara's glee over all of us going together. Well, she wasn't excited about Veronica and Rémy going with us, but was managing to be nice to her on our shopping trip. She still wasn't a huge fan of Veronica, and even less of her and Rémy together, but she was trying. When Rémy heard I had agreed to go with Jack, he announced we would all, of course, go to dinner together beforehand and then on to the dance in the limo he would rent. He said he wanted the full American prom experience. Jack balked when he learned we would be going with Rémy, but finally agreed when I said, wistfully, that I had never ridden in a limo. I had figured out he would do pretty much anything to make me happy, even if he wasn't particularly jazzed about it. I knew for a fact he didn't have the least desire to go to prom, but he knew I wanted to go—I'm still not sure why I wanted to go—so we were going.

I had three dresses over my arm I planned to try on. Tara looked at them and put them back on the rack, shaking her head. "Honestly, Ally! What are you going to do when I'm not around to shop with you?" She went through the rack, pulling three different dresses out and handing them to me.

"I'll probably dress like a homeless person. Does that make you happy? Black? I don't know if I want a black dress."

"You will look amazing in black. Trust me; it will set off your hair perfectly. Veronica, have you got something to try on? Good. Let's go." She marched to the dressing rooms like a general leading a charge.

She was right, of course. I ended up buying the second dress I tried on, a short, tight, black sheath. It had a halter-top, which showed my shoulders and upper back, something I thought Jack might appreciate. It made me feel pretty and sexy and Tara said I had to get it. So, even though it was more than I wanted to spend, I bought it. She and Veronica assured me that while it was sexy, it wasn't trashy. Tara found a deep pink dress that swirled around her knees in a fun, flirty manner. I was a little jealous because I have never been able to wear pink. Veronica settled on a deep blue strapless dress that highlighted the fact that she was quite well endowed. I was sure Rémy would be a huge fan. After a brief stop in the food court for recaffeination, we headed to a shoe store to complete our outfits. I found some strappy black heels that I knew would be crippling me by about thirty minutes into the dance, if not sooner. But my dress demanded high heels, so I bought them. By this time Grams had given up the illusion of my credit card being for emergencies only and gave me a monthly spending limit. I think she was actually glad I had finally decided to show a modicum of interest in fashion, rather than phoning it in as I had for the previous sixteen years of my life. This shopping trip was certainly maxing out this month's limit.

The following Saturday was prom. The three of us girls decided to get ready together in Veronica's palatial bedroom and the three boys would pick us up from her house. Veronica had every kind of cosmetic and hair appliance that has ever been made. She was even better at makeup application than Tara; I certainly benefitted from her artistry that evening. She and Tara worked together to coax my hair into an elegant up-do, made possible by the fact it had grown out enough since December. Veronica loaned me some sparkly earrings I hoped were not real diamonds, but probably were, which completed my look.

"Oh, my God, Ally," Tara gushed. "You look amazing. Veronica, we are miracle workers!" She high-fived Veronica.

"Thanks," I said sarcastically. "So, you're implying it took a miracle to make me look like this?"

"Oh, don't be cranky. Look in the mirror." She

pushed me in front of Veronica's full-length closet mirror.

I didn't recognize the sophisticated young woman staring back at me. She looked like I had always wanted to look: sleek, elegant, and so put together. I stared in disbelief as Tara hugged me from behind. "Thanks, you guys," I whispered. "You *are* miracle workers."

Tara kissed me on the cheek. "I know, right? Jack is gonna flip!" She laughed. "Okay, the boys are here; Mat just now texted me. Let's give them a minute and then we can make our grand entrance. Veronica, kudos on having a great curved staircase for that purpose."

"Yeah, we had it installed for the occasion," she murmured.

Tara looked at her, surprised, and then tipped her head in respect at the snarky comeback. We each glided down the stairs, one after the other, as per Tara's orders. The boys were waiting downstairs with Veronica's mom and stepdad, turning as we made our appearance.

"Holy—" Mat began. Jack backhanded him lightly, nodding his head toward Veronica's parents. Mat cleared his throat and stepped forward to greet Tara, leaning down to kiss her cheek and present her with a wrist corsage. Rémy picked up Veronica's hand, kissing the back of it in true Rémy style.

Jack stepped forward, took my hand and spun me around slowly, saying, "Wow. Just wow." He leaned forward to kiss my cheek. "I have a lot more to say about this later," he whispered. As he placed a corsage on my wrist, I got a chance to look at him fully. He was wearing a black tuxedo with a stark, white shirt. He looked amazing. Actually all three of the guys did; they could easily be posing for a spread in *GQ*.

Veronica's parents took quite a few pictures since they had promised to take plenty to share with Tara and me. They took a few with our cell phones, as well, so we would have some immediately. Once we finished the photo shoot, we were off in the limo to dinner at Seasons Rotisserie and Grill, where Rémy had made reservations. We soon found out by reservations, he meant he had booked a private room. I was beginning to realize Rémy was quite wealthy and loved to spend money. He told us to order anything we wanted; dinner was on him. Jack and Mat objected to this, but Rémy charmed them into accepting his generous, yet ostentatious gesture. He ordered an assortment of appetizers for us to start with as we perused the menu. I settled on honey-poached artichoke ravioli while Jack ordered prime rib. I tried to be conservative about how much I ate so I wouldn't have a food baby sticking out of my dress, but it was hard. The food was so delicious and Rémy insisted on ordering a sample platter of desserts, insisting we had to try some of each. Jack was going to have to roll me out of there.

Prom was held at the Albuquerque Convention Center and it was lovely to be dropped off by the limo right in front of the doors. As predicted, my feet were already killing me, and I was glad to not have too far to walk. There were several other high school proms being held that evening, but we finally found the ballroom for Oso Grande High School and entered into an old-time circus theme, complete with big top and three rings. There were decorations all around for the various freak shows one might expect at a 1930s circus and fake campfires interspersed throughout the room. It was absolutely horrifying.

I stood staring at one of the tissue paper campfires as Jack enveloped me from behind. "What are you looking at, querida?"

"I'm trying to figure out why they would have open flames so near a totally wooden circus. It makes no sense to me." I could feel him shaking with laughter. "God, Jack. This is atrocious. I'm so sorry I dragged you to prom."

"I think I actually dragged you, babe. I had to trick you into going with me. Besides, God-awful decorations aside, I wouldn't have missed seeing you in that dress for the world. You look absolutely amazing tonight." His hands smoothed over my bare shoulders as he leaned down to press his lips to my exposed skin. "Please, never get rid of this dress. I'm going to dream about it for the foreseeable future."

I turned in his arms. "You, sir, also look amazing tonight." I gripped his lapels and pulled his face down to mine. "I'm going to dream about you in a tuxedo for the foreseeable future." I kissed him, lingering for a few sweet moments.

"Come on, Ally," he said against my lips. "Let's dance."

We danced in a group with Tara, Mat, Veronica, and Rémy, having more fun than I ever expected to.

After the first set, I sank gratefully into a folding chair and eased the instruments of torture, otherwise known as shoes, off my aching feet.

"Babe, they do killer things for your legs," said Jack as he pulled one of my feet into his lap and began massaging it, "but you need to ditch them. Most of the other girls have already." He pointed to a pile of high heels in the corner. I was happy to acquiesce, as were Tara and Veronica.

We spent an enjoyable evening, dancing nearly every dance. Rémy was a fantastic dancer and pulled the rest of us along with him, not allowing us to sit out. Jack and Mat both held their own in dancing, Tara and Veronica were both great, and I was simply along for the ride.

"I've told you before you have other qualities, which more than make up for your dancing deficit," he said as he held me close in a slow dance.

"Oh yeah?" I challenged. "Why don't you name a few? I'm feeling like a complete klutz right now."

"Hmm, let's see," he pondered, his hands caressing my bare back. "Well, you chose me as your boyfriend, so you clearly have excellent taste."

I laughed. "Anything else?"

"I'm thinking. Oh, you have great taste in prom dresses."

"That's it? You can't do any better?" I pouted.

"I'm just getting started. You also smell divine." He nuzzled my neck as he said this. "And you are a pretty good kisser."

"What? Pretty good? You—" I pulled back, offended.

He laughed and pulled me back for a lingering

kiss. "Sorry," he said. "My mistake. You are a great kisser," he teased.

I smiled at him and leaned my head into his chest, breathing in his magical scent. "I love you, Jack Ruiz."

"I know," he replied. "And I love you too, Ally Moran. Happy prom, sweetheart."

We all stayed until the very end of the dance and then Rémy had the limo driver drive us to Nine Mile Hill to look at the city lights. We went out for breakfast at about 2:00 a.m. at the Frontier, a 24-hour restaurant across the street from the university. Jack and I shared one of the enormous cinnamon rolls swimming in butter sauce, which the restaurant was famous for.

I was the first one dropped off. Jack and I spent a few precious moments at my front door, sharing cinnamon-flavored kisses until Mat hollered out the limousine that they needed to get the other girls home before dawn.

***

Two weeks later, I stood in front of my bedroom closet mirror trying to get my mortarboard to sit at the proper angle on my head. Honestly, after hundreds of years, was this the best hat design they could come up with? There was no way to make it look attractive, not to mention the fact it was bright scarlet, which clashed horribly with my red hair. I paused in the act of jamming in yet another bobby pin and gave it up as hopeless. "Ugh! I look ridiculous!"

"No, you don't. Stop feeling sorry for yourself. Here's your gown." Grams carried in the freshly ironed, matching bright red graduation gown. "Are you about ready? We need to get going or we'll be late. You look beautiful, by the way." She carefully set the gown on my bed and came to hug me from behind. "I can't believe you're graduating from high school today." I saw her chin tremble. "Are you sure you don't want a senior year? I'm sure we could work something out."

I smiled at her in the mirror. "Yes, I'm sure, Grams. High school is so last week."

She laughed, as I had hoped she would. "Let's go."

***

An hour later I was sitting three rows in front of Jack, due to the alphabetical nature of our seating arrangements, listening to the valedictorian urge us to follow our dreams, forge our own pathways, blah, blah, blah. I craned my head around to look at him to see if he was as bored as I was. He looked up and winked at me. His aunt and uncle were hosting a joint graduation party for us later this evening because I had insisted Grams and Mom were too busy with wedding plans to throw me a graduation party. Trina couldn't stand the thought of me not having a party, so she insisted on expanding Jack's to include me.

"Jack," I had tried to apologize. "I'm so sorry. I never intended to horn in on your party."

He had stopped my lame protests by simply

kissing me until I shut up. "Shh. I think it's a great idea. We have the same friends, anyway. This way we combine our families. It's probably time they started getting to know each other, don't you think?" He had moved my hair aside to kiss my neck, which sent shivers all over my body, making it very difficult to concentrate on what he was saying. It finally sunk in.

"Wait, what are you saying, Jack?" I pulled away from his hypnotic lips to question him.

He smiled, brushing my hair behind my ear. "Well, I'm not proposing yet. But it's coming. Just thought you should know."

I threw my arms back around him, pressing my face into his neck.

"Hey, why the tears, querida? Is the thought of marrying me so horrifying?"

I laughed, as he obviously meant me to. "No, of course not." I kissed him. "And I'm not saying yes, yet. But it's coming. Just thought you should know."

***

"Alethiea Grace Moran." I walked across the stage, accepted my diploma, and shook hands with the principal, vice-principal, and school board representative. The cheers and clapping I heard were from Jack's family, for the most part.

I resumed my seat and impatiently waited for Jack's turn. "Jackson Iván Ruiz." I added my whistle to the clamor from his family. A few minutes later, "Tara Lynne Scott." We had all done it: Jack a couple of years late, Tara and me a year early, but we had done it.

As soon as we recessed and were free of the New Mexico Public Education system forever, I found Tara and Jack. I hugged Tara, practically squeezing the life out of her, before turning to Jack to do the same. "You did it, Jack. You did it. I'm so proud of you. I love you so much."

He kissed me softly before pulling back and saying, "I know. I love you too."

***

The party was in full swing and Grams and Manny had certainly hit it off. Jack's father, Marcos, was present and I spent a few minutes getting acquainted with him, trying not to show my resentment since he was the reason Jack and I had broken up for more than a month. To be fair, I knew deep down the real reason was Jack's response to his father, not Marcos himself, but it was so much easier to blame him. I made a concerted effort to be nice to him, however, because I didn't want him thinking his son had a shrew for a girlfriend.

"So, Ally," Marcos said, "Jack tells me you will also be attending the University of New Mexico. What are you planning to study?"

"Well, sir, at this point, I'm planning to get a double major in English literature and education."

"Please, call me Marcos. That's wonderful. You want to teach English? At the high school level?"

"Yes, that's the plan." Why was it so awkward and difficult to talk to my boyfriend's father?

"Well, I, of course, think literature is wonderful thing to study, although I recommend you broaden your scope beyond English literature. Be sure to take some classes in world literature, as well. Perhaps you could take one my classes sometime," he suggested.

"Yeah, sure. That would be great." I looked around, hoping to find an excuse to get out of this conversation. Hopefully, I would not always feel so awkward talking to Jack's dad.

Mat was introducing Tara to all of his vast extended family and Megan came to appropriate me, claiming Jack had been hogging me lately. When she finally got bored and went off to the den to watch a movie with some of her cousins, I began to look around for Jack, who seemed to have a habit of disappearing at his own parties. I figured he was in his bedroom, trying to find a few minutes of peace and quiet, but I ran into Rémy and Veronica before I had a chance to find him.

"Congratulations, Ally," Veronica said as she hugged me. "I can't believe you're not going to be there next year. What am I going to do without you?" Her eyes were actually shining with unshed tears as she pulled away.

"Thanks, Veronica. You'll be fine next year," I said weakly, but I wasn't sure if I believed it. Her former friends continued to shun her, not that it was any great loss, but I knew she would struggle without any sort of support network. I suddenly wished I had talked to her about joining Tara and I in taking extra classes in order to graduate early. "Veronica," I hesitated, "have you ever thought about getting your GED? You could join us at UNM this fall. I don't know, it's probably a stupid idea. Never mind."

"No." She shook her head. "It's not a stupid idea. It's a really good idea. I'm not saying dropping out of high school is a good idea for everyone." She laughed tightly. "But under the circumstances, it might be the best option for me."

"Well, I think it is an excellent idea," said Rémy. "This way I would not be dating a high school girl any longer." He leaned down to kiss her on the cheek.

"Well," I said awkwardly when she turned and met his lips. They didn't look like they were going to surface any time soon. I left to find Jack. Rémy called to me as I walked away.

"Ally, I need to talk to you later. Can I call you tonight?"

I stared at him a moment before nodding tightly. We had yet to discuss our plans to get me to France to meet his grandmother, the Oracle. "Sure, Rémy. Call me later."

As expected, Jack was in his bedroom, taking off his jacket and tie. I leaned against the doorframe and watched him until he saw my reflection in the mirror.

"Hey, gorgeous." He smiled. "What are you doing up here? Did you get bored at your own party?"

"I'm looking for my boyfriend. He seems to have disappeared. Have you seen him?"

"Hmm. No, I haven't. Sounds like an idiot, though, to leave a beautiful girl like you all alone. I think you're better off without him. I could give you a much better time."

"Ooh, that sounds like an offer I can't refuse," I said as I pushed away from the doorway and sauntered across his bedroom to where he was standing. I stood in front of him, running my fingers up his chest naughtily. "Well? What have you got?"

He captured my wandering hands and held them against his chest. "Let's see," he said, nipping my chin lightly. "I might have a little something here somewhere," he continued along my jaw all the way to my earlobe, taking it gently between his teeth, then soothing it with his tongue.

I groaned and he laughed, continuing his path toward my lips. "This boyfriend of yours sounds like a real tool. Why don't you let me take his place?" He kissed each side of my mouth.

"Okay. I like the way you kiss. I guess I'll go out with you." I turned fully into his kiss, opening my mouth under his. Not that I have a whole lot of previous experience to draw on, but Jack was an amazing kisser.

"I'd say 'get a room', but you already have," Mat drawled from the open doorway. "Jesus, you two. Don't you have any sense of propriety? I was sent to find you. Mom will shit kittens if she finds you up here making out."

We broke apart and Jack leaned his forehead against mine, panting slightly. "Get lost, Mat. I'm kissing my girlfriend."

Mat laughed. "Yeah, I can see that. Fine, I'll go, but I'm leaving this door open, kids. You two better be back downstairs in no more than five minutes. I assume it would take even you slightly more than five minutes to do anything really interesting, Jack."

"You stupid f—" Jack began, but I grabbed his face and pulled him back in for more kissing.

"Let's not waste our five minutes on him," I said against his lips. I could hear Mat laughing all the way down the hall.

***

Mrs. Hayes had finally scheduled a long-delayed funeral for Ashley. She had wanted to wait until Ashley's remains were released to her, so we gathered on a bright, sunny Tuesday morning, a few days after graduation, to commit Ashley Hayes to the earth. It seemed disrespectful to bury her on such a beautiful day, but spring in Albuquerque rarely produced dismal, rainy weather, which would have better suited the occasion. Mrs. Hayes had opted for a simple graveside service rather than a church funeral and Jack and I stood together at the grave, solemn, but glad Ashley finally had justice. Brian stood next to us, looking grim. Mr. and Mrs. Graves were there, as well as Scott and his wife. He had tears running down his face as he held Anna close to his side. It was beautiful to see how he expressed his love for one woman while mourning another. I wasn't sure I fully understood it, but I knew I was glimpsing true love at its deepest level.

"Almighty God," intoned the minister. "Into your hands we commend your daughter, Ashley Hayes and her child, in sure and certain hope of resurrection to eternal life through Jesus Christ our

Lord. Amen."

"Amen," we all echoed.

"These bodies we commit to the elements," he continued, "earth to earth, ashes to ashes, dust to dust. Blessed are the dead who die in the Lord. Yes, they will rest from their labors for their deeds follow them."

We lingered after the service to speak to Mrs. Hayes. I hoped to be able to speak privately to Scott, as well. He might think I was crazy for what I wanted to tell him, but it was a chance I was willing to take.

"Oh, my dear," Mrs. Hayes pulled me into a tight, perfumed hug. "I can't ever begin to tell you how much it means to me to finally know what happened to her. Thank you so much." She was crying, but then so was I.

"It's okay, Mrs. Hayes. I did it for Ashley. She deserved to be at rest. I'm glad I could help." I hugged her again before she walked away to talk with Mrs. Graves.

Jack pulled me into his arms and whispered against my hair, "Are you all right? Let me get you out of here."

I wiped my eyes and looked up at him, smiling weakly. "I'm okay. I really want to talk to Scott Alder, okay?"

He looked at me, trying to judge whether or not I was up for it. "Fine, come on." He took me by the hand over to where Scott and his wife were standing.

"Ally," Scott said. "Thanks for everything. The detective told me you believed in me the whole time, especially when he didn't."

"I knew it wasn't you, Scott. Um, is there any way we could talk privately for a minute? Please?" He looked at his wife and they seemed to have a silent conversation for a few seconds before he gently released her hand and led me a few feet away.

"What is it?" he asked.

"Scott, you might think I'm crazy for what I'm about to tell you, but I feel like you should know." I took a deep breath. "I'm, well, I'm sort of psychic." I winced as I saw the disbelief on his face. I pressed on. "You don't have to believe me, but Ashley got in contact with me; that's how I got involved in the investigation. I won't bore you with all the details, but I saw her while I was unconscious in David Moore's house. She appeared to me and helped me escape. She wanted you to know how happy she is for you, you know, with Anna and all. She's really glad you finally found someone to love." He was staring at me with wide eyes. "And you guys had a daughter. She's with Ashley now. Ashley said she's beautiful," I ended on a hushed whisper as I saw tears slip down Scott's cheeks. "That's all." I turned and walked back to Jack.

***

We sat on my couch a little while later, holding each other, both of us thinking about how Ashley's story had ended. "Jack, did you see how much Scott loved her? And yet he really loves Anna too. I'm so glad he found someone else to love."

"Yeah. Jesus, Ally, I don't know what I'd do if you were taken from me. I don't know how he managed to survive. I don't think I would." I could feel him swallow hard.

I turned in his arms to take his face in my hands. "That is about the most amazing thing you could ever say to me, you know." I rested my head against his chest and breathed in his essence.

CHAPTER EIGHTEEN

"Is this the promised end?"
–Shakespeare –King Lear (5.3.265)

The weekend after school let out for the summer was set for Mom and Brian's wedding. I had hosted a bridal shower at our house two weeks ago, which turned out really well. Most of the guests were teachers from Mom's school, and Tara and Grams had helped me put the whole thing together, finding those silly games always played at showers. Although I wasn't too keen on all the wedding fuss, I wanted Mom to have the full-on wedding experience including bridal shower and bachelorette party. She was the greatest mom ever and I wanted her to have every single one of her dreams.

We had one minor setback at the final dress fitting. Although Mom had picked a dress she thought would have plenty of room to allow for the pregnancy, and she had bought it a size bigger than she normally wore, her boobs didn't cooperate. They just kept getting bigger. Mom stood there on the raised dais in the bridal boutique, crying hysterically because the dress was way too tight across the bust. It looked fine everywhere else since her baby bump was really quite small and confined to the front of her body.

"Jen, it's all right, darling," Grams said. "We'll figure something out. Ally, where is the seamstress?" She directed this last question to me, somewhat urgently.

"I'll find her, Grams." I was glad to escape. I found her in the back of the dress shop, gathering her materials for the final fitting. "Maria, we need some help out there." We both hurried out to find Mom sitting on the edge of the dais with her head in her hands, sobbing.

"I'm too fat! I can't wear this dress! I'm going to look terrible next Saturday! The wedding is off! I have to tell Brian the wedding is off, that's all." Maria tsked, ordered her to stand up, and examined the bodice of the gorgeous wedding dress. She clucked her tongue and told us she would go and get her mother, the only one she knew who could handle something like this. Long story short: Maria's mother, an ancient woman who spoke absolutely no English, was a fabric miracle worker. She managed to add extra panels to the front bodice of Mom's dress, which didn't take away from the beauty in any way. Mom's newly enlarged breasts fit in perfectly and the finished product was stunning. She looked absolutely beautiful and I knew Brian would be bowled over. Crisis averted.

Brian hosted the rehearsal dinner at Yanni's, a local Greek restaurant. It was fun and very classy.

Jack and I were the youngest there, but we had a great time anyway. I loved how comfortable he was with my family, able to enjoy himself and make sure I had a good time, as well. We all enjoyed meeting Brian's parents and six brothers, a few of whom lived in Albuquerque. Yikes! I hoped Mom knew what she was getting into by marrying into such a fertile family. It seemed quite likely I would have more siblings down the road; Mom was only 36, after all.

The wedding day dawned bright and clear. The three of us girls spent the morning at the Mark Pardo salon, getting our hair done as well as facials and a mani/pedi apiece. It was fun and I could hardly wait until Jack saw me, primped and polished, with an elegant updo and wearing the great bridesmaid dress Mom had found for me. I know: nobody ever really likes the bridesmaid dress, but this one was different. I'm not saying I had deluded myself into believing I could ever wear it again, but I still felt great in it today. Jack would not see me until I was walking down the aisle, and I well knew how much he appreciated a sexy dress.

The wedding was set for four o'clock, but we arrived at the winery by two. It was a wonderful venue, with beautiful grounds I imagined Jack and I getting lost in later in the evening. I helped Mom get ready, making sure her dress hung perfectly. "You look absolutely stunning, Mom. Brian is not going to know what hit him."

"Thank you, sweetie. I know it's ridiculous, but I'm nervous," she said as she smoothed her dress. "I'm thrilled to be pregnant, you know, but I have to admit I wish I wasn't showing quite so much at my wedding."

"Don't worry about it, Mom. Your little baby bump is adorable," I rubbed her tummy as I said this. "Besides, everyone is going to be so busy staring at your giant rack they won't even notice." She laughed and hugged me.

"Ally, sweetheart. I love Brian and I'm so happy to be having his baby, but I wish we had done things in the proper order. I wish I had been a better role model for you. I'm sorry."

"Oh, Mom," I choked out. "You are an amazing role model. You have taught me how to be a strong, independent woman, and that's what is truly important. Now stop making me cry! My mascara is going to run."

"Okay, I'll stop. I just want you and Jack to be more careful than Brian and I were. Please promise me," she urged.

What was it with adults assuming teens were automatically having sex because we were dating? "Mom, Jack and I are not sleeping together. I promise. We are planning to wait quite a while before we take such a big step."

"Really?" she asked.

"Really. Now let's get you out there and married, okay?"

"Okay." She nodded.

The appointed time finally arrived and I gave my mom a final kiss on the cheek before I turned to head up the aisle. Jack was sitting on the near end about halfway up the bride's side, and his jaw dropped in a gratifying manner when he saw me. I winked at him as I walked by. I reached the front of the chapel and took my place as my mother and Grams began their approach. The look on Brian's face as he watched my mom walk toward him was awe-inspiring. You could see the love shining out of his eyes and I felt really good about this marriage. They exchanged traditional vows and wedding rings, were pronounced man and wife in a shockingly short amount of time and then Brian pulled her close for the bridal kiss, which went on and on until we all started clapping and wolf-whistling. They broke apart, Mom blushing and Brian looking disgustedly smug. I sighed and realized I now had a stepdad. This was going to change things.

Mom had eschewed the traditional bridal party table, opting for a more modern family table so Grams could sit with us as well. Mom had thoughtfully included Jack as my dinner partner, probably figuring I would have deserted otherwise. Brian's brother, the best man, gave his toast and then it was the maid-of-honor's turn. I had been working on it for several days, but I was incredibly nervous as I stood up to take the microphone from the best man. Jack gave me a wink and a slight push when I hesitated.

"Okay, um, hi everyone. I'm Ally. I'm the maid-of-honor. Um, obviously." I gave an embarrassed chuckle and looked around, panicked. I met Jack's steady gaze and he nodded his encouragement. I could do this. "So, Jen is my mom and I want to say how proud I am of her. I mean, she bagged herself a great guy." There was light laughter following this.

"But seriously, I am really happy to welcome Brian into our family. Mom was pretty cagey about him at first, but she finally brought him around to meet my grandmother and me. We didn't manage to scare him off, which speaks to his determination. He must really love her to put up with us." Grams and Mom both smiled at me, while Brian put his arm around his new wife and pulled her in for a kiss. I smiled at them; they were really sweet together. "I've had an opportunity to get to know Brian pretty well over the last few months as we worked on a, um, *project* together." He raised his eyebrows at me knowingly. "I know first-hand Brian is an honest, hardworking cop and will make my mom a great husband. I couldn't bear to give her to anyone else." I was horrified to realize a tear had slipped out without my express permission. I wiped it away and must have looked surprised at its appearance, because many people chuckled in sympathy. "Anyway, let's raise our glasses to Jen and Brian, or as I call them: Mom and Dad."

"You did great, sweetheart," Jack said, kissing my temple as I sat back down. I had to get back up a few minutes later for the bouquet toss. Mom was very funny about looking back to be sure to not aim it anywhere in my direction. Tara ended up with it and the horrified look on her face was priceless. I saw Jack punch Mat playfully on the shoulder as Mat looked embarrassed. I tried not to cringe as Brian kneeled in front of Mom to pull off her garter, accompanied by "Hot for Teacher" by Van Halen. I had to look away when he started to use his teeth.

"Hey, are you all right, querida?" Jack asked,

reaching over to wipe away yet another darned tear as I watched my mom and Brian dance their first dance as man and wife to Tom Odell's "Grow Old With Me."

"Oh, I'm fine, just a bit weepy and sentimental tonight. My mom looks beautiful, doesn't she?"

"It runs in the family," Jack answered.

I smiled at him. "You are really sweet, Jack. I'll be fine." The DJ was starting the general dance music. "Dance with me?" He smiled and stood, holding out his hand. He led me to the dance floor and pulled me into his arms, my favorite place in the entire world. We danced until the end of "I Was Made for You" by She & Him. As it ended, Jack bent to kiss me sweetly.

"I love you, Ally."

"I know."

***

I got up very early the next morning to go with Jack to the airport as he left for basic training at Ft. Leonard Wood in Missouri where future Army Corps of Engineers trained. He had been accepted into the ROTC program and had been informed he would actually be gone for ten weeks of training. I was devastated when I heard this; it was nearly the entire summer! I'd managed to keep my opinion to myself and I was rather proud of this newfound maturity. I was scheduled to leave the next morning for a month in Ireland, which would definitely help pass the time, but once I got back, I knew the time would crawl by until Jack returned.

He had said his farewells to his family the night before so I could drive him to the airport, a sweet gesture I appreciated. I picked him up with plenty of time to spare and helped him load his duffel bag into the backseat of my VW. "You want me to drive, querida?" he offered. I shook my head, unable to speak, so he simply nodded and climbed in the passenger seat. I drove around the block and pulled into a church parking lot and turned off the car. "Ally?" he asked. I clenched the steering wheel tightly, trying to control my emotions, but unable to hold in a sob.

"I'm sorry, Jack. I was trying to be so mature and in control about all this, really I was. But I'm going to miss you so much," I ended on a whisper.

"God, Ally. Come here." I leaned over the gearshift and he pulled me into his arms. I kissed him with all the love I could possibly instill in a kiss, mixing it liberally with the salt of my tears. He pulled back and wiped my cheeks with his thumbs. "It's okay, babe, it's okay. I'll be back before you know it." He kissed me again. I nodded and collected my wits to finish driving him to the airport.

Our farewell scene, right before the security check, was fairly calm and collected, all things considered. He turned and flashed me a beautiful smile before he entered the security area.

I drove home, making it all the way to my driveway before falling apart.

***

Grams dropped me off at the airport the next morning since Mom was on her honeymoon in Hawaii. Cassie was also on her honeymoon, having married Gregory the week before my mother's wedding, so I would be flying to Ireland on my own. I assured Grams she did not need to come in with me and could simply drop me off at the departures curb. I hugged her goodbye, promising her I would miss her desperately, and wheeled my suitcase to the Delta counter. After checking my bag and clearing security, I headed to one of the eating areas to get a bite of breakfast. It was very crowded and I had to share a table with a gentleman reading a newspaper.

I sat down with my breakfast burrito and asked, "Find anything news-worthy?"

Rémy folded down the page of the *Albuquerque Journal*. "In this rag? No. I prefer to read *Le Monde* for a more European perspective, but they don't carry it here," he smirked his old familiar smirk. "Are you ready?"

"Yes. Let's go."

"Oui. Let's go," he agreed.

As we left the eatery, I threw away the unused ticket to Galway and pulled out my boarding pass to Washington, D.C., with a connection to Paris and followed him to our gate. Rémy had given me the ticket a few days before. We had worked out weeks ago our plan for me to go to France to meet with the current Oracle while she was still living. His family had made all the arrangements, insisting I keep everything secret from everyone, a decision I found extremely difficult. Rémy impressed upon me the need for all the subterfuge, assuring me the Irish Seer Council and my family would not understand and would attempt to keep me from the Gaulish clan. I had reluctantly agreed, knowing I would have to pay the piper when I returned to Albuquerque. I hadn't even told Jack. I hoped he would forgive me.

So here I was, about to fly to France with a 22 year-old Seer who had been masquerading as a foreign exchange student all semester. I really, really hoped it was not the worst decision I had ever made.

The End

ACKNOWLEDGEMENTS

As always, lots of love and kisses to my family for their patience and indulgence while I was absorbed in my manuscript. I couldn't do this without your love and support. Thanks to my mom and Cat, who have conversations with me about my characters as if they were real people. Special thanks to Mom, who took me to France; I wouldn't know about Rouen if it wasn't for you. Thanks to my bestie, Carol, for reading everything and listening to me rant for hours on end. You have made this adventure such fun! Thanks to my students for giving me great ideas for conversations and fashion. Michelle and Stephanie, I owe you for the amazing wedding story. Be careful what you tell me because it will end up in a book!

Special thanks to my readers. I can't tell you how much it means when one of you tells me you enjoy my stories.

ABOUT THE AUTHOR

Amy Reece lives in New Mexico with her incredible husband and two ridiculous mutts, Greta and Sodapop. When she's not writing, she's teaching high school English and social studies or maybe wandering through a thrift store in search of the next lucky teapot for her vast collection. She is an unrepentant bookaholic and has overflowing bookshelves in nearly every room of her house. Her favorite authors include J.R.R. Tolkien, J.K. Rowling, and C.S. Lewis–must have something to do with initials! She loves to travel and is hoping to need many research trips for future writing projects.

Blog:
https://amyreece.wordpress.com/

FaceBook:
https://www.facebook.com/areeceauthor

Twitter:
https://twitter.com/AReeceAuthor

Pinterest:
https://www.pinterest.com/alreece12/